Escaping the Grind

Escaping the Grind

From the Chronicles of Carlson

NICHOLAS ADAM

iUniverse, Inc.
New York   Bloomington

Escaping the Grind
From the Chronicles of Carlson

iUniverse books may be ordered through booksellers or by contacting:

iUniverse
1663 Liberty Drive
Bloomington, IN 47403
www.iuniverse.com
1-800-Authors (1-800-288-4677)

Because of the dynamic nature of the Internet, any Web addresses or links contained in this book may have changed since publication and may no longer be valid. The views expressed in this work are solely those of the author and do not necessarily reflect the views of the publisher, and the publisher hereby disclaims any responsibility for them.

ISBN: 978-1-4502-3383-5 (sc)
ISBN: 978-1-4502-3385-9 (dj)
ISBN: 978-1-4502-3384-2 (ebk)

Library of Congress Control Number: 2010929445

Printed in the United States of America

iUniverse rev. date: 06/09/2010

To GG

ACKNOWLEDGEMENTS

This book would not have been possible without the generous support from the following individuals:

- Former athlete of mine and now journalist for Omni TV, Andrew Ng, who politely informed me that my excessive use of the words "however" and "therefore" was very annoying
- My aunt Janet, who gave me the perspective of a middle-aged woman
- Former students and athletes Joseph Lee and Damian McMullen, who helped me remember what it felt like to be a twenty-something
- Nikki Minchin and Nancy Kolodzie, who told me which sections of the story dragged, which flowed, which were poignant, and which were hilarious
- Sherry Hinman, for her editing advice
- Josephine Newman, who taught me how to be free from anxiety, and Carson Petrie, who taught me how to run free
- Old friends Carla Gugliemo and Leah Taylor, who helped me develop my female characters
- Poppa Joe Kolodzie, for sharing some of his stories teaching sex ed
- My mom, Ronda Lynne Carlson, who every day shows courage when coping with environmental hypersensitivity and neuropathic pain
- All my current and former students, for providing me with joy and stress, both of which make for good material

Enjoy

PROLOGUE
Before the Real World

The man tried to crush my hand with his sausage-sized fingers …

Why did I listen to Dumb and Dumber?

My privates are numb despite cycling the final fifteen kilometres to the summit out of the saddle. The Coquihalla was so steep in this stretch that I barely averaged six kilometres an hour, though madly spinning in my easiest gear. I've had more than one anxiety attack. I have no idea where Eric and Teagan are.

After witnessing a number of steaming, smoking automobiles pull over, I thought, *If a three-hundred-horsepower four-by-four can't make it up this monster without breaking, how can I? It's thirty-three degrees and so humid that my sweat doesn't evaporate.* I chose to walk. Miraculously, my cramping thighs willed the rest of my lanky body to the summit rest stop.

There, a foul-smelling bathroom sat adjacent to a parking lot. I stumbled in, desperate for liquids, and thrust my dehydrated mouth beneath the cold faucet. A rusted sign by the tap read, "NOT FOR DRINKING," with small print saying, "Surface runoff—may contain mercury, cyanide, and arsenic." I didn't care.

I also didn't recognize myself in the mirror. Brown stubble, now at the itchy stage, did not mask my gaunt cheeks and translucent skin. My sandy mane, plastered to my cranium, made me look like a kid with a fever. Goose pimples covered my forearms and sunburnt, throbbing calves. Basically, I smelled like a hockey bag and looked like a serial killer.

No one will take pity on me. I've asked several people for a lift to Merritt, another sixty kilometres down the toll highway. However, my appearance frightened everyone away, even the van full of stoned teenagers.

Here now I rest, slouching against the exterior concrete walls of the rank bathroom, updating my diary. The majestic Rocky Mountains surround me, but I'm too exhausted to enjoy the view. Why didn't I listen to Uncle Willie?

"Whatever you do, boys," advised the old man this morning, "don't take the Coquihalla." I assured my concerned relative there would be no need to call my father back in Toronto. D'Souza, Teags, and I would comply.

"It's too steep, especially after the tunnel," he continued. "Those avalanche chutes are there for a reason. Some cars can't even make it."

"We appreciate your advice," said Eric.

"Aye, cheers mate," said Teagan.

They pedalled away. Uncle Willie then pulled me so close I could tell his morning brew was a double-double. "Trust the brown boy more than the Irishman."

"We'll be all right," I said.

"I don't need to call your father?"

"Please, no; he'll worry." I gave Uncle Willie a hug. "Thanks for everything."

I hopped onto my bike and then caught up to my friends down the road.

"Bollocks," said Teagan. "Willie's a gobshite. That other route is for pussies."

"Teagan," I said, "my uncle's lived in the Okanogan his entire life. I think he would know."

"Dude, you're being conservative," said Eric, pointing to the grubby map of British Columbia we'd been using. "Look how much shorter this is."

Eric was right. Taking the Coquihalla would save at least ninety kilometres of riding.

"True," I said. "We could get back on schedule."

"We'd feckin never be off schedule if ye didn't write so many love letters!" barked Teags. "I'm surprised we feckin left before noon today."

"Ha, ha, ha," I said before giving him the finger. "At least I have a woman."

"Touché," said Teags.

"Besides, it wasn't my fault D'Souza got us lost that day."

"Yer right about that one, mate."

"Dudes! Stop fighting. Let's just go," said Eric. He pedalled off on his $6,500 Devinci road bike. Teagan and I followed—to our supreme regret.

Thank God we bought greasy foot-longs before leaving Hope. Nowhere on this beastly Coquihalla can we obtain sustenance. On our previous two days of cycling (Thursday: Vancouver Airport to Harrison Hot Springs; Friday: Harrison to Hope), finding food was no concern. We simply stopped every thirty to forty kilometres for a rest and a bite. Now, my double-meat-extra-cheese-and-mayo sub has to fuel me until Merritt.

I'm certain Eric is already there. Teagan and I didn't train for this trip like he did. Riding a seventeen-pound carbon-fibre bike doesn't hurt either. Even though Eric's been carrying one of my saddlebags (I packed too much), he's still always ahead of Teags and me.

Speaking of my scrawny, freckled friend, Teagan's probably an hour behind Eric and still cursing me for being slow. "Why'd ye bring a feckin mountain bike?" he asked, twenty-five kilometres into today's ride. "We told ye it'd be too heavy to climb these mountains. I'm goin' ahead. Ye mind?" He didn't wait for a response.

Alas, dear diary, I must now continue, probably to my impending doom. In the event that my feeble condition causes me to plummet off the Rocky Mountains, I've decided to write my obituary:

To whoever finds my rotting corpse: Be happy that my decomposed tissue is less odiferous than the B.O. I had in my last hours of life.

Carlson "Chud" Veitch. June 12, 1974–July 18, 1998
A recent graduate of teacher's college, Carlson was to become a secondary school teacher this fall (if he ever got hired). The poor sod died painfully, never knowing the

joys of telling horny teenagers what to do. After swerving his cheap bicycle to avoid a mountain goat, young Veitch tumbled off British Columbia's Coquihalla Highway to his demise.

Surviving Carlson is his big-hearted father Wilbur, long-lost sister Kate, beautiful girlfriend Lisa, and wise Uncle Willie (who had warned Veitch not to take the Coquihalla). To those left behind, please ignore the fact that Carlson died doing something idiotic and take comfort knowing that he joins his beloved mother Mary and hyper-spastic dog Lady-Bear in heaven.

Since the body is too mangled, visitation will be closed casket. It occurs on Monday, July 20, between 2 and 4 PM, with the funeral to follow. Make donations to Queen's University, York University, or the newly created Carlson Veitch Memorial Fund for wayward cyclists.

6:17 PM

I'm alive! Mercifully, the soggy sub sandwich kicked in to raise my blood sugar and fuel my ride. Better still, much of the remaining journey was downhill. I actually had fun, especially when bombing down the last section at close to the one-hundred-kilometre-per-hour speed limit.

If only I knew the whereabouts of Teagan and D'Souza. I'm at the meeting point, the local Clown (McDonald's) restaurant. I used my calling card and the pay phone here to leave a message on Eric's cell. Knowing Eric, mind you, he probably wouldn't think to check for messages.

6:35 PM

Just wolfed down two Super Size meals, so why is my stomach still growling? I'm sitting outside, hoping for a glimpse of Teagan or Eric. Country music now fills the air, origin unknown.

6:42 PM

Just engulfed a hot apple pie.

The music is louder. A portly gentleman with crooked teeth, thick glasses, and a furry salt-and-pepper beard told me it's the third day of the Merritt Mountain Country Music Festival. His name is Nathaniel.

6:51 PM

Nathaniel told me the story of tonight's lineup. Marty Stuart got sick with the flu, so a local B.C. girl will croon in his place. Her name is Bobbi Smith, and she'll sing before tonight's headliner, Travis Tritt. Sensing I was parched, Nathaniel waddled to his car and brought me back a two-litre bottle of Merritt Mountain spring water. We shook hands and the kind man was off.

7:03 PM

Bought two soft ice cream cones. Returned outside. Flipped through tourist pamphlets. Found elevation profile of today's ride.

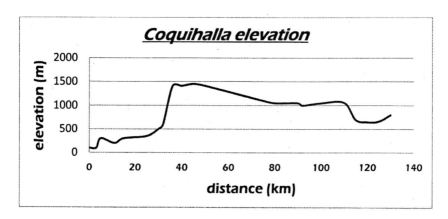

The vertical section thirty-five kilometres in is what nearly killed me. Still no sign of Dumb and Dumber.

7:11 PM

Bobbi Jones now sings. I must admit she's good. Usually, I despise country.

7:13 PM

I see Teags and D'Souza coming toward me off the highway. Somehow, my sorry ass beat them here.

9:30 PM

Here's the story:

After leaving Hope, Eric zoomed ahead and mistakenly turned east. Teags and I were too far behind to notice he'd erred. D'Souza rode 25.4 kilometres toward Penticton before realizing his goof. This put Eric about fifty kilometres behind Teags at the time he ditched me.

Teagan and Eric confessed that the steepest part of the Coquihalla left them shattered and barely able to walk to the summit, let alone ride. Nobody granted them pity rides either.

Teagan couldn't find decent shade at the summit rest stop, so he pedalled farther to find some. He took a nap just off the Coquihalla, in the shadows of the spruce trees lining the adjacent river. I overtook him during this slumber. Eric caught up to Teagan shortly after he resumed his ride.

After Teags and D'Souza fueled up at Clown, we searched for a room. From roach motels to campsites, B&Bs, and five-star resorts, fans of the music festival had filled all vacancies.

We bumped into Nathaniel in the Holiday Inn lobby. He'd forgotten his water bottles and was back to fetch them. "There's nothing unless you go to Kamloops," he said. "I'd drive you boys but I have to look after my wife and kids. Best of luck."

None of us wished for another eighty-kilometre ride, especially in the dark. We chose to crash on an inconspicuous hill behind Clown.

Mosquitoes attacked Teagan and me throughout the night. Somehow, Eric was immune.

"Bloody hell!" said Teags.

"Midges?" I whispered. Eric appeared to be sleeping.

"Aye," replied Teagan. I heard him slap one against his neck. "Vile creatures."

Eric ripped a big fart and deadpanned, "That should keep them away."

"I thought you were asleep," I said.

"Shite," said Teagan. "Get yer arse examined."

"How many ice cream cones did you eat?" I asked Eric.

"Three," said Eric.

"Aren't ye feckin lactose intolerant?" asked Teagan.

"Yes," said Eric. "But have you been bitten in the last minute?" D'Souza was right. His noxious emissions protected us.

Sunday, July 19

"Do ye have te write yer feckin love letter just before we wanna leave?" barked Teags. It was already 11 AM and I'd just mailed my latest postcard. "We'll feckin never make it to Kamloops at this rate. And ain't yer sister expectin' the lot of us on the twenty-seventh?"

"Dude, just write to Lisa *after* we finish our ride for the day," said Eric. "Or you can use my cell and call her."

Compared to yesterday, today's three-hour jaunt to Kamloops was heaven. The entire route was flat or downhill.

Kamloops means "the meeting of waters," and for good reason. Both the North and South Thompson Rivers join here, dividing the picturesque city in half. Near downtown, the Canadian National and Canadian Pacific rail lines meet and so do three major highways. It's no wonder Kamloops is the official Tournament Capital of Canada.

After last night's sleep on the hill, we chose to splurge on accommodations. Our room has two queen beds and a cot. Usually we take rooms with only one queen bed and a cot. The hotel has a pool and offers a buffet breakfast.

We spent the afternoon lounging poolside and playing cards. I now lead the series in rummy, whereas in 9-5-2, we're tied at four. Between games, we read or drifted off for a snooze in the soothing sun.

During dinner, Teagan complained that he hadn't been laid during the trip.

"Christ, Teags," said Eric. "We've only been here four days. We're not all playboys like you."

"Nice te see a little spark in ye," replied Teagan. "See those titties o'er there?"

How could we not? The woman attracted more than just *our* glances. Along with a great rack, she had a perfect olive complexion.

Teagan covered his bony shoulders with a golf shirt. He stood up and walked toward the beauty.

"Come on, Teags. She must be thirty-five," said Eric.

"She's way out of your league," I said.

What is it about Teagan that women find attractive? Are they suckers for his accent? Does he display a certain charm I don't see? He must at least censor his vulgarities.

Within minutes, Teagan had her laughing. Drinks arrived. Teagan sipped his traditional rum and Coke while the beauty preferred a colourful martini. She removed her T-shirt, revealing a skimpy bikini that barely held her perfectly shaped breasts. Teagan winked at us when she flung back her salon-quality black hair.

"I can't take this," I said to Eric.

"*SportsCentre* should be on soon," said Eric. "And that means Tour de France highlights."

"Let's go."

Last night, Eric was ecstatic to discover that his idol, Jan Ullrich, had won stage seven of the Tour. Ullrich now wears the *maillot jaune* as overall leader of the tour. There are fourteen more stages, including three in the Alps and two in the Pyrenees.

Personally, I'm more interested in baseball. Sosa and McGwire's chase for the record has got me watching for the first time since the Jays won the World Series.

"Think Sosa or McGwire hit another homer?" I said.

"Who cares, dude. They're both juiced. I want to see Tour highlights."

"You don't think Ullrich is doping?"

"That's blasphemy! He just knows how to use his domestiques in the peloton."

"Do they really make a difference?"

"I'll be your domestique tomorrow. And you'll see how much difference it makes with somebody blocking the wind."

We were back in our room. Eric flipped on the tube and found *SportsCentre.* To Eric's disappointment, anchorman Darren Dutchyshen said that Ullrich had lost his lead in the Tour de France today. This blow was somewhat softened by the news that neither Sosa nor McGwire hit a home run today.

"There are more stages," said Eric. "He'll get the yellow back."

Eric turned off the tube and then asked me, "If I let you use my cell to phone Lisa tomorrow, will you help me with my entrance essay?"

"That was random," I said.

Eric's mind is so full of unrelated ideas that it's sometimes difficult for him to organize his thinking. "No problem," I said. "Is this for the med school in Australia?"

"Yes, and oh yeah, your dad left a voice message for you on my cell."

"Today?"

"Um, the day we were in Harrison Hot Springs."

How fitting.

"Eric, that was three days ago!"

D'Souza was always late for kinesiology lectures. The class of 1997 even bought him a watch before convocation so he wouldn't be tardy. The plan failed. The students for our year were already in alphabetical order and on our way to Jock Harty Arena before my scatterbrained friend arrived.

"Dude," said Eric. "I'm sorry."

He played me the message. Poppa Wib was so wound up with excitement that his already rapid speech cadence was elevated to the tempo of an auctioneer: "Hey-big-guy-Leaving-this-message to-say-that-on-July-30-you've-got-an-interview-with-a-former-colleague-of-mine-Mrs.-Kelly-Turner-for-a-science-position-at-Kipling-Secondary-Bye."

My first interview for a real job!

12:18 AM

Can't sleep. I keep worrying about what to say to Mrs. Turner.

How will I compensate for my lack of professional experience? What if she figures out that during my placements, my associate teachers did all the class discipline and, because of that, I have no idea how to manage a group of teenagers by myself? If I told her about my love of working with younger people and my passion for promoting fitness, would that be enough? Would a display of my anal-retentive organization skills cover for my weaknesses?

2:13 AM

Still awake. Still thinking about job interview. Shouldn't have taken the afternoon nap. Periodic leg cramps don't help either. At least D'Souza isn't farting.

Teagan just came in, went inside the bathroom, and turned the tap on. He didn't even notice me writing in my diary using my penlight to see.

2:18 AM

Teagan now out of the bathroom. I didn't hear the toilet flush. What was he doing in there? There had better not be a steamer in the porcelain. Teagan just collapsed on the cot and mumbled, "Ahhhhhhhhh."

2:19 AM
Teagan already snoring.

Monday, July 20

As Eric and I awoke, Teagan was fiddling with his bike. "I'm going te eat," he said. Teagan appeared to have a black eye. We caught up a few minutes later.

At the buffet, a grand assortment of fruit, cereal, cooked meats, eggs, and bread awaited us. We loaded our plates with high-calorie bacon, eggs, and sausages. Teagan sat in a dark corner. We joined him.

Indeed, Teagan did sport a shiner. "Feck you," he said to the laughing D'Souza. "Don't ye say anything." We deduced that Teagan's plan to get lucky must have backfired.

"How was I supposed te know the woman was married?" said Teagan. Eric and I burst into hysterics. "Hairy fecker was big, too. Came back and kicked me bike this mornin'. Feckin broke a spoke in me wheel."

After breakfast, we returned to the room. Teagan arrived last, his pockets filled with muffins. "For the road," he said. Eric and Teags forbade me to write a postcard to Lisa before we cycled the 133.8 kilometres to Sicamous.

The black-eyed Irishman, the absent-minded brown boy, and the lovesick neurotic continued our picturesque ride along Shuswap Lake. Today's high-fat breakfast made it a slow one, as we all suffered from different versions of gastrointestinal distress. Teagan puked, I had cramping problems, and D'Souza blew farts. We vowed to load up on carbohydrates instead of bacon and sausage at the next buffet.

Sicamous lies past the Salmon Arm portion of Shuswap Lake. Salmon Arm is also a town, named for the plentiful salmon present in the lake when settlers first arrived. Apparently, they used pitchforks to pluck the salmon from the water and even used the fish to fertilize crops. Sicamous is also the Houseboat Capital of Canada. We're staying in one now.

Teagan is snoring. About ten minutes ago, he got up, went to the bathroom, and turned on the tap, only to emerge five minutes later just like last night. No toilet was flushed, and he didn't leave a steamer. I checked the toilet for shit last night. I don't know what the hell he was doing. Come to think of it, he did the same thing when we stayed at the roach motel in Chilliwack. Whatever "it" is, Teagan was out before his head hit the pillow, so "it" works.

Eric's now tossing and turning beside him, but nothing seems to awaken Teags.

I just got off the phone with Lisa.

"Chud," she said. "How are you?"

"Great," I said. "I kinda like this travelling thing."

"Now you know why I'm going to Peru."

"I'm going to miss you. I don't know what I'll do."

"I'll miss you too."

"I wish you weren't going."

"You know this is important. I have to do this for me."

"But what about us?"

Lisa changed the subject. "I got your first postcard this morning."

"I'm writing one every day."

"You're a sweet man, Carlson. So, is everything on schedule?"

"We're a bit behind."

"Will you make it to Kate's on time?"

"I hope so. I don't want to pay the penalty for changing my flight home. Look, I was just calling to say hello and the boys are trying to sleep, so I should go."

"Good night, then."

"Miss you."

"Me too."

I just heard Eric mutter, "Screw this." Now he's off to the bathroom with the tap on, presumably doing "it." I hope "it" isn't what I think it is.

Tuesday, July 21

I remembered to ask Teagan about "it." We had stopped for a snack inside the forested peaks of Mount Revelstoke National Park. High-calorie muffins were essential to fuel the 72.4-kilometre climb to Rogers Pass.

"I was snapping off," he said, without a hint of shame. I spit out a few blueberries from my muffin.

"Ye gotta do something about the MSB."

"MSB?" I asked.

"Feckin massive sperm buildup, ye dumb shite."

"Just be happy he turned the tap on," said Eric, laughing. I recalled Eric visiting the bathroom after Teagan.

"Wait a minute. You too?" I asked Eric. He nodded.

Feeling self-righteous, I said, "Well I don't need to do that until after Lisa leaves."

"Easy for you to say. You probably had sex with her the night before we flew here."

"Yeah, so?"

"Dude, I'm on a bit of a dry spell, remember?"

"Carlson," said Teagan, "ye can't feckin tell me you'll make it the rest of the trip."

"Yes," I said. "Yes I can."

"Twenty bucks says ye can't make it."

"This is not an episode of *Seinfeld*! We're not repeating the contest."

"Is that a yes or a no?"

We're now at the centre of Glacier National Park, at Rogers Pass, 1,382 metres above sea level. Our ride up Mount MacDonald felt effortless because of the view. Though the air was twenty-three degrees Celsius, glaciers were only steps off the highway, slowly melting away. What's more, a quick glance upward revealed snow-capped mountains, which completely surrounded us.

If this is what travelling is like, I'm hooked.

I'm writing from inside Glacier Park Lodge, located at the summit of Mount MacDonald. Eric's watching *SportsCentre*. McGwire hit his forty-third homer and Ullrich is back in yellow, so we're both happy. Teagan is trying to fix his bike. He broke another spoke and the front tire is wobbly. Since we can't find a repair shop up here, Teagan hopes he can safely coast down the mountain to Golden, our destination for tomorrow.

An hour ago, we played rummy. I won the first three games. Teagan refused to play anymore because he can't compete against my "bloody feckin card counting."

I have no ideas for Eric's essay yet.

<u>Wednesday, July 22</u>

I almost gave into "it" last night.

Despite practising the breathing exercises my therapist recommended, I couldn't sleep because I kept dwelling on my relationship with Lisa.

How am I going to survive months without seeing her? I can visit on the holidays, but financing the flight requires employment. I'll be penniless after this adventure. I may be forced to work with my dad at the driving range. What if she wants to break up with me?

She hinted at a breakup in April, stating, "Six thousand kilometres is an awful long way, Carlson."

Maybe I'm being paranoid, but what if my perceptions are true?

Shortly after resuming our adventure (79.2 kilometres today to Golden), we rescued a vagabond named Christian. Somehow, his waiflike physique had managed to tow a mountain bike and two cargo trailers up Rogers Pass. Cycling down, though, was the real dilemma. Christian's brake cables snapped four days ago when he was in Penticton. The plucky fellow couldn't afford the repair costs. Christian used the soles of his work boots, now completely smooth, to slow down! Teagan gave him spare brake cables, and together with Eric, fixed his bike.

Sporting a 1980s mullet and full beard, Christian was halfway through his two-thousand-kilometre ride to Saskatoon. He hopes to find work there. Though at least fifteen years our senior, Christian's lifelong possessions fit inside the first trailer, probably less than two cubic metres in volume. The second cart was a tent-covered child trailer. We were all amused and relieved that Christian wasn't towing a child. Instead, it housed his dearly beloved Rottweiler, Chico. The dog and Christian share the tent at night and subsist on tuna and white bread. We took a couple of photos, gave them a few of today's stolen muffins, and were back on the road.

D'Souza cycled to the lead as customary, with Teagan shortly behind. When I arrived, Eric had already found lodgings, and Teags was off somewhere repairing his bike.

We're staying in the cramped, dusty attic of a bed and breakfast. Eric couldn't find a vacancy elsewhere. In fact, Mrs. O'Leary, the stern proprietor, initially refused him the claustrophobic room. "Young man, there's barely room for two," she'd snipped. "And I have enough brekkie to prepare already." D'Souza had to promise we'd help with dishes before the old bag relented.

Mrs. O'Leary needn't have worried. Teagan spent the night in Anne-Marie's room. We were watching TV in the common room when Teags and I first viewed her slender, toned thighs. Eric was too enthralled with the Tour—Ullrich is still in yellow—to notice. Teagan wasted little time. "Ye got beautiful legs," said the charmer.

Using the Internet at the B&B, I've learned that Canadair offers a flight to Lima, Peru, on Boxing Day. I phoned Lisa using Eric's cell.

I asked her if it was okay for me to come down. She hesitated but then agreed and suggested we visit the Amazon or Machu Picchu. Why did she pause before giving me an answer? Does she want to break up with me in the interim? Or worse, forever?

I dare not leave before Boxing Day. It would break my father's heart. Kate doesn't usually come home, so I can't leave Poppa Wib alone on Christmas Day. I wish Kate would just forgive Dad about Mom's death. Unless they haven't told me something, it wasn't his fault.

Thursday, July 23

Teagan's gone. Anne-Marie took him away. Eric and I rode 83.1 kilometres over the Kootenay Rockies to Lake Louise, Alberta, without Teagan's foul language and crass comments. Witnessing the awe-inspiring, shadowy peaks of Kicking Horse Pass just wasn't the same.

"She's a feckin great lay," Teagan had bragged. "We're gonna hitch te Squamish and do some climbing." We understood. A promise of sex and rock climbing was too much for him to resist.

Before Teagan left, Eric had a suggestion for us: "Teags, why don't you switch bikes with Carlson?"

A brilliant scheme!

"He'll be able to draft off me using your road bike, and you'll probably need his mountain bike if you do any off-roading in Squamish."

Teagan nodded. Then Anne-Marie interjected, "There's some kick-ass trails in Whistler, too."

The lustful pair caught their first ride after breakfast. How Teags will get back to Calgary in time for the flight home is a mystery.

Teagan's obsession with rock climbing began two years ago, soon after arriving in Canada. He'd just started postgrad studies in exercise physiology at Queen's when Eric and I first met him.

About to commence our final year as undergrads, D'Souza and I were back early to train for cross-country running season. Sick of being the fastest of the slower training group—affectionately branded the "Fast-Slow Guys"—we desperately wanted the label "Slow-Fast Guys" or better yet, "Fast-Fast Guys."

During a punishing thirteen-kilometre run, Coach Pereira followed us on his mountain bike. Unusually caustic that year (who wouldn't be after a double-knee replacement?), he barked orders, especially during the final sprint down Earl Street.

"Drop your arms! Keep your hips forward!" he screamed.

After the run, Coach made us lift weights.

At one point, Eric and I feebly attempted to bench press two plates for ten reps. During my seventh rep, I began to weaken. Just then, we heard "Feckin shite, bollocks, feck, feck, feck!" in a strange accent. Distracted, Mr. Absent-Minded neglected to spot me. My pectorals slowly gave out, and the cold barbell, loaded with 135 pounds, descended toward my neck.

"Er-ic," I wheezed. "He-elp." Noticing my peril, Eric's brown skin actually turned crimson. Embarrassed, he lifted the bar to safety. "You little shit!" I screamed. "The bar nearly crushed my windpipe." I cuffed him on the shoulder.

"Dude, I'm so sorry."

Quickly forgiven, Eric and I ceased working out and went to investigate the commotion.

Around the corner from the free weights was a climbing wall. It was there we first met the man from Ireland. Teagan's scrawny physique made Eric and me feel like Schwarzenegger. Attempting to traverse the wall with no hand chalk and wearing Docs, Teags was doomed. After losing a foothold, then a handhold, his bony ass tumbled onto the mouldy blue safety mats. "Feck!" he bellowed once more.

"You okay?" questioned Eric.

"Yeh, just feckin frustrated," responded Teagan.

Eric told him about the Queen's Climbing Club. Since then, Teags has been to Joshua Tree, California, with them twice and can flash a 5.11d on the Yosemite decimal system. To "flash," dear diary, means climbing a route without falling, and "5.11d" is an advanced climb where the hardest move on the route only has one small handhold or foothold. It's a level reserved for the ridiculously talented or perpetually unemployed.

Since Teagan left early with Anne-Marie, Eric and I got stuck doing the dishes. Choosing to dry, Eric didn't have to endure Mrs. O'Leary's beak constantly peering over his shoulder. Somehow, the old bat could find the tiniest particle of dirt through thick glasses and cataracts. "Young man, you missed another speck on this fork!"

<u>Friday, July 24</u>

Teagan's bike is FAST—why did I bring a mountain bike in the first place? On the brisk 58.9-kilometre ride to Banff, we passed a wild moose. Its large snout reminded me of my father. I sent him a moose postcard with the message:

> Remind you of anyone?
> Love, your son, Chud

In fact, I got a little obsessive with the postcards.

To Lisa from the secluded Emerald Lake:

> Lisa,
> Wish you were here cuddling with me.
> XOXOXO Love, Chud

To my high school friend Megan from the top of Sulphur Mountain:

> Megan,
> Guess who felt at home here with the stink?
> How's the boyfriend?
> Carl

To Uncle Willie from Bow Falls and the Hoodoo Pillars:

> Uncle Willie,
> We should have listened to you. The Coquihalla
> nearly killed us. Don't tell my dad, ok?
> Carlson

To my old friend Rick from the Banff Hot Springs Hotel:

> Rick,
> Lots of bikini-clad women here. You should have taken a break from your 80-hour work weeks on Bay St. and come. Stop buying condos, cars and other toys and use the money for travel instead.
> Carl

To my sister Kate, from the Columbia Icefield:

> Hey sis,
> Eric and I should arrive on schedule. We got behind but will skip the rest day.
> Your bro,
> Carlson
> P.S. You'll be happy to know that Teags isn't coming.

Saturday, July 25

What a thrill. Eric and I dreamed we were pros riding the Tour de France. Drafting off each other like we were in the peloton, we averaged 40.2 kilometres per hour for the 144.3-kilometre ride to Calgary. If D'Souza and I could do these rides twenty days in a row without stopping for food, without a one percent downhill grade and without a slight tailwind, we'd be Jan Ullrich's domestiques on Team Deutsche Telekom.

Only a few kilometres from our hotel in the Southwest (Calgary is a modern city divided into quadrants), Eric and I rode past the bobsled tracks used in the '88 Olympics. We stopped for pictures and also inquired if the city offered rides to the public. They do, just not in July. Next time, Eric and I will brave the two-man sled and maybe even try speed skating at the oval.

<u>Sunday, July 26</u>

Chinook winds and a three-hundred–metre elevation drop helped Eric and me complete today's monotonous 181.1-kilometre ride to the cattle town of Brooks, Alberta. Dead prairie dogs (*Cynomys gunnisoni*) and wheat were the only things to look at for nearly six hours.

Sometimes, I drifted mentally and let D'Souza pull away. Consuming my mind were thoughts of Lisa and worries about what to say in my upcoming interview. Eric, typically, didn't notice my absence. I'm sure he just imagined himself riding alongside Ullrich on the cobbled Champs-Élysées in Paris.

<u>Monday, July 27</u>

Medicine Hat, near the Alberta-Saskatchewan border, is where my older sister Kate lives and works. Today's 131.8-kilometre ride here was another bore. I secretly wished for a flat tire so I could give Eric a valid excuse to stop and put a temporary end to the tedium. I counted twenty-seven dead prairie dogs before first viewing the city from the highway. Since the Trans-Canada is so straight and flat here, you can see forever. It was another eleven dead rodents before we arrived at Kate's front door.

She wasn't home but left us a note, written in her faultless cursive:

> *Chud and Eric,*
> *Welcome to Medicine Hat. I'm sorry but I was called*
> *in for an extra shift. The key is where we discussed.*

Eric and I took several minutes to locate the elusive key. Kate had left the details of its hiding spot on Eric's voice mail. "Inside the frog's mouth" was all he remembered. Kate has fourteen porcelain frogs on the front porch of her bungalow and an additional twelve in the garden!

We eventually located the key inside a purple frog beneath the juniper bush.

Kate had left us a second note on the fridge:

Make yourselves at home; there is lasagna in the fridge.
Kate
P.S. Sometimes the microwave short-circuits so use the oven if you wish.
P.P.S. My boyfriend Drew may be around later before he picks me up at work.
P.P.P.S. He's a little scary looking, but don't worry.

Indeed, Drew's appearance is frightening. However, his sunken brown eyes, acne-scarred skin, square jaw, and barrel chest mask the timid man within. "Hi, I'm Drew," he said in a soft-spoken tone. I extended my hand. Drew's handshake was weak, like a wet noodle, and he squeezed my fingers instead of my palm. This is one mistake I won't make when meeting Principal Turner in three days.

After a cold lasagna dinner, Drew gave us a tour of Medicine Hat. Oil is the main industry in "The Hat," supporting its sixty thousand residents. However, there's more to this place than black gold. We're in Canada's sunniest city, so it's no wonder that eight golf courses and over one hundred kilometres of trails are found here. Most of these trails link to the Saskatchewan River, which snakes its way through downtown. The highlight was a visit to the World's Largest Tepee, a mammoth structure standing twenty stories high.

After the tour, we picked up Kate from Sunnyside Care Centre, a nursing home.

"Be prepared for polyester," said Drew, as we walked inside. He wasn't kidding. Seemingly all of the residents wore blue or brown polyester pants.

"There must be a lot of static cling," said Eric. "I'd hate to be the one doing their laundry."

"We use powerful fabric softener," responded Drew. "I know. I do their laundry sometimes."

Drew walked us down the main foyer. A random resident called out, "Nu-urse." We weaved amongst an endless number of fogies using walkers and canes.

"Usually I do maintenance work here," continued Drew. "But sometimes they need an extra hand down in laundry."

"Is there a bed-care wing?" asked Eric.

"Yes," said Drew. "I draw the line at cleaning shit off their clothes, though."

"Nu-urse," called another resident from within a room.

"What's bed care?" I asked.

"Where people go to die," said Eric. "They're often incontinent."

We passed the smoking room. Three women surrounded a single man, who appeared to enjoy the attention. One of the women, cigarette dangling from her mouth, adjusted a dial on the man's oxygen tank. A long plastic tube ran from the tank and through a nosepiece on his face.

"Emphysema," Eric commented.

A second woman noticed Drew and knocked on the glass to get his attention. Drew waved, and we continued down the hall until we reached an elevator. We rode up to Special Care, a wing of the nursing home where the residents with Alzheimer's live.

"All the women have poodle perms," I remarked.

Drew punched in a code outside the door to Special Care. It clicked open. "Get in quick or some of them will try to escape," he said. I pushed Eric through the door and followed close behind.

Kate greeted Drew with a kiss, me with a hug, and D'Souza with a handshake. "I need another half hour or so," she said. "Drew?"

"Yes, hon."

"Take Eric and my little bro to play cards with Mr. Harris while I finish up."

"Anything for you, baby."

"He's whipped!" I whispered to Eric.

"Dude," he said, "you think you're any different with Lisa?"

According to Drew, Mr. Harris once figured out the exit code and escaped. The octogenarian found his way across the U.S. border to Butte, Montana. Butte is about one hundred kilometres south of here. The local police found Mr. Harris at a gas station pay phone, trying to order tacos.

Drew led us around the U-shaped wing. We passed a common room. There, a gaunt old woman watched pro wrestling on TV.

"That poor man," she said. "They're beating him up just because he's a Negro." Eric explained that the show was scripted and choreographed, but the thin woman didn't get it.

"Nu-urse," she called out.

Drew introduced us to Mr. Harris, who was playing solitaire.

"I'll see you guys in a bit," said Drew.

He walked back down the hallway. Several residents swarmed around him, like a bunch of five-year-olds chasing a soccer ball. They knew he had the exit code.

For a man with dementia, Mr. Harris sure was a card shark. Eric and I played 9-5-2 with him. Often looking confused, he would pat down his white hair and squeeze his Popeye-sized forearms like a nervous tic. However, it was all a ruse, for the instant Mr. Harris sensed our pathos, he'd strike and win most of the tricks. The old fart defeated us within forty-five minutes.

The experience with Mr. Harris inspired me to finish Eric's essay. Mr. Harris became Hannu Mikkola, a fictional senior citizen with dementia. The essay details Eric's relationship with the eighty-one-year-old immigrant from Finland. Included are the 9-5-2 story and a modified version the Butte, Montana, misadventure. I changed Medicine Hat, Alberta, to Kingston, Ontario, and Butte, Montana, to Watertown, New York, and made Eric the hero. I'm sure the University of Sydney Medical School will never know that Carlson Veitch was the ghostwriter.

Tuesday, July 28

Eric's mission is to ride the entire width of Canada. He pedalled away after breakfast. Kate and I, plus her twenty-six porcelain frogs, wished him good luck. Eric's going to need it. He's got another 5,800 kilometres before reaching Cape Spear, Newfoundland.

Teagan never arrived at Kate's, so I guess things went well with Anne-Marie. Or maybe he got run over like one of the eighteen prairie dogs I counted on today's ride back to Bassano. Hopefully, he'll meet me at the Calgary airport tomorrow.

Despite a satisfying lunch in Bassano (double cheeseburger), I didn't want to get back in the saddle. My crotch had just awoken from a state of numbness, and I was pissed off.

Before leaving Kate's, a bitter argument with her had triggered my emotions. We had a big row over Mom's death. Kate can't let go of her anger at Dad for supposedly letting it happen. She wants me to ask Dad about the lawsuit, and I want her to bury the hatchet and come home for Christmas for the first time since she moved west.

I had used my anger to fuel the ride to Bassano, but it was time to stop dwelling. When Brita offered me a ride to Calgary, I didn't hesitate to accept.

Brita was an elegant looking older woman who reminded me of my mother. She kept saying, "You have much to learn, young one," when I opened up to her about my frustrations with Kate. I felt a little bit like Luke Skywalker absorbing the wisdom of Jedi Master Yoda.

When I was a Star Wars–obsessed kid, Mom used to explain things to me using Jedi lingo. After she suffered another blackout, I asked her, "Are you going to die?"

"I might die," she said, snuggling her weakened, ninety-pound frame around me. "But I am your 'Force,' and I will always be with you."

<u>Wednesday, July 29</u>

Home.

Teagan never made it to the Calgary Airport, but I'm not worried. The man travelled to five continents before his twenty-fifth birthday. He can look after himself.

Poppa Wib picked me up from Pearson Airport at 8:51 PM. He had some banana bread ready—Mom's old recipe—in case my blood sugar was low. Dad also noticed me fidgeting. Who wouldn't fidget after being cramped up on a plane? We stopped at Centennial Park so I could go for a run. I love my father.

I've decided not to shave my beard because it's past the itchy stage and I've never had one before.

Job interview tomorrow!

<u>Thursday, July 30</u>

Kelly Turner, principal of Kipling Secondary, is a tiny woman, but everyone respects her. The secretaries, custodians, and teachers all straighten up and work a little harder when she's nearby.

"Carlson, it's a pleasure to meet you," she said, offering a firm handshake. "Please come into my office." There was no bullshit with this lady. I felt comfortable around her. Unfortunately, Kelly will retire mid-September.

Her replacement seems like a dick. Mr. Damian Glenn's laconic personality was less than endearing. He merely nodded at me when I said hello. In addition, the man tried to crush my hand with his sausage-sized fingers during our handshake, as if it was some sort of contest. I resisted the squeeze the best I could.

At least Mrs. Turner tried to appear interested during the interview. I know I babbled far too much, but Mr. Glenn did nothing to hide his boredom. He yawned at least three times and was constantly looking at his gold watch, like he had somewhere better to be. At one point, however, I caught Mrs. Turner shooting him a disciplinary glance. He stayed focused after that.

My casual appearance (disheveled beard, khakis with Birkenstocks, and a collarless dress shirt) probably didn't help either. Mr. Glenn couldn't have been impressed. Not a single bristle of his salt-and-pepper hair was out of place. He wore a stylish, silver, three-piece suit, but the matching tie was so tight that some of his neck fat spilled over the top of the collar. Yes, ties are like a noose around the neck.

I left the interview feeling it was a bit of a bust. Hopefully, it wasn't too obvious that I often had no idea what I was talking about. And why didn't I emphasize my passion for promoting fitness to kids? Maybe I won some points with my polished answer to the cooperative learning question.

Lisa came over tonight. She gave me a kiss hello and then quickly complained that my beard was making her itchy. Further affection was to be withheld until I removed the patchy fur. Dutifully, I ran downstairs and shaved my facial hair. However, in my haste, I cut myself above the Adam's apple, and the tiny wound refused to stop bleeding. Imagine trying to have a serious discussion with the one you love while constantly dabbing a shaving cut.

"This is hard for me to do, Chud. But it's necessary." I knew what was coming.

Lisa looked me in the eye and into my soul. She started crying, but I knew she was resolved in her decision. Lisa insists that we officially break up on August 2, the day she flies to Peru. "If we're truly meant to be together, we'll know when you visit after Christmas."

Friday, July 31

Poppa Wib now works part time at the 7th Street Driving Range. Located within walking distance from home—we live at #355, 6th

Street—I stopped to visit after my long run (a Fast-Slow-Guy time of 1:31:11 for twenty kilometres). Dad was out in the tractor collecting golf balls.

As a joke, I bought a small bucket and aimed my shots directly at him. Eventually, after a few slices (the wind off nearby Lake Ontario exaggerated this effect), I hit the bull's eye. My perfect 250-yard drive hit the cage protecting Dad inside the tractor. Poppa Wib saw it was me and looked pretty pissed. I ran back home to avoid a lecture.

When Dad got home, I had roast beef and potatoes ready for dinner, but he still gave me an earful. "I-taught-an-extra-two-years-to-help-you-through-university!" he yelled, with his typical rapid cadence. "I-set-up-an-interview-for-you. I-retired-at-the-exact-time-to-make-a-spot-in-the-system-for-you-and-this-is-the-thanks-I-get!" I gave Poppa Wib some extra gravy, but the meal was still pretty quiet after his rant.

"Sheesh. Sorry, Dad," I said. I can't understand why he was so irritated. It was just a little prank.

AUGUST

"What's a hard-on, Daddy?"

<u>Saturday, August 1</u>

"Carlson," said Mr. Damian Glenn over the phone. "You were unsuccessful in your interview."

"Oh," I replied, deflated.

"You are qualified but just not the right fit. Good-bye."

How curt, I thought. A little sugar-coating would have been nice. He knew it was my first interview.

School begins in thirty-six days. I don't want to be a supply teacher. The students eat them alive.

I saw Lisa for the last time until Christmas holidays. It was awkward and tense. Her parents threw a lavish going-away party and, amidst all her friends and relatives, I had little time to see her. The going-away sex wasn't so great either. I finished early. Must have been the MSB.

<u>Sunday, August 2</u>

Lisa off to Peru.

My therapist might disagree, but I think one day of wallowing in self-pity is okay.

<u>Monday, August 3</u>

Now I know why Dad was so livid a couple of days ago.

To get my mind off Lisa, I helped Poppa Wib at the driving range. My first job was to go out in the tractor and collect golf balls. I figured he would give me something more mundane to do, like sweeping, so this was quite exciting. Watching the spiral pickers scoop up the range balls and hearing the rhythmic "plut-plut-plut" when they hit the collector cage detached my thoughts from love.

33

I was chasing a groundhog *(Marmota monax)* with the tractor when the first missile struck. *CLANG.* Then two more: *CLANG-CLANG.* My ears immediately began ringing after the three golf balls smashed off of the protective cage. Grabbing them in pain, I looked back to see a trio of teenagers laughing and pointing at me. Worse, the sound from the impact reverberated through the metal cage and caused my bones to vibrate. Startled, I instantly knew why Dad had been so pissed.

I have since apologized profusely to him.

Tuesday, August 4–Thursday, August 6

No job interviews.

No Lisa.

No word from Teagan and Eric.

No anxiety relapses, but I've made an appointment with my stress therapist for the eleventh. All I do is skulk around the house and watch the news and eat potato chips.

Today for example, I learned that the provincial Tories plan a $6 billion tax cut for Ontario big business, and I consumed three different canisters of Pringles.

Friday, August 7

Today's news:

Bombs destroyed U.S. embassies in Dar es Salaam (Tanzania) and Nairobi (Kenya). The attacks killed 224 people and maimed more than 4,000 others.

Don't think I'll be travelling to East Africa anytime soon. Still, I wouldn't mind climbing Kili in Tanzania one day. Plus, running with the Kenyans in the Great Rift Valley could be cool. Maybe I'll be fast enough to keep up with their twelve-year-olds.

Today's potato chips:

One bag of salt and vinegar Miss Vickie's (too greasy); one bag of Humpty-Dumpty Sour Cream & Onion (too salty); and one cylinder of no-name, no-flavour imitation Pringles. I hope Dad doesn't notice the grease stain I got on the seat of his favourite recliner.

Saturday, August 8

President Clinton is using yesterday's attacks to deflect attention from his alleged infidelity (oral sex with White House intern Monica Lewinsky). Maybe he and Teagan are related?

I'm getting sick of chips. Maybe it's time to get off my sorry ass.

Sunday, August 9

Poppa Wib woke me up at noon today, his proboscis protruding into my face. "Get-up. You're-wasting-the-day."

Every time I sat down and moped, he gave me a new chore. Today, I cleaned the grease stain from his recliner, removed twenty-three dandelions from the lawn, cleaned the eavestroughs, vacuumed the house, mopped the floors, dusted the light fixtures, scrubbed the basement windows, and did three loads of laundry.

Today's news:

Exiled Saudi millionaire Osama Bin Laden is the suspected ring leader in Friday's attacks.

I abstained from potato chip consumption today. Hopefully I don't relapse tomorrow.

Monday, August 10

Teagan woke me at noon today. "Get off yer feckin arse," he said, disrupting my peaceful slumber. Teags grabbed my wrist and— *thump*— pulled me onto the hardwood floor.

"Ow! What the hell!?" He dragged my limp carcass, like a mop on a dirty floor, toward the bedroom door.

"Mate, if ye don't get up, I'm gonna pull ye down the feckin stairs."

"Okay, okay. I'll get up. When did you get here?"

"Yer dad picked me up from the airport an hour ago. Said ye'd been a bit of a dry shite."

Over brunch, Teags explained that things had soured with Anne-Marie ("I couldn't handle the woman when she was on the feckin dot"), so he came back. Poppa Wib and my fair-skinned freckled friend already had the next three days planned for me: after my appointment with Ronda Lynd tomorrow, I'm driving Teagan back to Queen's. There, I'll apply for two teaching positions (Dad's already highlighted the postings for jobs in Kingston), party with Teagan, and do some running with my arthritic ex-coach Pereira.

Tuesday, August 11

Ronda, my stress therapist, helped me design the following plan:

Carlson's Plan
1. *Run every morning before 10* AM *(to regulate my eat-sleep cycle).*
2. *Phone Kelly Turner. Arrange an appointment and ask how to improve my interview skills.*
3. *Enter the Orillia triathlon on August 22.*
4. *Find one new job posting a day, anywhere in Ontario, and apply for it.*

5. *Take away the dwelling factor. When I obsess over getting Lisa back, treat it just like an anxiety attack: "Anxiety is like being stuck on an elevator. All you have to do is take your finger off the 'door close' button and step off."*

And the following list:

> *Seven things to do when I catch myself dwelling*
> I.   *Play golf with Poppa Wib.*
> II.   *Exercise.*
> III.   *Read about swim technique for upcoming triathlon.*
> IV.   *Draw cartoons about my adventures in the Rocky Mountains.*
> V.   *Work on my résumé.*
> VI.   *Hang out with Megan and Rick and play poker.*
> VII.   *Phone Teagan/visit Kingston.*

I'm in Kingston now. I shared the above information with Teagan. He said that getting laid would be a much easier solution.

<u>Wednesday, August 12</u>

Teagan is still puking his guts out after finishing his first "beer mile" (chug a beer + run a lap × 4: if you puke, you run a penalty lap). He earned three penalty laps of the Richardson Stadium track but still finished in 14:12. Joel and Jeff, two former Fast-Slow Guy teammates of mine, fared better, crossing the line in 6:11 and 6:12 and without penalty. I was five seconds behind. The big story besides Teags was Fast-Fast Guy Matt nearly breaking that elusive five-minute barrier. Matt finished in 5:02 and then proceeded to run a drunken fifteen kilometres just for fun. I swear he'll be the Canadian marathon champion one day. While Matt ran, Joel, Jeff, and I took Teagan back to his Aberdeen Street home.

We teased him about his ineptitude.

"My grandma could do better," I said.

"You're a disgrace to the Irish nation," said Jeff.

Teagan flipped us the bird over his shoulder while puking into the toilet.

Thursday, August 13

I woke Teagan up from his hangover this morning.

"Get off yer feckin arse," I said, grabbing one of his freckled forearms. *Thump.* I pulled him onto the floor.

"What the feck are ye doin?" he screeched. "I'm hung over. Leave me alone."

"How does it feel, you bastard?" I responded, suppressing laughter. "Mate, it's time to get up and finish your thesis."

Teagan's dissertation defense is in six weeks. After that, he flies off to Asia for a few months before returning to begin a PhD.

I applied for two jobs in Kingston before driving home.

Friday, August 14

This morning, I phoned Kelly Turner to ask for advice on interview skills.

"I'm impressed with your initiative," she said. "If you can come in immediately, I'll be able to see you."

Within minutes, I was at Kipling Secondary. I walked past Damian Glenn in the main foyer. He wore another fancy three-piece suit, though it didn't distract from the adipose on his neck. I hope he didn't notice me staring.

"Hello, Mr. Glenn," I said.

He nodded. "Mr. Veitch. I see you shaved the rat off your face."

I chose to ignore this slight, though I really wanted to comment on his fat neck.

Once in the main office, Kelly greeted me with a firm handshake. "Carlson. Nice to see you again. I see you've shaved your beard."

Mrs. Turner is like a younger, pint-sized clone of Mrs. O'Leary (the stern proprietor from the B&B in Golden). She whisked me to her office and gave me the frank advice I needed to hear.

"All prospective employers must determine the following about a teacher-candidate. "First, experience. Second, knowledge of curriculum. Third, class management skills. Fourth, competence with special needs children. Fifth, involvement in extra-curricular programs. And sixth, organization. Preparing for these common questions will swiftly eliminate your tendency to babble.

"And next time, Carlson, wear your best suit and tie." We shook hands. "Say hello to Wilbur for me," she said.

I hope somehow I can work for her in September, even if it is only for two weeks before she retires.

Saturday, August 15

Today, amidst hordes of screaming children, I practiced my pathetic front crawl at the 10th Street pool. I just can't get my breathing correct. How am I going to survive the 750-metre swim? Why am I doing this triathlon?

Sunday, August 16

I heard them arguing over the phone like they always do. Kate probably yelled at Dad for not reacting to Mom's symptoms sooner.

Dad said he did everything he could at the time, apologized a thousand times over, and begged Kate to come home for Christmas.

Dad handed me the phone. "See-if-you-can-talk-some-sense-into-her," he said, before storming outside.

"Did you ask him about what I said?" asked Kate.

I was only six when Mom first showed symptoms of formaldehyde toxicity, so I don't remember many details. Kate was twelve, so her memories still burn. I only recall Mom getting smaller, then going away and never coming home.

I could now see Dad in the backyard. He was madly swinging his golf driver at the open air. It looked like he was swatting at a swarm of mosquitoes, but I knew he was just pissed off.

"He doesn't want to talk about it," I said.

"So you didn't ask why he dropped out?"

Kate wanted me to ask Dad why he'd dropped out of the civil action lawsuit against the Canadian government and Rowland Insulation. I knew it was because Poppa Wib ran out of money, so I hadn't probed the issue. The subject of Mom's death was delicate enough.

"No."

"If he'd just listened to Mom sooner, maybe she'd still be around."

"It's in the past, Kate. I love you both, but I'm not going to be dragged into the middle. Why can't you forgive him?"

Monday, August 17

Eric is here.

After 4,500 kilometres of cycling, there's no subcutaneous fat on his body. Along with ridiculously defined abs, his pectorals have cross-striations when he flexes. Too bad it takes five hours of cardio a day, extreme dieting, a Nazi death camp, drugs, or liposuction to achieve this look.

"How were the Prairies?"

"Boring," he said. "But at least they were safe."

Eric told me that when riding between Kenora and Sudbury, being forced off the road by ignorant transport truck drivers was a daily occurrence.

"Dude, I wanted to pack it in so many times. But I kept thinking of Terry Fox running all that way on one leg. There was no way I was quitting."

Eric continues his journey tomorrow.

Tuesday, August 18

Four more job applications.

Wednesday, August 19

Bill Clinton finally confessed. On national television, he admitted to having an "improper physical relationship" with Monica Lewinsky and that he'd "misled people" about his sexual affair with her.

Thursday, August 20

Another terrible workout in the pool. My legs keep sinking. At least I was smart enough to go during adult swim hours this time. There were no screaming rug rats splashing water down my esophagus. Instead I was continuously lapped by fogies on a senior citizen swim team.

Job interview Monday!

Bill Clinton's approval ratings have soared.

Friday, August 21

Saving Private Ryan was brilliant. Dad and I saw it after our ninety-minute drive north to Orillia. We're back in the hotel now.

He's already asleep. It took him less than thirty seconds after returning from the bathroom. I hope to God he wasn't doing "it." I won't inquire tomorrow.

Between Veitch Sr. and Veitch Jr., the topic of sex is almost as awkward as the topic of Mom's death. Dad taught sex ed to other people's kids for thirty-five years, but he never had the "birds and the bees" talk with his own. I remember seeing a commercial about teenage pregnancy when I was ten and wondering why it was such a big deal. After all, it was God who made her pregnant.

Kate explained how things really worked. I had the worst case of "shrink-dink" for days after that revelation. It was also Kate who explained to me what a hard-on was.

Poppa Wib took Kate and me to see *Cocoon*, the movie about the old fogies finding the fountain of youth. When Wilford Brimley said to his buddies, "I've got a hard-on," I was perplexed.

"What's a hard-on, Daddy?" I asked Poppa Wib. There were snickers from the teenage boys sitting in front of us. I knew they were laughing at me, but I didn't know why. Kate dumped popcorn all over their heads.

"Shut up, you jerks. He's just a kid." The boys slunk down in the theatre seats and never made a peep after that.

Dad never answered my question, so after the movie, Kate enlightened me. Everything else I learned about sex was from Rick and Megan in junior high.

Most of it was wrong, especially the part about the supposed aphrodisiac properties of a Spanish fly pill. Terry, the class bully, dropped one in Megan's ginger ale once when she wasn't looking, and it didn't make her horny.

Why am I writing about sex? Shouldn't I be focused on tomorrow's race?

1:12 AM

I'm nervous and I can't sleep. My hands, dear diary, shake the same as Captain Miller's did in the movie.

Whose idea was it to enter this triathlon anyway?

Saturday, August 22

I dare not move. My chafed nipples and inner thighs bleed with the slightest friction. I feel like a new mother who's just breastfed quintuplets. Layers of gauze do little to prevent my wounds from reopening. If I'm ever stupid enough to complete another triathlon, I'll wear the proper clothing. Poppa Wib is nursing my exhausted body back to health with banana bread and green tea.

Details tomorrow.

Sunday, August 23

Triathlon start

It was a donnybrook. At the sound of the horn, me and 492 others sprinted off the beach and into the lake like a herd of stampeding water buffalo. My goggles didn't make it past the first few strokes. They now lie somewhere on the bottom of Lake Simcoe. Once I finally got my stroke rhythm, if I even have one, things didn't improve. I was continually elbowed and kicked, with one such blow narrowly missing my nuts.

I shouldn't have rushed. My weary pectorals could only move me fast enough to come in 412th on the swim leg. I refused to do the breaststroke or hold onto the rescue kayak like some of the other stragglers, but I was relieved when my nineteen minutes and sixteen seconds in the water were finally over.

Transition one

Even with my blurred vision, Teagan's bike was easy to spot. It was one of the last remaining on the racks, and Poppa Wib was pointing to it.

Bike

The skin on my inner thighs rubbed together with every pedal stroke and became raw and blistered. Why did I wear my skimpy running shorts instead of bicycle tights? Worse, my front tire developed a slow leak after I hit a bump too hard (I was sipping water at the time). Consequently, my bike split was 59:50—a pathetic 30.1 kilometres per hour—though still good enough for 225th.

Transition two

As I bent down to slip on my socks and running shoes, my quads cramped. I collapsed to the ground and screamed in pain. It was at least a minute before the spasms stopped. I chose to ditch the socks, another decision I would soon regret.

Run

At first I thought there was water in my shoes. However, I soon realized the sloshing sound was actually burst blood blisters from the soles of both feet. These latest wounds, combined with intermittent thigh cramps, reduced my running speed to a pedestrian (for me) 4:59 per kilometre rate. My run split was 34:20, placing me 213th for that split of the race.

Why do I do such crazy, stupid things?

Monday, August 24

Thank God I covered my cracked nipples with petroleum jelly and gauze. Otherwise, they may have bled through my dress shirt during the interview. However, because of the chafing between my thighs, my gait was hindered.

Principal Joseph, a Clint Eastwood look-alike, noticed my hobble as I approached to shake his hand. I explained the story. The leather-faced man was impressed. Unfortunately, the rest of the interview was a bomb. I forgot everything Mrs. Turner taught me.

Tuesday, August 25–Friday, August 28

Three more applications.
Three more interviews.
Three more rejections.
At least I feel more comfortable "tooting my own horn" and bull-shitting through the standard questions.

Saturday, August 29

Dad thrust open the curtains in my room and then sat beside me in the blinding sun. He stared at me with a peculiar look on his face.

"You've-been-asleep-for-ten-hours," he said, before poking my shoulders. "Time-to-get-up.

"So, how is Lisa?" he asked. He'd been up to something.

"Huh. I dunno," I replied. "What?"

"I forgot to give this to you yesterday."

Dad handed me a postcard and then walked out of my room. I'm sure he read the whole thing.

Dear Chud,
Have you found a job? How is Poppa Wib?
This postcard photo is of Belen, a floating town on the Peruvian Amazon. The populace lives in huts constructed on high stilts or floating wood. When the river is high (our spring), their huts rise upward along the stilts. People travel around in canoes just

like Venice. Belen is essentially part of Iquitos, the
city where I now work.
     You would adore Iquitos. Everyone walks
or bikes and Peruvians are hospitable. However,
your body may melt from the heat and pollution.
It is usually 30 C by 9am and the motorized
rickshaws emit excessive exhaust.

Lisa XOXOXOXOXO

Five pairs of XOs. Does this mean she misses me?

Sunday, August 30

Eric phoned from Cape Breton Island. He's just finished cycling
the 298-kilometre Cabot Trail and plans to whale watch for a few days.
After that, he'll ferry to P.E.I. and circle the red sand island before
continuing to Newfoundland.

D'Souza explained why I got dizzy between the swim and the
bike. "Dude," he said, "water is nine hundred times denser than air, so
changing between them throws off your balance."

Stinging eyes from swimming without goggles didn't help, either.

Monday, August 31

Megan told Rick and me she thinks her boyfriend is about to pop
the question. I learned the news of her impending domesticity during
a round of golf. After this shocker (Megan always said she'd be the last
of us to get married), Rick told Megan and me that he's just bought a
condo and this will be his last round on the links for a while. He needs
to save money.

We were always the three amigos back in high school. What's going
to happen now?

SEPTEMBER

"They were a little too revealing, sir."

<u>Tuesday, September 1</u>

Dear Lisa,

If I ever get a job, I'll buy my plane ticket to Peru with the first paycheque. Despite filling out 10 applications and completing five interviews (including one today), I still don't have a job. Maybe I should apply for an overseas position; any openings at your school?

Poppa Wib (he says hi by the way) keeps reassuring me that something will come up. He's enjoying his work at the driving range and now wants to invest in the stock market using E*TRADE. He should probably learn how to use the Internet first. Dad's still running and is still a nosy bastard (he read your postcard before I did) but I love him. I only wish Kate would bury the grudge and come home for Christmas.

I hope all is well. Keep sending me updates. I wish I were there with you.

Love Chud XOXOXOXOXO

<u>Wednesday, September 2</u>

I hope Eric didn't have to witness the plane crash. A Swissair jet carrying 229 people crashed near Peggy's Cove, Nova Scotia. All aboard were killed. Eric is supposed to be whale watching around that area now.

<u>Thursday, September 3</u>

Eric phoned to say he wasn't near the crash and asked me to forward the message to his parents.

"Dude, will you please just do this for me? If I call, they'll just harass me about getting a job or getting a girlfriend or getting into med school. They'll just want me to fly home early. You know what they're like."

"What am I supposed to say?"

"Just tell them I lost my phone and I sent you an e-mail."

"Don't they have e-mail?"

"They can't even turn on a computer."

Mr. D'Souza said he appreciated my phone call, and he seemed to believe my little white lie. "You tell him I'll pay for his flight home tomorrow," he said to me before yelling to his wife, "Geeta, Eric lost his phone again but he's okay!"

Friday, September 4

Two more interviews.

Two more rejections.

I'm doomed to become a lowly supply teacher, tormented daily by adolescents. School begins on Tuesday.

Saturday, September 5

Dad suggested I phone Kelly Turner and ask for any last-minute openings. Initially, I spoke with future principal Damian Glenn, who said nothing was available. However, I insisted on speaking with Mrs. Turner.

"It's a good thing you phoned today," she said. "There's some shuffling occurring within the school board. Something might come up. I'll let you know."

YES!

Sunday, September 6

Kelly didn't phone.

Monday, September 7

My first real job starts in less than twelve hours! Kelly phoned with the news after dinner.

"It's only for one semester," she said. "But you'll be working at Kipling Secondary until January 29, 1999."

I'm to meet future principal Damian Glenn at 8 AM tomorrow. He'll give me my schedule and my room keys, and handle any paperwork.

My current emotions fluctuate between excitement (I won't be a supply teacher until at least February) and panic (I have no idea what I'll be teaching).

Poppa Wib sensed my apprehension. "The number one rule of teaching is to stay calm. If you can survive the first day, you can survive the semester."

Tuesday, September 8

"Hello, my name is Carlson Veitch. I'll be your PE (or science) teacher this semester."

That's how I began each class. I was nervous, but spitting out these first two sentences was easy. Before continuing my introductions, at least one kid had his (or her) hand up in the air. Without fail, this kid asked a curveball question. To complicate matters, my stupid nose would always begin to run.

Thus, in period one (fitness), when a bubbly redhead asked, "Are you married, sir?" my answer was, "Uh, no, (*sniff*) I'm not married."

"Anyways," I'd continue, "I just graduated (*sniff*) from university this spring."

Dad later scolded me for offering this information. "Those kids don't need to know you're a first-year teacher."

The same kid then asked another question. "Do you have a girlfriend?"

"Uh, yes, (*sniff*) I have a girlfriend."

"Are you going to be mean?"

"Uh, no, (*sniff*) I'm not mean."

Dad later told me I should have said yes.

"Good," said the carrot top. "Because most of the teachers here are mean."

In period three (science), when the boy with thick glasses asked, "Do you know when we're getting our yearbooks?" my answer was:

"No, (*sniff*), I don't know the answer to that." (*Sniff*).

"Cause I heard it might be a while 'cause Mrs. McKee was in charge and she had a nervous breakdown."

"Uh, that's a little personal, (*sniff*), don't you think?"

In period four (PE), when the kid with oversized feet asked me, "Can we call you Carlson?" my answer was, "Uh, no, (*sniff*). Mr. Veitch, please."

By this time I was asking myself, Why did my hay fever sensitivity choose today to rear its ugly head? I hope I don't get branded with "Mr. Sniffly" as a nickname.

"Can we call you Mr. V?" the kid would then ask.

"Uh, yes, (*sniff*) Mr. V. is fine," I said.

"What about sir?"

"Yes, (*sniff*) you can call me sir."

After my introductions, we spent the remainder of each class reading through course outlines and signing out textbooks. Every couple of minutes, I felt the clear snot leaking from my left nostril and onto my upper lip. There were never any Kleenex. Thus, in the science class, I was forced to use brown paper towels, and in PE, I'd just turn around to the whiteboard and secretly (at least I hope) try to wipe the moisture from beneath my nose.

<u>Wednesday, September 9</u>

As of this morning, I still had no mailbox in the staff room. To rectify this, I asked the secretary in charge for help. I went during my prep (period two).

With her blue polyester pants and poodle perm, the head secretary looked like a resident from Sunnyside Care Centre.

"Who are you in for?" she asked.

"I don't know," I replied.

"I see."

"I was hired two days ago."

"You'd better see Mr. Glenn, then."

Great. Interaction with Noose-Neck.

Mr. Noose-Neck's office sat adjacent to Mrs. Turner's. His door was closed. I peeked inside and saw he was on his computer. He looked busy, so I didn't knock.

Mrs. Turner's door was open. Though she shuffled through a sea of paperwork and was talking on the phone, Kelly spotted me and waved me inside.

"Hold on," she said to the phone. "Carlson, have a seat. How is everything going?"

It's a bit overwhelming. "Fine."

"Is there anything you need?"

"Actually, I don't have a mailbox yet."

"You're covering for Janis McKee. Check her box." She then yelled out the door, "Mrs. Smith?"

The poodle perm woman responded, "Yes, Mrs. Turner?"

"I need you to put Carlson's name on Janis McKee's mailbox."

"Yes, Mrs. Turner."

"By the end of the day."

"Yes, Mrs. Turner."

"Thanks," I said.

"You are more than welcome," replied Kelly. "I know how difficult it is for a first-year teacher. So how is your father doing?"

"Good," I said.

"Glad to hear that. Say hello for me. Now if you'll excuse me."

I walked to the staff room. When I saw the stack of papers in the mailbox labelled "Janis McKee," I felt a twinge of panic. I found the following:

1) Three class lists
2) Three revised class lists (as of 9:12 this morning)
3) Yesterday's audit trail
4) Five pages of updates to the staff handbook
5) A union update from Jane Crowley, about the proposed Bill 160 (Education Quality Improvement Act) by the Conservative government
6) An add/drop list (some kid named Marco was added and then dropped and then added to my Grade 9 PE class)
7) A textbook inventory list (from Sara Ross, head of the science department)
8) Notice of a teacher evaluation for Janis McKee (I recycled this one because it wasn't for me)

I wish I hadn't asked.

Thursday, September 10

My teaching career lasted two days. It was Jozef the custodian who broke the news to me. The short, muscular man was cutting up cardboard boxes outside. After driving into an empty parking lot, I was puzzled as to everyone's whereabouts.

"Excuse me," I said. "Do you know where everyone is today?"

"No school," he replied. "Strike."

Jozef's accent sounded Polish. I know because he sounded like Babcia and Dziadzia, my maternal grandparents.

The radio confirmed Jozef's story: "Teachers across the province met for a rally at Queen's Park today, protesting the proposed changes to education caused by Bill 160."

It would have been nice to find out from a more official source.

Friday, September 11

Jane Crowley, head of the teacher's union in my area, phoned me this morning, wondering why I wasn't picketing the school board.

"Your name is on the list," she said. Her voice sounded like that of an old lounge singer who'd inhaled too much second-hand smoke.

If my name was on the list, why didn't anyone phone me Wednesday night?

"You won't receive any strike pay unless you picket," she said.

I drove to the school board immediately.

Upon arrival, I felt lonely, despite being surrounded by thousands of other teachers. I didn't know anybody, and no one knew me. So it was quite a relief when I recognized Jane's croaky voice. She carried a clipboard, which I presume held an attendance list.

"We might be here a while," I heard her say to a tall, heavy-set black woman.

"At least this way I'll keep up with my walking program," joked the woman. "I lost twenty pounds this summer."

I walked closer to the pair. One of them reeked of perfume. I tapped Jane on the shoulder.

"Excuse me," I said. "I'm Carlson Veitch. Are you Jane?"

We shook hands.

"I'm Jane," she said. "Why weren't you at the rally yesterday? How do you expect the union to give you strike pay when you don't protest?"

"Jane," said the black woman, "Kelly hired Carlson on Monday night."

"Oh," said Jane.

"Give him a break."

Jane walked off with her clipboard. The scent of perfume remained.

"I'm Sara," said the rotund black woman. "I'm your science department head." Sara shook my hand. "I'm sorry I didn't get to meet you on Tuesday."

"It's okay," I said.

"And don't worry about Jane," said Sara. "She's trying to quit smoking."

Saturday, September 12

Megan would never let Rick or me get away with such folly. I guess she has a different set of rules for her fiancé Derek.

The four of us played euchre at Rick's new condo. It's a one-bedroom, six-hundred-square-foot condo on Queen's Quay. He paid an extra $10,000 to face the waterfront rather than the CN tower.

Derek was my partner, and winning was the last thing on his mind.

"Hearts are us," he'd say if hearts were trump, or "crazy clubs" if they were called. I wanted to smear the lasagna leftovers on his red cheeks. Ever since Megan, Rick, and I were teens, we've always played cutthroat rules with all games and, thus, in euchre, "a card laid is a card played." However, every time Derek made a mistake, Megan defended him and insisted he be allowed to correct his error. Naturally, my team lost.

Sunday, September 13

We are an army of 126,000 pissed-off educators. Our campaign of civil disobedience is the largest teacher strike in North American history. It's no wonder.

In 1995, Minister of Education John Snobelen was filmed stating that the Progressive Conservative government planned to "bankrupt" and create a "useful crisis" in the education system as a method of instigating its reform. Snobelen (a high-school drop-out) and his boss Mike Harris (the premier of Ontario and a failed elementary school teacher) plan to slash approximately $1 billion from the Ontario education budget.

In the last three years, while following their "Common Sense Revolution" election platform, the Tories have been cutting social services in order to fund a $6 billion tax cut for businesses. The proposed education reforms are detailed in Bill 160 (the Education Quality Improvement Act). We're fighting to prevent this bill from being passed into law.

Monday, September 14

Sara introduced me to Gary Berg, head of the physical education department. Gary has a large belly and walks with the lumbering gait of an old football player. He looked like a bear shuffling along the sidewalk.

"Are you sure you want to be in this profession?" he asked, before taking a bite of his apple fritter. "When me and your dad started teaching, the kids would stand up and greet us when we entered the classroom. Now, they're all mouth with nothing important to say."

Tuesday, September 15

I witnessed my first drive-by tomatoing today. Actually, I witnessed two, and both attacks were from a woman riding shotgun in a BMW.

"My fucking kid should be in school!" screamed the woman, before firing her first volley. Jane Crowley was the victim.

"Ignorance," croaked Jane, wiping the tomato from her thigh. "I'm sure those people are enjoying the tax cut."

The BMW returned a few minutes later. This time, the woman gave us the finger before flinging more of the rotten fruit in our direction. These latest came straight toward me. I used my picket sign, "Defending Public Education," to block.

Sara was not so lucky. The tomatoes ricocheted off my sign and struck her on the cranium. Looking to see if she was okay, I noticed tomato guts plastered between rows of her braided hair. At least it neutralized the smell of her overpowering perfume.

Sara laughed it off. "I'm going to go home and make love to my husband," she said.

Wednesday, September 16

Sara must have noticed me staring at the brunette's shapely body. "Carlson," said Sara, "try not to be so obvious."

"Huh?"

"Women can tell when you ogle."

"What?"

"Let me introduce you."

Sara put her arm around me and pulled me toward the woman. It felt like junior high when Megan forced me to ask Suzanne Chase for my first slow dance.

"Lauren," said Sara to the woman. "This is Carlson. He's in the science department, too."

"Cool," said Lauren. "Are you the guy who ran here this morning?"

"Yeah," I said.

"You have nice legs."

I wanted to tell her, *Those chic glasses make your deep blue eyes look gorgeous. You have a beautiful, shapely body. Your wavy hair pulled back like that with the two long bangs hanging down on either side of your forehead is really sexy. If I didn't have you to look at, walking circles around the school with this picket sign would be less bearable than it already is.*

Instead, a restrained "thanks" left my mouth, and I walked away.

Why do I get tongue-tied around attractive women?

Why do I have to be so hung up on Lisa?

Should I even be thinking about Lauren when I'm in love with Lisa?

Thursday, September 17

Protest at Queen's Park

"I'm sorry for being aloof yesterday," I said to Lauren.

"That's okay," she said. "I just won't tell you how nice your legs look anymore." I think (hope) she was joking when she said that.

We boarded the yellow bus and sat together near the back. During our ride from Kipling Secondary to the protest downtown, I learned a little more about her.

Lauren grew up in Windsor and also went to university there. She's now in her fourth year of teaching and has just started a "two over three." With this arrangement, Lauren teaches full time for two years before taking the third year off. However, she earns 67 percent of her salary for the entire time.

I also learned that Lauren coached the cross-country team last year but did so with little running experience. Basically, she told the kids to run, did the paperwork, and took them to races. She invited me to help her coach this year when the strike ends.

The conversation flowed until I stupidly asked Lauren if she planned to watch "Dr. Death," Jack Kevorkian, perform the assisted suicide on *60 Minutes* tonight. There was some awkward silence after that. Luckily, it was only a few more minutes before we left the bus.

Tens of thousands of teachers surrounded the legislative buildings. Every few minutes, the crowd erupted into spontaneous chants of, "We won't back down! We won't back down!" It was like being at a hockey game screaming, "Go, Leafs, Go!" only now, the enemy wasn't the Habs but the Conservative government.

"Look at that!" said Lauren.

Someone had created a huge paper maché model of Mike Harris's head. It was the size of an Easter Island monolith, and four teachers carried the likeness around on a four-by-eight plywood sheet. Harris's mouth was agape, holding an apple. He looked like a roasted pig at a Macedonian wedding.

"We won't back down! We won't back down!"

That's how the first of five union leaders began his speech.

We couldn't see, so Lauren suggested we climb one of the maple trees for a better view. She asked for my help getting up. I don't know if she truly had difficulty climbing or just pretended so I'd have to touch her. Regardless, I didn't mind looking at her round behind.

"We won't back down! We won't back down!"

Every speech began and ended with this chorus. The energy was powerful, like when the Pope spoke at Exhibition Stadium. Every union leader vowed to maintain the alliance until the Conservatives capitulated.

"Bill 160 will not be passed into law!"

Friday, September 18

Dear Lisa,

Remember when the Jays won the World Series? You, Megan, Rick, me and the rest of Toronto flooded Yonge St. in celebration. Remember when you didn't get accepted to the "Semester Abroad" program? You were devastated.

Imagine experiencing both within twelve hours and you understand the emotions of a high school teacher in Ontario right now.

Yes, I finally got a job teaching high school, but we went on strike after just two days, protesting Bill 160. Premier Hairy-Ass spilled his rhetoric to the citizens of Ontario, claiming we were holding the students of the province hostage. His crony, John "Snowball-head" even threatened to fine us. However, the unified force of all five teacher unions swayed public opinion.

All five union leaders spoke at Queen's Park yesterday, to raucous applause. The Tories were sure to crack within days. Each leader promised not to back down, yet within hours, two of them did.

All elementary teachers are back in the classroom today but are confounded as to why their leaders seemingly gave their secondary school brothers and sisters the Judas kiss. Without the alliance, the high schools had no fighting power, and we go back to work on Monday.

Poppa Wib figures someone cut a deal. He's certainly glad to be retired from the profession but feels sorry for me; "I taught for 35 years and was only on strike for one day."

It's been a strange two weeks.

Love Carlson

XOXOXOXOXO

I miss you

Saturday, September 19

D'Souza finished his ride, dipping his carbon fibre Devinci bike in the Atlantic this morning. I hope he remembers to clean the seawater off his $6,500 machine.

He phoned me at 1 AM while on the plane home to Ottawa. Poppa Wib was pissed the call woke him. He asked me, "Doesn't that East Indian boy have any sense of time?"

I was still awake, so I didn't mind chatting with Eric.

Sunday, September 20

Highlights of my brilliant long-term plans:

Period One (Grade 12 Fitness)
Each morning during announcements, students record a lifestyle log (nutritional intake, sleeping patterns, resting heart rate [RHR]) and then document their exercise routine (sets × reps × weight) during the subsequent workout.

Period Three (Grade 10 Science)
I've already assigned dates for student presentations during the biology section of the course.

Period Four (Grade 9 Boys PE)
Here I will emphasize skill circuits rather than drills. This facilitates cardiovascular fitness through continuous motion yet still develops technique. I've designed skill circuits for basketball, volleyball, soccer, badminton, and football.

Pretty good for a rookie teacher.

Monday, September 21

Mr. Sniffles returned to the classroom today. Is this runny nose thing a nervous habit? Should I call my ENT?

My students were impressed that I had the entire semester planned. Maybe this means none of them noticed my post-nasal drip.

Flo-Jo, women's world record holder in the one-hundred-metre dash, died of a heart attack earlier today. Many, including yours truly, believe her death at age thirty-eight was caused by steroid abuse. Florence

Griffith-Joyner broke the women's one-hundred-metre record in 1988, a year after Canadian Ben Johnson broke the men's.

At the Olympics in Korea, both Flo-Jo and Ben won Olympic gold. However, Ben got busted for steroids and was forced to relinquish his medal. Flo-Jo tested clean. At least Ben's not six feet under right now.

Tuesday, September 22

My students are angels.

"It's just the honeymoon period, son," warned Poppa Wib. "They'll start testing you soon." Dad can think whatever he wants, but I happen to believe their angelic behaviour is a result of my superior class management and organizational skills.

Eric phoned. "Dude, I told you Flo-Jo was juiced," he said. "Ben was only the pariah." Eric then hung up. He phoned back thirty seconds later. "Oh yeah, I got into medical school," he said. "I'm leaving for Australia in a couple of weeks. Thanks for your help."

Eric's classes start in January. He's going to fly down under next month, however, and travel before meeting his grandparents in India for Christmas.

I'm jealous.

Wednesday, September 23

I am not Moses. Thus, parting the sea of students blocking my entrance to the parking lot this morning was difficult. Where did they all come from?

There were never this many before, and I swear most of them were smoking. Smoking is not allowed on school property. I'd report every last one of them if I knew any of their names.

I tooted my horn. This had little effect, as most of them just looked at me and then continued puffing. Eventually they did shuffle out of the way. One creature, a six-and-a-half-foot colossus with an ugly red goatee, was the last to give way.

After I parked, I noticed a pair of ominous looking boys approaching. They butted out their cigarettes. I noticed they were twins yet did nothing to distinguish themselves from each other. Both boys had long, dark hair with pork-chop sideburns hidden beneath. Both wore black AC/DC T-shirts and ripped, baggy blue jeans.

"Sir," said one, "are you helping Ms. Weeks with cross-country this year?"

"Yes," I replied. I was taken aback by his politeness.

"When's the first practice?" asked the other.

"Tonight."

"We'll be there."

I wondered how a pair of smokers could possibly endure a proper cross-country workout.

"Don't worry," one said. "This is our last smoke until the end of the season."

My "skimpy" racing shorts created quite a stir when I walked outside to practice. The comments ranged from "holy super-developed legs" (Lauren) to cat whistles (some of the girls) to "that teacher must be a faggot." This last comment came from somewhere within a group of older boys. I suspected it was colossus boy from the parking lot this morning.

Three kids showed up to practice: Stephanie, the short stick-like blonde who is in my period one, and Stanley and Edward, the twins from the parking lot.

"Don't worry, sir," said Stanley. "More people will show up."

The boys didn't run well, stopping to wheeze and cough every few minutes. Stephanie kept up fine but wouldn't stop talking about the merits of veganism.

<u>Thursday, September 24</u>

Colossus has a name; it's Jimmy Frame, and he joined my Grade 12 fitness class this morning.

"I heard there was a rookie in here," he said to his friends before approaching me. "I'm gonna be your best friend," he said sarcastically. *Oh shit*, I thought.

I wore medium-length shorts to practice today. Thus, no lewd comments from the hall. I was careful, mind you, to flex my gastrocnemius muscles a little extra hard when I met Lauren on the field.

The twins wore white tank tops and baggy shorts that hung past their knees. They lagged behind again today but didn't stop.

Stephanie was pleased I didn't wear the skimpy running shorts. "They were a little too revealing, sir," she said, before spitting out more facts about veganism.

All three classes are still on perfect schedule.

<u>Friday, September 25</u>

All three classes are now completely off schedule. How can this happen in one day? Now I have to adjust everything.

I think I now know why Dad's nose grew so big. Marco Costa, a little pinhead on a four-foot, seven-inch frame, hit me on the snout with a stray volleyball. The little puke wouldn't admit to it, but I know he's responsible. He was the only student not following instructions during the skill circuit, and I witnessed him serving from the wrong side.

"I'm going to have to call your parents," I said to Marco.

"Go ahead," he replied. "They won't do anything."

Mouthy bastard.

"We shall see."

I left a message on what I think was Mr. Costa's answering machine. Since there was no outgoing message, I'm not sure the number was correct. I'll need to verify with Mrs. Smith on Monday.

Just waiting for Megan and Derek to pick me up now; we're headed to Eric's cottage in the Kawarthas for the weekend.

Saturday, September 26

Too many shooters ... drunk now ... damn you Rick ... damn you worse Teagan ... we're at Eric's cottage ... world spinning ... combo of booze and vicious wipeout from tubing ... Megan crazy bastard driving Eric's two-hundred-horsepower boat ... pulled four tubers behind ... made big wave pool ... slung us on whip-turn through middle ... everyone flew off but me ... stupid enough to hang on and challenge Megan to take me through again ... didn't survive whip through wave pool that time ... suffered unintentional enema ... Derek has it on video ... bastards keep playing it over again and laughing at me... vision too blurry to see video clearly ...

Sunday, September 27

Derek showed us the wipeout video. I hit the six-foot wave at nearly forty kilometres per hour and did a single twist, double backflip before hitting the water. If I hadn't done a face plant, my routine would've garnered a perfect ten from any Olympic judge. Derek also showed clips of me running around the campfire, wearing nothing but a jockstrap, and then jumping into the water. Of this I have no recollection. Teagan says I can no longer tease him about the time the hypnotist at Stages Nightclub made him run through the dance bar in his tighty-whiteys and hump the bar stools. I have the video of Teagan's "Stages" incident to blackmail him if he ever gets too big for his britches.

A run through the cottage roads reduced my acidic hangover to a tolerable level. However, my head started throbbing again on the drive back home. Megan started bitching about the heavy traffic. A long string of cars followed one driver who travelled just under the speed limit.

"This is pathetic, inching along like snails," said Megan.

"Step on it if you're going to pass," replied Derek.

"When it gets like this, they should just pull over and let people pass."

"You're a pro, Megan."

"They have such a thwarted sense of egotism. They're on such a steady, controlled pace it's like, inside, they're on a power trip. PULL OVER!"

Monday, September 28

Somebody should throw Marco in a locker. That's what would've happened when I was in Grade 9. Not because he's small but because he's an asshole. For your information, dear diary, Poppa Wib calls this phenomenon "small man syndrome."

I checked with Mrs. Smith, and the number I called on Friday was indeed correct. Thus, either Mr. Costa just hasn't gotten back to me yet or Marco erased my message.

Marco knows his antics piss off teachers and students alike. He's recruited Julio, a tall, muscular classmate, as a bodyguard. Julio could easily pass for a senior. Mind you, the absurdity of seeing Marco and Julio side by side offsets my irritation. Both are fourteen, yet Julio is a foot-and-a-half taller and a hundred pounds heavier. Julio has a five o'clock shadow by noon. Marco has adolescent boy peach fuzz for a moustache and three whiskers on his chin. Grandma Veitch has more facial hair.

<u>Tuesday, September 29</u>

I finally spoke with Mr. Costa about his pinhead son. Mr. Costa never received the message. This means Marco did, in fact, delete it before his father could listen. Regardless, Marco was right when he told me his parents wouldn't do anything to him: Mr. Costa denied his beloved son was capable of misbehaving in the manner such as I described.

I returned home in time to watch a disturbing news clip with Poppa Wib. Jared High, a thirteen-year-old boy from the States, killed himself after weeks of relentless bullying from his peers. I can only imagine what Marco says to other kids like Jared behind his ignorant father's back.

<u>Wednesday, September 30</u>

It was as if I didn't exist.

It didn't help that Mrs. Malone, the absent teacher, neglected to leave seating arrangements or a lesson plan. Thus, it was impossible to pinpoint who was doing what. For attendance, I had students write their names on a sheet of paper. Hopefully, the idiots who signed in as Chewbacca or Buffy the Vampire Slayer were smart enough to write their own names as well.

Only two or three kids listened to me while the rest threw paper airplanes and erasers or walked freely around the classroom. Several of the delinquents were farting, and others kept swearing. I felt like a lion tamer.

Reluctantly, I called in Principal Noose-Neck for assistance. However, he just played "buddy-buddy" and socialized with the kids. I was hoping he'd scold them. It was no surprise, then, when the malcontents resumed their animalistic behaviour the minute he stepped out the door.

I even tried teaching some of the more receptive students how to solve a two-step equation. This was difficult since most didn't have paper, a pencil, or a textbook, and none could add two and three without a calculator.

How did these kids graduate from elementary school?

Thank God I'm not a supply teacher. They face this delinquency daily. It's a wonder more aren't driven to psychosis. Thinking of Lauren's big, bouncing boobs was the only thing that got me through.

I feel kind of guilty writing that last statement, but it's true. Should I feel like a dog because I'm thinking of Lauren's tits instead of Lisa's thighs?

OCTOBER

The only thing preventing me from marking is my addiction to Minesweeper on my PC.

All I said was, "The cloaca is an all-in-one hole," before losing my Grade 10s to hysteria. Only Donna MacLean kept a straight face.

Andrew Yates wanted clarification. "You mean frogs and birds shit, piss, spunk, and screw each other out of the same hole?" he asked.

More laughter. Donna cringed at the immaturity of her classmates.

"I don't appreciate your language, Andrew—"

"Sorry, sir."

"—but yes."

My "tube vs. sac" systems of digestion lecture would wait for another day. I didn't think anyone but Donna could handle knowing that the mouth and the ass in sac-system animals such as jellyfish are one and the same.

I gave Andrew a detention (cleaning chalk boards) as punishment for his colourful language.

Friday, October 2

Why did these kids take a fitness class if they hate running? Only Jamal the beanpole and Stephanie jogged the track for warm-up before hitting the weights. Frustrated by the lack of effort from the rest, I picked up a dew worm. Jamal and Steph chuckled when Jimmy and the rest of the class actually ran away from me while I chased them with the slimy *Lumbricus terrestris* dangling from my fingers.

"Don't chase me with that fucking worm, sir!" said Jimmy. I considered disciplining him for his language, but watching the mutant sloth run away like a scalded mule was sweet revenge for his previous lethargy.

"Get 'im, sir!" said Jamal, as Jimmy weaved past. Jimmy eventually ran off the track and attempted to hide behind the portables, but I kept on his tail. I could easily have caught up and thrown the worm into his goatee, but Jimmy was running, and that was the purpose of the warm-up.

We passed Noose-Neck, who was poking his fat neck into one of the portables. I don't think he noticed me chasing Jamal with the worm, but if he did, he should be happy because I'm getting his starting centre in shape for basketball.

Postcard from Lisa!

> Dear Chud,
> I'm thrilled you're at Kipling Secondary. I hear Kelly Turner is brilliant. However, I'm sorry to read of the conflict with the Conservatives. I don't envy you. My principal is from Windsor, and most of the teaching staff are expatriates from Canada, the U.S. and the U.K.; we followed the strike action closely and were rooting for you guys. The consensus is that education cutbacks by right-leaning governments are now a worldwide phenomenon.
> Do you still plan on a visit after Christmas? If so, I can't meet you in Iquitos until December 28. A local couple on the support staff plans to adopt me over Christmas.
> Love Lisa
> XO

Only one XO?
Last time I got five. Does this mean anything?

Sat 26 Dec 1998				
Toronto (YYZ) Depart 12:46 PM Terminal 3	to	Atlanta (ATL) Arrive 3:02 PM Terminal SOUTH	1,173 km (729 mi) Duration: 2hr 16min	Flight: **7432**
Atlanta (ATL) Depart 5:14 PM Terminal SOUTH	to	Lima (LIM) Arrive 10:48 PM	5,142 km (3,195 mi) Duration: 6hr 34min	Flight: **435**
Total distance: 6,315 km (3,924 mi)				
Total duration: 8hr 50min (11hr 2min with connections)				
Sun 3 Jan 1999				
Lima (LIM) Depart 12:23 AM	to	Atlanta (ATL) Arrive 8:10 AM Terminal SOUTH	5,142 km (3,195 mi) Duration: 6hr 47min	Flight: **436**
Atlanta (ATL) Depart 9:56 AM Terminal SOUTH TERMINAL	to	Toronto (YYZ) Arrive 12:16 PM Terminal 3	1,173 km (729 mi) Duration: 2hr 20min	Flight: **7433**
Total distance: 6,315 km (3,924 mi)				
Total duration: 9hr 7min (10hr 53min with connections)				

<u>Saturday, October 3</u>

> Dear Lisa,
> First paycheque yesterday! I spent it all,
> and then some, on my plane ticket. I can't wait.
> Attached is a copy of my itinerary.
> Love Carlson
> XOXOXOXOXO

<u>Sunday, October 4</u>

D'Souza phoned to ask if he could spend Thanksgiving with my Dad and me. He'll fly from Toronto to Sydney via LAX on Monday night and needs me to drive him to the airport. Poppa Wib said to phone Grandma Veitch, who in turn said it's okay as long as Eric helps with the cooking.

Teags invited himself over as well, though not as tactfully as Eric. He then asked me if my aunt Pamela would be in attendance.

"Yer aunt is feckin hot."

I told the Irish bastard he was welcome for Thanksgiving provided he didn't hit on her.

<u>Monday, October 5</u>

Jimmy conveniently arrived after the warm-up this morning. "I ain't running, sir," he said.

Maybe I should have found another worm to chase him with. "Your loss," I said, and enjoyed the morning jog with Jamal and Steph.

Poppa Wib says I'm too nice to my students and should've chased Jimmy with another worm. Dad is of the "don't smile till Christmas" mentality.

I argued he was being old school.

"That method doesn't work anymore."

"One day," he said, "you will learn."

I hope he's wrong about this one.

Tuesday, October 6

I owe the twins a pizza. Edward puked after his third hill repeat and Stanley after number four. I'd promised them a slice if they ever threw up from training. Stephanie and two new recruits (a pair of Grade 9 girls) made it up the Centennial Park ski hill without throwing up.

Steph believed the puking was due to poor nutrition and didn't have a problem telling them so. She also lectured me on the sins of offering pizza as a reward.

Two homophobes beat up a college student, Matthew Shepard, because of his sexuality. It's all over the news. Dad and I watched it on TV. Police from Laramie, Wyoming, found Shepard tied to a fence and left to die.

Maybe this will have some sort of an impact on Marco, Julio, Jimmy, and the other boys who use the terms "gay" and "fag" so loosely.

Wednesday, October 7

Mr. Donahue and his drama students led an antibullying assembly today. Their poignant skits focused on homophobia, racism, and body image. Jimmy, Marco, and Julio were oblivious to the message.

During one performance, Jimmy snoozed in the back corner. Worse, I even saw Noose-Neck walk by him several times yet do nothing to wake him. Noose-Neck could have at least nudged Jimmy on the shoulder.

Talk about enabling poor behaviour. Does this mean the starting centre on the basketball team gets special treatment?

Meanwhile, Marco kept poking the girl in front of him, and Julio suffered from giggling fits. After repeatedly shushing the pair, I instructed Marco to sit beside me. The little pinhead created a scene.

"That's not fair," he squeaked. "What about Julio?"

"Marco," I whispered. "Move here, right now."

"Answer my question first."

"Marco, you are not in charge."

"This is gay. Other people were talking."

"I didn't say you were the only one."

"Then why are you picking on me?" This last statement was audible to the performers on stage.

I imagined throwing Marco in a garbage can and then flinging the can at Jimmy's head. This way, the pinhead would be kept quiet and the colossus would be awake.

"Keep your voice down," I whispered. "And move!"

Jimmy woke from his slumber.

"Chill, sir, I'm going," whispered Marco.

I noticed Jimmy smiling.

Marco finally moved but stepped on Tim's feet while making his way toward me. It was intentional, and Tim was ready to retaliate. However, Julio stared him down. Marco knew Julio had his back, so he slapped Tim across the cheek and then raced to sit beside me.

"I'm here, sir. Happy now?" asked Marco, acting innocent.

"Mr. Veitch," said Tim, "Marco slapped me."

"You're a rat," said Julio.

I turned to Tim, said, "I saw it," and then turned back to Marco. "Come with me."

"Wha'd I do?"

I stood up and motioned for Marco to follow. "Marco. Now!"

"Whatever!" Marco kicked his chair.

I imagined myself choking Marco, much like Homer Simpson would strangle Bart. Is it a sin, dear diary, when I have such thoughts?

Mr. Donahue's performers paused to watch Marco stomp out of the gym. It was as if we were part of the act. I followed Marco and passed Noose-Neck on the way.

"Mr. Glenn," I said, "I'll need your assistance."

Noose-Neck nodded, and the three of us walked out of the gym.

I heard muted laughter from Jimmy's seating area. Stephanie later told me the cause of the commotion: Jimmy had pointed my way and called out, "Bully!" Of course, his posse of nincompoops found this amusing.

Once outside the gym, I said to Noose-Neck, "Can you escort Marco to the office, please? I'll be sure to call his father again." Noose-Neck took Marco to the office, and I returned to the gym.

Following the assembly, my Grade 9 PE class helped Jozef and the other custodians clean up. We had to stack 1,192 chairs on trolley carts, which were then stored beneath the gym stage.

Marco arrived from the office, smiling and licking a sucker. I heard him whisper to Julio. "Mr. Glenn is a doormat. He just gave me a talking to."

That's it? After opposing my authority and disrupting the whole assembly the kid only gets a "talking to" and earns himself a sucker?

During cross-country practice, I wanted to confide in Lauren and tell her that looking forward to practice with her was one of the only things getting me through the day. Instead, I told Poppa Wib. I also admitted I was growing disillusioned with the teaching profession. Dad put his arm around me and said, "Just survive the first year, son."

Poppa Wib then treated me to a movie. We saw *There's Something About Mary* at the Megaplex. It was the perfect antidote. When Ben Stiller's character got his nut sac stuck in the zipper I almost died laughing, and by the time Mary used his semen for hair gel, my abs were sore from over an hour of constant laughter. My problems didn't seem so bad after all.

<u>Thursday, October 8</u>

Why does the nicest kid in the class have to be the one who breaks the treadmill? Jamal was only trying to help. It was Jimmy who kept fooling around. Why couldn't he have had this mishap?

Instead of pumping iron, Jimmy the Jumbo-Dumbo pretended to be a Harlem Globetrotter. When he thought I wasn't looking, and even when he knew I was, Jimmy dribbled the red medicine ball between and around his legs.

"Sorry, sir," he'd mutter, before fooling around again only seconds later. I kicked him out to the hall and gave him a lecture.

"Don't yell at me, sir," he mumbled. "You just have to ask me nicely and I'll do it."

I imagined cutting off his repulsive red goatee and then shoving a dozen worms down his throat.

I regained my composure and told him, "I did ask you nicely, and it didn't work. You are to remain out here until I come get you."

"Whatever."

I walked back inside the weight room just in time to witness Jamal's misfortune. The poor guy was just trying to clean up and accidentally dropped the medicine ball. It rolled to the edge of the moving treadmill on which Stephanie was running. After the ball collided with the belt of the treadmill, it was sucked beneath. The machine screeched to a halt, and Stephanie stumbled off backward. Within seconds, the sharp stench of burnt rubber diffused throughout the room.

Jimmy heard the commotion and came inside.

Stephanie got to her feet and then glared at Jamal. Jamal looked like a puppy who'd just peed on Mom's new carpet.

"You idiot!" she screamed at him.

"Ahhhhhhhhhhhhhhhhh!" I yelled. "Jamal!"

"I'm so sorry, sir," he said.

"Want me to get a custodian?" asked Jimmy. Before I could respond, he flew out the door.

As the rest of the Grade 12s watched, Jamal and I flipped the treadmill on its side.

"Maybe we should unplug it, sir," suggested Steph.

The medicine ball had wedged itself between the tread and the frame. It was completely collapsed and resembled a giant red blood cell.

"This machine costs hundreds of dollars," I said to the class. "See why I get mad when some of you dribble the medicine balls?"

"Jimmy's not here, sir," said Stephanie.

"It was an accident, sir," said Jamal. "I swear."

"You, I believe," I said to Jamal. "We still have to fix it, though."

Jimmy soon arrived with Jozef and Noose-Neck. Jozef said something in Polish that only Nathan (who snickered) understood. Babcia and Dziadzia only taught me pleasantries in Polish, like *Djien kuye* (thank you) and *Dobranos* (good night), but I think Jozef said "fucking hell." Jozef noticed my strange reaction to his comment.

Noose-Neck dismissed the rest of the class while Jamal, Jozef, and I tried to free the medicine ball.

"Carlson, you Polish?" asked Jozef. I nodded.

"Your first name is Carlson?" asked Jamal. He was amused to know my first name. "Isn't Carlson a last name?"

"Yes, Mr. Jamal Eugene Wright, Carlson usually is a surname."

He winced when I spoke his middle name.

"Point taken, sir."

The medicine ball popped free.

"You go to Poland before?" asked Jozef. "Krakow beautiful. You see salt mines, too."

The ball struggled to return to its spherical shape. It was like watching a raisin trying to become a grape. Jamal was relieved.

"See you later, sir," he said.

Friday, October 9

"I'm glad you made us puke on Tuesday," Stanley told me. "Kill-Hill seemed so easy after that." The twins finished eighty-eighth and ninety-first out of 291 in the junior boys' 5.2-kilometre race. Today's cross-country race was at Centennial Park, where we'd trained three days earlier.

Edward wasn't talking. "He's pissed 'cause I beat him," said Stanley.

"You guys did that off of six workouts and less than two weeks after quitting smoking," I said. "Imagine if you kept that up for a year."

Stephanie placed seventeenth out of 318 senior girls. She should qualify for OFSAA. Her protégés, two Grade 9s named Shauna and Melissa, survived their first race. Shauna was fifty-fifth out of 215, and I owe Melissa a pizza.

Between races, I marked some of my Grade 10 bio tests. All but Andrew Yates correctly explained the difference between a "bag" and "tube" system of digestion. However, Andrew did remember everything about cloacas.

"Cloacas are all-in-one holes," wrote Andrew. "Liquid and solid excrement (See? I used the right word, sir) and eggs and sperm come out of the cloaca, and sperm can also go in to the female from the male threw the cloaca." Andrew also drew accurate and explicit pictures of bird, frog, and snake excretory systems.

"See? I even used examples like you told me, sir," he wrote underneath the labels.

The drawings were so good that I wanted to photocopy them for future classes. However, I was afraid if Andrew got wind of this, it would just encourage him.

<u>Saturday, October 10</u>

Teagan arrived at Mimico Station on schedule, carrying a large backpack full of travel gear. After defending his thesis earlier in the week, my Irish friend was ready for his Asian adventure.

"Gonna fly standby te Bangkok. Can ye take me to Pearson when ye drop off D'Souza?"

"If we ever find him," I replied.

D'Souza was already a half hour late. We waited another fifteen minutes before driving home. Eric was already there. He'd gotten off the train at Union Station instead of Mimico, didn't see us, and then took a thirty-five dollar cab ride to the now old New Toronto.

Grandma Veitch had D'Souza peeling potatoes and carrots by the time we arrived. Teagan immediately focused his attention on my newly divorced aunt Pamela. Grandma thought this was cute and thus absolved the Irish charmer from any kitchen duties, leaving Dad, Eric, and me to pick up the slack.

Poppa Wib stooped over an open oven, checking the temperature of the roast beef.

He saw me and said, "I don't know who is worse: my mother or your friend Eric. I can barely smell the beef."

"Was Grandma farting again?" I asked. Dad nodded. I turned to Eric and said, "She can hardly hear and has no sense of smell."

Dad continued, "She thinks no one notices."

"I was kind of wondering," said Eric.

"Try not to react," I said, before joking, "That shouldn't be difficult for you."

"We'll be ready to add the veggies soon," said Poppa Wib.

"Just have to finish chopping the garlic, Mr. V.," said Eric. "The carrots and potatoes are ready over there."

Dad added the root vegetables to the roast and then left the room.

D'Souza told me the recipe called for seven heads of garlic. I told him my grandmother must have meant seven cloves. I reminded my friend that Grandma Veitch was also part blind due to cataracts and had probably misread the instructions. Eric kept insisting that Grandma wanted seven heads, and I eventually complied.

Grandma squealed with delight after biting into the beef. "I taste it."

So did the rest of us. In fact, we kept belching up garlic gas well into the night.

Sunday, October 11

Every time I blow my nose or scratch my face, I smell garlic. No matter how much I wash my hands, the stink remains. Grandma Veitch's famous roast turkey and stuffing wasn't the same. Each time I took a bite, all I could smell was garlic. I tried eating with dishwashing gloves to mask the aroma, but the rubber scent was just as bad. I even tried to eat without my hands, but Grandma scolded me for bad manners.

This comment occurred mere moments after Grandma tooted at the table. Teagan spit up some of his stuffing before Aunt Pamela explained the situation.

Grandma then cut me the smallest piece of pumpkin pie. By the time she served D'Souza, Aunt Pamela, Poppa Wib, Teagan, and herself, only a sliver was left. "It serves you right for such poor manners at the table," she said.

Aunt Pamela left after dessert, and Teagan hitched a ride with her. She agreed to drop him off at the airport a day earlier than he'd planned. I told Teagan not to hit on my aunt, but Teagan just laughed at me. Poppa Wib was more persuasive.

"Lay one finger on my sister and I'll hunt you down in Nepal and chop off your testicles," he warned.

With this threat, Teagan turned whiter, if that's even possible, and nodded to my dad before walking out the door.

Grandma, Eric, and I played Scrabble while Dad cleaned up. Eric got pissed because Grandma kept challenging his words and winning.

She'd hunch over the game board, slide her glasses toward the edge of her hook nose, and stare him in the face before saying, "I challenge," in her Grandma voice.

I didn't fare much better. Grandma kept stealing the triple word scores I set up for myself.

Monday, October 12

Holiday Monday

No more excuses. Grandma's back at the retirement residence and Eric's on a plane to Australia. The only thing preventing me from marking is an addiction to Minesweeper on my PC. Breaking my high score on the expert level is far more appealing than marking volleyball theory tests.

Tuesday, October 13

When someone flips you the bird, it's normally considered an insult. Teenagers, however, are a different breed. My Grade 10s, for example, cackled at the sight of Dan giving them the finger from the TV screen. His video presentation began with a close-up on his hand, counting down from five to one. Dan's middle finger was the last one standing.

Worse, Noose-Neck witnessed the whole thing. He arrived unannounced a few minutes earlier while Kristy concluded her disorganized presentation on beetles. I don't know why Noose-Neck was there, only that he scribbled himself a note after the opening shot of Dan's video.

"Daniel, please see me at the end of class," I said, attempting to assert my authority in front of the vice principal.

Noose-Neck scratched something else in his notebook and left shortly afterward. I imagine he wrote something like, "Carlson must preview student videos" and "the young teacher is an imbecile."

Even worse, during period four, Noose-Neck strolled into the gymnasium just as Marco Costa crashed into the wall. Unbeknownst to Noose-Neck, Marco had been misbehaving earlier. The pinhead kept riding the trolley (which previously carried exercise mats) on his stomach like Superman. I sat Marco in the corner as punishment. The rest of his classmates completed a cardio circuit during his time out. Immediately after serving his penalty, Marco ran full speed at an unsuspecting Tim, who was stretching. Noose-Neck walked in during Marco's sprint.

Tim evaded the attack, and Marco's head nearly hit the concrete wall. Fortunately for Marco, he turned just enough to take the impact on his shoulders. His rubber, prepubescent body landed on Tim anyway.

Retaliating, Tim shoved Marco back into the wall. This time the pinhead smacked his cranium and was cut open. Julio was the third man in. He tackled Tim from behind and then delivered three shots to his head.

Somebody in the class yelled, "Fight! Fi-ight!" and the rest of my Grade 9 boys surrounded Julio and Tim. I pushed my way through the mob, separated the combatants, and walked them over to Noose-Neck.

He scribbled another note and then took Tim, Julio, and Marco to his office.

It was only Tuesday.

Wednesday, October 14

Mr. Costa came to his son's defense and was adamant that Marco be spared punishment. Noose-Neck caved. Consequently, though Marco had instigated yesterday's fiasco, he only got another "talking to" from the principal. No wonder Marco's recidivism rate is high.

Julio's parents speak little English but understood that he is suspended for fighting. However, they don't comprehend how Julio became involved in the first place.

Tim received a three-day suspension. At first, Tim's dad blamed me. "That other kid deserved it," he said, and, "Why didn't you stop him from attacking my son?" I explained that my recommendation was to suspend Marco but the decision was Mr. Glenn's.

Tim's dad calmed. "I'm sorry for bitching at you. This just isn't right."

Dad drank a double-shot of vodka with me after I related the events of the past two days. "Your Dziadzia used to feed me these when I was stressed about your mother's illness," he said.

Only two days until the weekend.

Thursday, October 15

Marco asked me why his volleyball test smelt like garlic. I knew it was because the garlic oils still saturated my fingers, but I lied. I said it was his mother's Italian cooking. He believed me.

Friday, October 16

Noose-Neck blindsided me; his Tuesday visit was an official teacher evaluation! Bastard never warned me about it, and he only based his assessment on my worst moments.

After a decent practice with the cross-country team, I checked my mailbox to find his scathing report. He makes it sounds as if I'm a buffoon.

> "Carlson is incompetent when handling special needs children … an ADHD student was allowed to run free in the gymnasium and dive into a concrete wall … likely due to poor communication with parents …"

Noose-Neck can't even control Marco … how can I?

"Carlson is not involved in any extracurricular activities."

Outright ignorance. How could he not know I coach cross-country with Lauren?

"… weak class management … even top students sense Mr. Veitch is a 'doormat' and walk all over him … allowed to dribble medicine balls in the weight room … safety risk … student broke a $1000 treadmill …"

Yet he walked by a sleeping Jimmy Frame in an assembly without so much as giving the Jimmy a nudge.

"… constantly needs assistance when covering for other teachers or during assemblies …"

Perhaps if Mrs. Malone had left a seating plan and a lesson plan this wouldn't have happened.

"… allows pupils to make rude gestures …"

Okay, I should have previewed Daniel's video. Rookie mistake. But this makes it appear like I never call students on their language.

"… extremely disorganized …"

I'll have to show Noose-Neck my semester long, day-by-day lesson plans.

"… Carlson displayed his own immaturity … chasing a student with a worm …"

I thought he hadn't seen that one. But hey, this comment comes from the guy who plays "buddy-buddy" with students instead of disciplining them.

"... I doubt that experience will make Mr. Veitch into a competent teacher ... he shouldn't be in this profession ..."

I guess I have no redeeming qualities whatsoever.

Maybe it was better that I couldn't find Noose-Neck. If he hadn't left for the weekend, I'd be liable to charge into his office and thrust five hundred of his candies down his throat, causing a painful death by asphyxiation.

Sara Ross was also gone—probably a good thing, too, as I may have burst into tears if I saw her.

Only Jozef and I remained at Kipling Secondary. He was out back having a smoke. I contemplated asking Jozef how to say "fucking hell" in Polish. Instead I said good night with a simple *"Dobranos."*

Saturday, October 17

Dear Lisa,

It's hard to find reasons to continue. My incompetent principal, Damian Glenn, ripped me apart on an official teacher evaluation. With his assessment, no administrators from other schools will ever hire me, let alone give me an interview. Bastard didn't even warn me I was having an evaluation and worse, didn't have the balls to give me the bad news in person. He simply left the paper in my mailbox for me to find just before the weekend. I feel like I have no control. I wish I was in Asia with Teagan or in the outback with D'Souza.

Maybe I could handle Damian if I enjoyed teaching any of my classes. A puny kid named Marco ruins my Grade 9 boys' gym class every day. He compensates for his minuscule size with attention-seeking behaviour and a big mouth. Marco also sends his oversized Mexican henchman, Julio, to bully other students. Physically, the two of them look like Danny DeVito and Arnold Schwarzenegger in the movie *Twins*. The only time I enjoyed this class was when another kid got fed up with Marco's antics and pancaked him into the gym wall. Marco fell to the floor in slow motion; it was like watching a pickle slide down the inside of a pickle jar. Thus, I've become a sadist. If I ever make it to January I have to teach these fools sex ed.

You'd think that a senior fitness class would be better, but no. Like Marco, but opposite in physical scale, a 6'7", red-tempered basketball player named Jimmy Frame leads most of his classmates to delinquency. Only two of Jimmy's peers have redeeming qualities and actually care about their health. Most of the rest skip lessons, arrive late, sleep through the workouts, or loaf around the weight room.

This isn't what I signed up for.

I told Poppa Wib how disillusioned I feel about the teaching profession. He keeps telling me, "Just survive the first year." All I wanted to do yesterday was sob in his arms like I did when he told me my mom died. Hope things are better with you.

Love, Chud

XOXOXOXOXO

Sunday, October 18

Eric phoned me from Alice Springs, in the outback, at 4 AM, oblivious to the time zone difference. Dad woke me up, not thinking to tell Eric he could phone me back. Normally I'd be infuriated, but the whole teacher evaluation debacle had resurrected my insomnia. Hearing from an old friend was a welcome distraction.

D'Souza called from his cell while waiting for the bus to Ayers Rock. He plans to do a training run around the iconic nine-kilometre sandstone formation tomorrow morning. Normal human beings would take a standard walking tour of Uluru with the Aborigines. However, I wish I was running with him, and I wish I'd written the Hannu Mikkola entrance essay for myself.

After the call, Poppa Wib tried to make me feel better, even saying I could aim golf balls at him while he drove the ball piker at work. We settled for an afternoon matinee and saw *Rush Hour* with Jackie Chan and Chris Tucker. It was a hoot. Better still was the preview for the new Star Wars movie. I've waited nearly sixteen years since *Return of the Jedi*.

Monday, October 19

I hunted down Noose-Neck after school to discuss the scathing performance report he gave me. We sat in his office. I resisted my urges to grab some of his candy and choke him to death.

"Carlson," said Noose-Neck, "do sit down." His brimming ego overflowed more than the fat around his neck.

Dispensing with any pleasantries, I waved my evaluation in the air, and asked, "Wasn't I supposed to receive notice about this?"

"And what is *this*?" Smug bastard knew exactly what I meant.

"My evaluation," I asserted. "You picked me apart, you showed up without warning, you—"

"Stop," he said, raising his hand. "You see, this is where we get frustrated; I put a notice in your mailbox on the first day of school."

"How can you say that? I didn't have a mailbox on the first day of school!"

"Yes, you did. You had Janis McKee's box."

"What? You never told me that. You gave me three class lists and two keys on the first day. You never mentioned a teacher evaluation."

"I never said I *told* you there was an evaluation. I told you I put the notice in your mailbox."

"You're being unfair—"

"Am I?"

"And you've just contradicted yourself."

"How so?"

"First, you said the notice was in Janis McKee's mailbox, and then your next statement referred to the box as my mailbox."

"Semantics, Carlson." He took a candy from his tray and removed the wrapper. "Tell me, when you finally determined that her box was actually yours, did you not see a teacher evaluation notice?" He popped the candy into his mouth.

Pausing, I did remember an evaluation notice, but not for me. "It was addressed to Janis."

"There. You should have assumed the notice was transferable to you."

"Kelly'd just hired me the day before. It was the first day of my career! You think I was supposed to figure all this out?"

He deflected the question. "I warned Kelly not to hire you. If you weren't the son of Wilbur Veitch, she wouldn't have given you a second look."

"Don't bring my father into this."

"Fine, but the fact remains, you are an incompetent teacher, and my evaluation correctly reflects this."

"How dare you." I almost broke down. I wanted to attack Noose-Neck like a homicidal maniac. "All of my assessments in teachers' college were positive." His phone rang.

"Clearly, they were mistaken."

"You caught me at my worst and only when the kids were misbehaving—"

Noose-Neck answered the phone. "Mr. Damian Glenn speaking. Can you hold a moment?" Then he turned to me. "I'm sorry, Carlson, but we'll have to continue this discussion another time."

I've made an appointment with my therapist for Saturday.

Tuesday, October 20

Andrew Yates's tabby cat got stuck in the heating grate today. After his biology presentation on cats, he asked if "Jarman" could walk freely for the remaining twenty minutes of class rather than be relegated to his cage. I naively agreed. None of us noticed the obese feline wandering off during little Donna McLean's obsessively thorough presentation on fungal reproduction. When some of the class awoke to applause, and perhaps relief, at the conclusion of Donna's seminar (even I thought it was too long), the stupid furball began a piercing meow.

The kids throw contraband candy and snacks behind the heating grate when they feel me approaching. I'm sure Jarman was after the remnants. Or possibly the overweight tabby spotted a mouse? Kipling Secondary is getting old.

Nonetheless, the clapping must have frightened him, and no amount of bribing with kitty treats convinced Jarman to relax and squish his way out. Mortified, I contacted administration. Noose-Neck brought Jozef, who said another swear word in Polish. They unscrewed the grate from the brick wall and let Jarman out.

He was completely unharmed. However, the students let out a wild ovation for his rescue, and Jarman got spooked again. The dim-witted tabby left a small fecal deposit on top of the food remnants he'd so foolishly pursued.

Noose-Neck wasn't pleased.

The bell rang. "Don't forget to put the stools up!" I shouted to my students. Only a few students complied.

Noose-Neck said to me, "I see your class management skills have improved. I have better things to do than rescue tabby cats from water grates."

"I'd like you to re-evaluate me," I stated to him. "Give me another chance, with fair warning."

"I'm sorry," he answered, "but I can't do that."

"Then you need to change at least two things."

"Really, and why is that?"

"First of all, I am organized."

I showed him my day-by-day semester plans. Initially, he was nonplussed: perhaps my organization had taken him aback? After flipping through a few pages, he responded.

"Carlson, you must be flexible with teenagers. It appears as if you started off organized but are now unable to adapt to the children's needs."

"I also coach cross-country running, but you state that I'm not involved with extracurricular."

"Fine," he said. "I'll change that one." Noose-Neck walked out the door.

"*Co osiot*," said Jozef, looking at Noose-Neck.

I looked up the English translation of "*Co osiot*" on the Internet. Jozef must have assumed I understood that it meant "What an ass" and that he was referring to Noose-Neck. I have an ally against my nemesis! If only I knew more Polish.

Wednesday, October 21

Our dank, cramped basement science office used to be the girls' change room when Kipling Secondary was only one floor. Across the hall, the boys' change room now stores the chemistry supplies. Biology and environmental science materials are located on the second floor, and physics equipment is on the third.

I was at school early, fiddling with the electromagnet lab I had planned. No amount of tinkering could get the stupid magnets to work. Sara waddled in just before 8 AM, the odour of her newest fragrance preceding her.

All I could think about was how much I hated my job, so when Sara asked how I was, I became teary-eyed, spilling my guts about Noose-Neck's evaluation and my cynicism with the profession.

"Whenever I have a bad day," she said, "I just think, 'In a few hours I'm going to go home and make love to my husband.'"

"But I don't have a husband!" I blurted out, before realizing what I'd said. We both snickered at this comment. I felt better.

Sara helped me fix the electromagnet and told me that Janis McKee may extend her stress leave. If so, Sara will recommend that I stay on for the second semester. In addition, she'll talk to Jane Crowley if Noose-Neck doesn't give me a second chance.

The New York Yankees won the World Series today, completing their sweep of the San Diego Padres.

Thursday, October 22

The game: Wolf Prowl
The place: Heart Lake Conservation Area
The contestants: Mr. Veitch's Grade 10 science class
The champion and new record holder: Mr. Carlson Veitch
"Basically, the rabbits and deer search the conservation area for food and water tags while avoiding the wolves," explained Amanda, our group leader at the ecology centre. We were there for the day, with much of the morning spent playing Wolf Prowl.

She continued, "You win by collecting the most points. Herbivores get five points per food or water tag collected. Wolves earn points by touching a deer or a rabbit. If touched, herbivores must surrender one of their three meat tags, each worth ten points, to the hungry wolf. Wolves cannot catch the same meal twice in a row. If the herbivores run out of tags, they die. Donna and your teacher are the two wolves."

After a three-minute head start, Donna and I began the hunt. She found a tree with seven food tags and hid nearby amongst some fallen leaves, ready to pounce. My strategy was not so subtle: I simply chased after my prey until I caught them. Within thirty minutes, my point total was 220 and I'd caught everyone at least once, except Chad.

This boy actually ran like a deer. I chased him for at least five minutes before catching a break. It must have been longer, mind you, because by the time we reached the beach area, Andrew Yates knew I'd been chasing Chad toward the water and had gathered most of the class to watch.

"Go Sparrow!" the kids screamed (the kids tease Chad because his legs are as thin as a sparrow's). "Don't let Mr. Veitch catch you."

Chad lost a shoe in a puddle but kept running. I was within three metres. He ran a zigzag pattern. I lunged but must have missed by mere millimetres.

"Sparrow! Sparrow! Sparrow!" the kids chanted in cult-like fashion.

I dove at Chad and missed again, this time somersaulting onto the packed beach sand, splashing mud pellets on the frenzied crowd.

"Ohhhhhhh," they hummed in unison.

I finished my roll and landed on two feet. Surprised, Chad made his last play. His only escape route was to run into the water and hope I wouldn't follow.

Clever little bastard.

Refusing to submit, I sprinted after him. I knew from the Orillia triathlon that the key to a beach start was high knees. So I skipped over as much water as possible and finally tagged my prey.

"Boooooooooo!" murmured the crowd. Chad gave me the tag. I felt like the ultimate wrestling heel, Chairman Vince McMahon, and held the tag high, like a championship belt, to the menacing crowd.

"Boooooooo!"

I took a bow.

"Boooooooo!"

I shook Chad's hand and invited him to join the cross-country team.

"Do I get to miss school?" he asked.

"Ten minutes left!" we heard Amanda bellow.

"Next week is the big race—you'll miss most of the day," I said.

"Cool," said Chad.

"And if you do well there, the school will pay for a hotel room for you at OFSAA."

"What's OFSAA?"

"Provincial championships. I'll tell you more on the bus ride home."

Mr. Veitch wasn't finished with the rest of the class. I splashed my way out of the water and tagged more prey on the beach. Akeel did a face plant before losing his last tag to me. Bug-eyed Zoey (I think she has a thyroid condition) squealed before submitting. Even Andrew Yates screamed, and in a higher pitch than anyone. I doubled the previous record, finishing with 540 points.

Over lunch, gossip circulated that I had a tattoo. I neither confirmed nor denied the rumours. Instead, I chuckled. I was both amused by how fascinated the kids were about this mystery and confounded as to who would create such a story.

We spent the afternoon analyzing marsh water. Chad kept falling asleep, and Donna, his microscope partner, kept poking him awake. I suppose that examining amoebae, paramecia, and other protists isn't quite as exciting as having your Grade 10 science teacher chase you into a lake.

Andrew Yates livened the mood. He pricked himself with God-knows-what and then made a microscope slide with a couple of drops of his blood.

"That's so cool," said Akeel, looking at the dancing erythrocytes.

"Lemme see! Lemme see!" said students in a gathering crowd.

Was this a teachable moment, or should I discipline Andrew for his impulsive act?

I decided on both. When the erythrocytes stopped moving, the crowd dispersed, and the class resumed their boring search for single-celled creatures.

Amanda concluded the afternoon with a showing of her pet snake, Reggie, who was nearly five feet long. Amanda showed us Reggie's recently shed skin and reviewed the anatomy of the creature.

"Can I hold him?" asked Andrew.

Amanda instructed, "Just be careful of his—"

"—cloaca, I know. It's very sensitive."

Friday, October 23

Classes were a zoo today! Anytime I miss a day, I come back and have to potty train them all over. Worse, I received the following notes about yesterday:

From Mrs. Malone who covered period one: "Jimmy Frame went AWOL."

From mystery supply teacher who covered period four: "Marco and Julio sent to office for throwing badminton racquets: Class was barely tolerable after that."

Jamal told me his journals had gone missing yesterday.

Bill 160 officially passed into law today. Our existing teacher contracts become null and void on February 1, 1999. If I do get my contract extended or get another job in a different school board, I'll likely be teaching four out of four. About the only good thing is that my class sizes should decrease.

Saturday, October 24

"Fear manifests when one feels out of control," said Ronda. "That's all it is."

Sipping on chamomile tea, Ronda and I reviewed strategies on how to diffuse my growing anxiety. We sat near the expansive bay window of her living room. Soothing my frayed nerves was the bright afternoon sun. Ronda, now in her sixties, was marvelously fit. The English woman suffered from panic attacks for eight years before recovering. At one point, she was afraid to leave her house.

Since Mom's death, I've had periodic battles with anxiety. Once, after watching *The Terry Fox Story*, I was afraid for three months that I would get cancer. A couple of years later, Kate forced me to watch the thriller *Jagged Edge*; after that I was afraid I'd turn into a murderer. The psychiatrists did little for me, especially as a teen. All they'd do is prescribe Prozac and benzodiazepines (BZs) and tell me to come back in two months. The Prozac helped a little, but I was afraid of becoming addicted to the BZs so I rarely took them—only if I was having a massive panic attack.

I've been seeing Ronda for nearly ten years.

"You won't die, I promise you," said Ronda. "You won't lose control. You won't go crazy."

"But what if—"

"Retrain yourself to let go. If you're out of shape for running, it never takes as long to get back into shape, does it?"

"No."

"This is no different."

Ronda told me to lie down and practice my breathing exercises. "In for five seconds, hold for five seconds, out for five seconds." After practicing, she made me write down the following:

"Holding breath increases CO_2 $\rightarrow$ increased CO_2 slows the CNS."

"Let it come, then let it go."

"I watched my mother wither away and die. If I survived that as a seven-year-old, I can survive Noose-Neck, Jimmy Frame, and Marco Costa. I can survive being without Lisa. I can survive anything."

<u>Sunday, October 25</u>

D'Souza phoned to say he's started surfing lessons along the Gold Coast. Nice life.

Meanwhile, I'm playing peacemaker again. Dad phoned Kate to ask if she is coming home for Christmas. Kate hinted that the answer was no, and then their conversation degraded into another argument about Mom.

About the only good thing that came out of this was that Dad actually opened up to me about Mom's death. Mom died because the formaldehyde outgassing from UFFI (Urea Formaldehyde Foam Insulation) destroyed her health. That much I knew. However, Dad told me why they had put the UFFI in the house in the first place.

In the late '70s, the Canadian government was in an energy crisis and promoted UFFI with tax incentives. Since we'd just moved into Mom's dream home—a wood-framed century home with no insulation—we took the tax break. However, on December 17, 1980, barely a year after heavily promoting the product, Canada banned UFFI installation because of its potential for toxic outgassing. We were never informed by the government or Rowland Insulation, the company who installed the insulation, and thus didn't know that UFFI was causing Mom's rapidly diminishing health.

<u>Monday, October 26</u>

Jimmy Frame told me to fuck off today. The oversized clown arrived to my Grade 12 fitness class thirty minutes late, hat on sideways and jeans halfway down his ass.

"Can I have the keys to the change room, Mr. Veitch?" asked the colossus.

"Good morning, Jimmy," I responded. "You'll need to remove your hat and pull up your pants."

How does he waddle around "low-riding" his pants like that, let alone get up the stairs without them falling down and exposing his crotch? I can understand wearing baggy clothes, dying hair green, and body piercing, but this phenomenon of boys having their rear ends stick out is beyond my comprehension; it just can't be comfortable.

"Come on, sir, I just got here," whined number eleven, the starting centre of the basketball team. "Gimme the keys."

Holding breath increases CO_2 $\rightarrow$ increased CO_2 slows the CNS.

Refusing to be intimidated, I repeated, "Take off your hat and pull up your jeans."

"You're mean, sir," boomed Jimmy in his baritone voice, all the while tugging on his ridiculously long red goatee. He took off his hat, revealing a shaved white head.

"Pull up your pants!"

"They're called jeans, sir," replied the cue ball, now attracting the attention of a couple of students in the class. Jimmy pulled up his "jeans" half an inch, as if to comply. "That good enough?"

"All the way up, past your waist." The big thug yanked his pants past his nipples, like an elderly man with a beach ball belly at Sunnyside Care Centre. He waved to his other goon friends inside the class.

"They're past my waist, sir." Jimmy's attention-seeking behaviour was working, as half the class had stopped their abdominal crunches and begun to howl at number eleven's antics. "Can I have the keys now?"

Choosing to pick another battle, I took number eleven outside the classroom, effectively removing him from his audience. His training journals were a week late, and I asked for them again. After ruffling through his disheveled knapsack and then dumping its entire contents on the hallway floor, Jimmy eventually produced a pristine blue Duo-tang and tossed it to me.

He could have at least copied them in his own handwriting, but I guess that takes too much effort for a lazy plagiarist. Jamal, my top student, had reminded me this morning that his journals had gone missing before the weekend. Jimmy merely used white correction fluid to remove the two "A"s and one "L" from Jamal's name and replaced them to make "Jimmy."

I confronted the big thug: "This isn't your work."

"You accusing me of lying?"

"Yes, Jimmy. You didn't even use the same colour to replace the letters of Jamal's name. How dumb do you think I am?"

"Fuck off, sir."

Let it come. Let it go.

I buzzed Mrs. Smith to let her know I'd sent Jimmy to the office.

I can't help but contrast my miserable teaching situation with the joy of overseas adventure that Lisa, Eric, and Teagan must be feeling. I envision, for example, Teagan sitting around a fire in Nepal, drinking yak milk, while groping some gorgeous native women. Meanwhile, Lisa loves her teaching job in Peru, and Eric's learning how to surf in Australia. Why am I here?

Tuesday, October 27

Jimmy wasn't in class today, so I assume Noose-Neck suspended him for the mandatory three days. Marco, therefore, was the only pain in the ass I had to deal with.

The little pinhead was late, as usual; forgot his gym uniform, as usual; and didn't follow instructions, as usual. However, it didn't bother me too much because I wanted to laugh every time I looked at his new hairstyle. Marco had dyed his hair blonde and gotten a perm. It looked like he was wearing a wig made of fusilli pasta. Even Julio was amused.

Today was also the Metro cross-country finals. Unfortunately, Noose-Neck didn't let me go, letting Lauren supervise because there were only six competing athletes. Stanley and Edward gave me the news after returning to school. Both twins placed in the top twenty for junior boys. Melissa, for the first time this season, finished the race and even beat three other girls. Stephanie won the senior girls race and will join Shauna (fourth in midget girls) and Chad (fifth in junior boys) at OFSAA on November 7. I don't owe anyone pizza.

E-mail from Teagan:
(He's using this new free e-mail service called Hotmail.)

```
Carl,
What the @#$@# are you still
doing there? I'm surrounded by
beautiful Nepalese lassies,
drinking yak's milk by a fire.
Why don't you quit your job and
join me in Lhasa? I'll be there
next week. Think of all the
Tibetan lassies we could meet!
Cheers mate,
Teags
```

Wednesday, October 28

Apparently, Noose-Neck feels that, rather than a suspension, it's more appropriate that Jimmy merely write an apology:

Sorry for ~~swering~~ swearing and cheating Mr. Veech. I promise it will never ever happen again.
JIMMY.F. #11 #11 #11

Therefore, instead of being suspended yesterday, Noose-Neck had Jimmy in his office, munching on candy and writing this Pulitzer Prize–winning confession. You'd think that Noose-Neck would at least make the brute learn to spell my name right!

I wish Bill Parsons was responsible for the entire alphabet of students, instead of just the second half, or better still, that Mrs. Turner, who hired me, hadn't retired and Noose-Neck didn't exist.

Thursday, October 29

During my prep, I confronted Noose-Neck in his office. I wanted to know why he felt an apology letter from Jimmy was a sufficient consequence when the staff handbook mandates a three-day suspension. Noose-Neck said Jimmy wasn't suspended because of "family problems." I had no retort at the time, even though I felt this argument was inadequate. I just took a candy off his desk and left.

1 AM
My thoughts wander in circles. I worry that teaching will always be like this.

1:35 AM
I'm downstairs now, watching wrestling on TSN. I'd forgotten how much fun it is to observe grown men beat each other to a pulp. Moments ago, for example, much to the dismay of the crowd, The Rock dropped a theatrical "Corporate Elbow" on the pudgy face of announcer Jim Ross. Then, Stone Cold Steve Austin ran down the ramp to Ross's aid and kicked The Rock in the jewels before giving him a neck-crushing move called "The Stunner." Now, Austin is giving everyone in the crowd the finger. It must be a salute because the audience is cheering.

Finally, then, I have some solutions to my problems:

1. Give Jimmy the Corporate Elbow.
2. Give Noose-Neck the Stone Cold Stunner.

Friday, October 30

Halloween costume day

I dressed up as a student today, mocking the boys who "low-ride" their pants. How they manage locomotion is still a mystery. I couldn't walk two steps without my jeans falling to the floor. With this in mind, I wore suspenders and decided that boxers would be better than briefs.

Lauren was dressed as Catwoman. We were both checking our mailboxes in the staffroom when I first viewed her sexy costume. One look at her shapely body created a half-mast down below. Hopefully, Lauren didn't notice I was "happy to see her."

The most popular student costume was that of Buffy the Vampire Slayer. Thank God there was only one girl dressed as Xena. This outfit showed a lot of leg and thus, wherever the warrior princess walked, a trail of panting boys followed.

Even Jimmy wore a costume, dressing as some sort of Dutch opera freak. Noisy Dutch clogs adorned his size-seventeen feet, his hideous red goatee was braided, and he wore a clown wig on his melon.

Jimmy noticed my outfit and was quite amused. "Yo, sir! Sweet costume," he said, before clonking off down the hallway. Does this mean he likes me now? Does this mean he'll stop acting like such a turd?

Andrew Yates arrived to science class dressed as a mummy. Most of his torso and his entire right arm were covered in duct tape. Tensor bandages enveloped the rest of his body. Fearing the duct tape around his chest would make the boy overheat and die, I told Andrew to remove it. I couldn't handle explaining another strange incident to admin. If Andrew really wanted authenticity, I was willing to lend him more tensor bandages from the PE department.

Chad and Daniel, dressed as mustard and relish containers, asked to help Andrew. When will I learn? They must have been there when Andrew had wrapped his arm. They knew that beneath the duct tape was a layer of gauze Andrew had hastily applied. Some of the duct tape, therefore, was attached to Andrew's bare skin. Chad and Daniel tore a few strips off Andrew's forearms. In the process, they ripped some of Andrew's forearm hair directly from the follicles, leaving the poor boy in considerable discomfort.

Andrew's eyes watered, and he screamed like a girl at a horror flick.

The class erupted with laughter.

"That's how it feels when we wax," said Donna.

Saturday, October 31

My intention was to win money to fund my trip to Peru. Thus, I forbade Rick, Megan, and Derek from feeding me cheap Casino Rama alcohol. It would only cloud my judgment.

Rick and I played blackjack, while Megan and Derek preferred the slots. After an hour, I was up $50. They changed the dealer on me, so I switched to an adjacent table.

This table also offered a bonus game called Lucky Sevens. Hit a 7 and the house pays 7 to 1; hit 2 and it pays 70 to 1; hit 3 and it pays 700 to 1. All this for an extra Toonie. The odds of hitting triple seven are 2,197 to 1, so I decided that a 700 to 1 payout made no mathematical sense. I refused to play Lucky Sevens.

The elderly ladies sandwiched between Rick and me became apoplectic when I hit a triple seven. They'd been paying the extra Toonie for a couple of hours and had never even hit a double seven. Had I ignored my logic and thrown in the extra two bucks, I would have won $1,400, enough money to cover all meals, accommodations, and tour guides in Peru.

To celebrate my misfortune, I drank two beers. After Derek won $500 playing slots, I drank four more. Don't remember much after that.

NOVEMBER

How was I supposed to predict that a bumblebee would create such a commotion?

<u>Sunday, November 1</u>

My hangover is vicious. I feel like Eeyore from Winnie the Pooh; it's as if a rain cloud follows me around the house.

I wish there was a Lino's in Etobicoke like there was in Kingston. Back at Queen's, on the rare occasions Eric and I drank too much, the one hundred grams or so of triglycerides from a Lino's poutine was a more effective hangover treatment than any prescription pain medication. The fat seemed to settle our stomachs and soften our foul moods.

<u>Monday, November 2</u>

"Our dear principal is just protecting his assets," said Gary. I spoke with the old bear at lunch, detailing my frustrations about how Noose-Neck mishandled the Jimmy Frame issue.

He continued, "If Damian suspended Jimmy, that would make his star centre ineligible to play basketball. I want you to know that I don't agree with his decision, and Damian's gonna hear about it from me. Your dad would never have put up with this shit from an athlete or an administrator, so neither will I."

Speaking of Jimmy, he wasn't in fitness class today, and the other students were quite pleasant. I actually had fun and was able to join in the weight-lifting circuit instead of policing the room.

In contrast, half the students in my Grade 10 science class were incapable of quiet, independent work. Apparently having a major presentation next week does little to create a sense of urgency.

I wanted to yell "Shut up!" at the top of my voice. However, I held back, taking my father's advice: "The number-one rule of teaching is to remain calm."

<u>Tuesday, November 3</u>

Noose-Neck muttered something to me in the hall today. I think it was, "Fight your own battles, Princess," so I guess Gary had a talk with him. I was running late for my Grade 10s, so I chose to ignore the slur and walk away.

The students kept chit-chatting, so I thought, *Screw Dad's advice*, and yelled "Shut up!" at the top of my lungs. No one said a peep after that. I guess Poppa Wib was wrong.

Jesse Ventura won the Minnesota gubernatorial election. Thus, an independent candidate and a former professional wrestler will soon rule the North Star State.

<u>Wednesday, November 4</u>

My Grade 12s were too chatty in the health room today. I yelled "Shut up!" at the top of my lungs, but this time it backfired. Jimmy and his posse broke into fits of laughter, and even Steph and Jamal appeared to be suppressing giggles. Maybe Poppa Wib was right after all.

Lauren told me that Jimmy Frame is from an affluent family and his parents are "enablers." Thus, whenever a teacher or administrator contacts home, Jimmy's parents defend him with an angry diatribe. Lauren knows firsthand because she ran into a problem with Jimmy last month.

Jimmy kept staring at her breasts in class and, consequently, she sent him to the hall. On his way out, Jimmy gestured to his friends that he was grabbing Lauren's boobs. Therefore, Lauren sent Jimmy to see Noose-Neck and followed up with an incident report and a phone call to Mr. and Mrs. Frame. Noose-Neck gave no consequences, and Jimmy's parents stated that the fondling gesture could not be proven. Jimmy denied ever doing it, and none of the boys who witnessed the gesture would fess up. Worse, Jimmy's parents insinuated that Lauren was dressed "too provocatively."

Lauren concluded, "Jimmy's story to Mr. Glenn about 'family problems' is fabricated. He knows that if our dear Mr. Glenn were to question the issue with his parents, Mr. Glenn would get an earful and would ultimately bow to the pressure of Mr. and Mrs. Frame."

Thursday, November 5

I dreamt that Lauren was my science teacher and that she dressed provocatively. This blissful image, combined with Jimmy skipping class this morning, helped to make the day pass quickly.

Friday, November 6

Drive to OFSAA

Stupid "Tubthumping" song from Chumbawamba. I can't get the chorus out of my head. It came on the radio after we stopped for dinner in Kingston. The kids sang it all the way to Pembroke.

"Oh, I love this song," said Shauna.

"I get knocked down, but I get up again. You're never gonna keep me down!" sang Lauren.

"I hate this song," I said. "It was released over a year ago and it's still overplayed."

"I get knocked down, but I get up again. You're never gonna keep me down!" sang Shauna even louder.

Soon, the twins, Steph, and Melissa joined in. Chad slept through the whole ruckus.

"I get knocked down, but I get up again. You're never gonna keep me down!"

Melissa and the twins, though they didn't qualify, had come on the adventure just to support Steph, Chad, and Shauna. Lauren's father's van held eight passengers, and Gary said it was okay provided they chip in for gas and accommodations. The PE department is paying for coaches and qualifiers.

The hotel

After settling in, everyone went for a swim. Everyone, that is, except for Lauren. I was hoping to see her voluptuous body in a bathing suit, but instead she sat poolside and completed her marking.

When she glanced up, I made sure to flex my abs, in case she looked in my direction. After a while, though, Lauren got so immersed in her marking that she didn't look up at all. I got her attention by splashing some water on her. Unfortunately, most of the splash landed on the lab reports Lauren was correcting. She was not amused.

"Holy darn, which one of you did this?" Lauren screamed.

All the kids pointed to me.

"Mr. Veitch, this is your doing?"

"Uh, sorry, yes, it was me," I replied, my posture shrinking.

Melissa commentated, "Mr. Veitch is now receiving the famous Ms. Weeks evil death stare." The kids laughed.

"I think I'll just go to my room, then, to finish," snipped Lauren.

"I'm really sorry."

"Don't be surprised if I make you dry out the pages with clothespins and a blow dryer."

Lauren packed up her things and left the pool area.

"Mr. Veitch is in the sin bin," said Melissa.

"If you're trying to impress a woman, that's not the way to do it," said Steph. "I don't think she noticed your abs either."

Shit!

"Mr. Veitch is blushing," said Melissa.

"Shut up, Melissa!" I yelled. She giggled.

I swam underwater until I was certain I wasn't blushing anymore. When I came up, I apologized to Melissa for telling her to shut up and asked her for some pointers on my front crawl technique. Melissa is a competitive swimmer. I swam a couple of lengths.

"It's a miracle you don't drown, sir," she said. "You're kicking from your knees instead of your hips, and your head is too high. That's why you plow through the water."

I swam a few more lengths. This time, my head was lower and I could feel my bum out of the water. I couldn't figure out the kicking thing, mind you.

Chad and the girls retired to their respective rooms. Meanwhile, Stanley, Edward, and I commenced a hunt for earthworms.

On Monday, we're dissecting them in science class. This weekend's homework, therefore, is for each student to capture at least one lowly worm. In doing so, the students learn an awful lot about stimulus and response. An earthworm will sense the slightest vibration on grass and slip to safety in a fraction of a second. I was not so naïve, however, to believe that every student would catch his or her own worm—hence the reason for my hunting in the first place.

Stanley caught the first worm. The trick, he said, was to pin down one end with a thumb before the worm tries to squeeze down its tunnel. Then, you pull the rest of the body out. With this advice, Edward soon pinned down his first catch. However, when he pulled the tail out, the worm stretched too far and broke in half.

Steph came out to say good night and recognized what we were doing. "I see you still have an obsession with worms, sir," she said. "Good night."

Saturday, November 7

OFSAA cross-country

It's always a thrill to feel the rumbling vibration as 250 runners zoom past you. This effect was somewhat tainted during the boys' races because they all stank of B.O. The girls, in contrast, had no such effect because they always smelled like bubble gum.

Steph placed a disappointing eighty-first in the senior girls race, Shauna fifty-eighth in the midget girls, and Chad, the sparrow-legged beast, was our top finisher, placing thirty-first—not bad for three weeks of training. The kid must have a naturally high VO$_2$ (delivery rate of oxygen).

Back in Toronto, Lauren and I discovered that the worms had spilled in the trunk of the van. With all the shuffling of luggage, they must have escaped. The vehicle stinks. Lauren is pissed. So am I. Now I have to catch twenty-eight new worms tomorrow.

Sunday, November 8

I figured the morning dew would be prime picking time, so I woke up at 6 AM to hunt for worms. After an hour, I'd only caught two, so I asked Derek, a fisherman, for the location of the nearest bait shop. He told me that Bob's Fishing doesn't sell worms at this time of the year and that Nibbles is closed because it's Sunday.

I confessed my plight to Poppa Wib, who, after some belly laughs, helped me in the hunt. We even watered the lawn, but this didn't bring many to the surface. We only caught two. After dinner, we went out using flashlights. This time, Dad caught seven and I caught one. I'm twenty short then, so if the damn kids don't bring in their own tomorrow, they'll just have to share.

Monday, November 9

Only Donna McLean finished her homework. In fact, she dug up a dozen worms, bringing the class total to twenty-two worms for thirty-one students. I reviewed *Lumbricus terrestris* anatomy with them.

Andrew was confused when I explained that earthworms are hermaphrodites.

"What's a hermaphrodite, sir?" he asked.

"Something with male and female parts," whispered Donna.

"Huh?" said Andrew. "You mean they have a dick and a twat?"

The class erupted into laughter. *Here we go again.*

"Just like you," said Chad.

"Shut up, Sparrow!"

"Andrew! Chad!" I yelled. "Out to the hall!" The boys obeyed.

The remaining students calmed down enough for me to demonstrate dissection procedures. Then, I slipped out to lecture Andrew and Chad about their inappropriate language. They apologized, but I still assigned extra cleanup duty. I grouped them with Donna and divided the remaining students into pairs.

Twenty minutes later, the stench was overpowering, worse than a miasmic Eric D'Souza fart. We opened both doors, which helped, but loitering students from other classes kept poking their heads inside so I shut the doors and opened three windows. Two others didn't have screens, but I stupidly opened them anyway.

How was I supposed to predict that a bumblebee would create such a commotion? The insect floated into Room 213, unaware it had seconds to live.

"I don't have my EpiPen, sir!" cried Daniel. "If it bites me, I'll swell up and die!" He rolled his lab report into a tube and then took a mighty swing, one that would make homerun king Mark McGwire proud, sending the bee hurtling toward the front of the class. It ricocheted off my blackboard and then landed on my attendance binder. *Bzzzzzttt. Bzzzztttt. Bbzt.* Daniel sprinted to my desk and squashed the bee with three more thumps of his lab report. "Die, die, die!" he bellowed.

"Danny, I think it's dead," said Andrew. "You killed Mr. Veitch's binder, too."

"Sorry about your binder, sir," said Daniel. "I promise I'll buy you a new one."

"We'll speak after class," I said.

"Yes sir."

Thank God that's over.

I should have shut the unscreened windows.

"Andrew and Chad!" I screamed. "What the hell are you doing?" By this time, Andrew's worm was already in a parabolic free fall to the ground. Mind you, I suppose this particular *Lumbricus* was happy since a soft landing on the grass was preferable to death by dissection.

Chad froze, his worm dangling between a thumb and a slender index finger. Chad's worm curled into a ball. Andrew poked Chad. Chad dropped the creature.

Andrew peeked out the window, turned around to face the class, and then covered his mouth in a weak attempt to stifle laughter. Other students rushed to the windows and looked down to see what the fuss was about. They too reacted with concealed giggles.

"What?" I yelled. "What did you do?" The class was silent, sensing my fury. I raced to one window and looked down. Beneath us was Mrs. Malone, working on the yearbook. She became editor after Janis McKee went on stress leave.

Chad's worm had landed in Mrs. Malone's wild, curly hairdo. However, she just sat there by the picnic table, examining photos, oblivious to the worm now crawling through her untamed locks.

Oh shit.

I pulled my head back inside, slid down the back wall, and covered my eyes with my palms.

Noose-Neck will kill me if he finds out.

Sixty-two teenage eyeballs stared at me, anticipating my rage.

Serves her right, I thought. *Her hair looks like a bird's nest.*

I snorted. Unsure if this was my emotions turning rabid or me snickering in laughter, the kids remained silent.

If the old bag had left me a seating plan and some clear instructions when I covered her class, I might feel sorry for her about this.

Andrew, Chad, and Donna sensed I was about to rupture.

"He's gonna crack," said Andrew.

I couldn't hold it anymore. I knew it was unprofessional, but I couldn't help myself. I started into a frenzied laugh. It was infectious. My students exploded into fits of hysteria.

Every time I stopped, I'd catch a goofy smile on someone's face and then I'd burst again.

I have no idea how I'm going to handle this one.

Andrew, Chad, and Daniel's antics earned them a detention.

"But I have a bus to catch!" cried Daniel.

"No, you don't," said Andrew. "You walk home with us."

"You're such a rat!"

"It's settled, then," I said.

While the boys scrubbed benches and blackboards, I phoned their parents and somehow detailed the incidents without laughter. Andrew's mom demanded that she speak with him. Daniel, Chad, and I could hear Mrs. Yates screaming at Andrew over the phone.

"I'm grounded for a month, sir," said Andrew.

I repeated the process with Daniel and Chad.

"I got a week," said Chad.

"Me, too," said Daniel.

Now everything will be fine so long as no one tells Mrs. Malone.

Tuesday, November 10

Noose-Neck didn't haul me into his office, so I don't think anyone told Mrs. Malone.

11:51 PM

I just opened an e-mail from Teagan to see a picture of his scrawny, pasty-white arse running naked across some Himalayan trail. Beneath the jpeg was this message:

Flying from Katmandu to Lhasa (Tibet) tomorrow

And I'm stuck here dealing with worms.

Wednesday, November 11

Remembrance Day

Neither Marco nor Julio kept quiet during the minute of silence. Therefore, I kept both hooligans after class. The punishment was to stare at each other for one minute without laughing. Marco thought it would be easy, but he failed. Julio wasn't much better. After a few minutes, Marco said, "Screw this, I've got a bus to catch" and walked out.

Julio stayed back—a breakthrough—despite Marco's pressuring him to do otherwise.

I shook Julio's hand and wrote up an incident report for Marco.

3:31 AM

I am ravaged with guilt about the Mrs. Malone worm incident. I must confess to her, or I'll never sleep again.

Thursday, November 12

9 AM

No word from Noose-Neck about Marco walking out on my detention.

11:01 AM

I passed Mrs. Malone in the hallway several times but was too chicken to come clean.

12:01pm

I went to Noose-Neck's office during lunch. At first, I didn't think he was there. However, I knocked and realized he was hiding around the corner. Perhaps I was hallucinating, but I think he was playing Solitaire on his computer. I told him about Marco walking out on my detention.

"Can't you handle that boy?" he asked.

"I can handle him," I said, "but when Marco refuses my consequence, I need backup."

"Did you phone Mr. Costa and let him know Marco would be late coming home?"

"Is it your expectation that I call parents before every detention?"

"The child might have a bus to catch."

"I happen to know Marco walks home."

"Fine, if he doesn't serve with you today, I'll double it."

"Thank you."

"I'm surprised you didn't go behind my back again and sic Uncle Gary on me."

I left his office.

3:00 PM

Marco refused to stay for his detention. I submitted a second incident report to Noose-Neck.

3:15 PM

I confessed to Mrs. Malone. I was afraid she'd pull a Marge Simpson and find something in her hairdo to attack me. However, the old bag was confused. I presume, then, that the worm must have ricocheted off her melon and then fallen to the ground. Either that or it formed a symbiotic relationship with her bird's nest. Regardless, I didn't stick around to elaborate.

5:58 PM

Finally left for home, though the mountain of marking still wasn't finished. I don't know why I spend so much time writing comments for my students. They never take my advice on how to improve anyway. Maybe if I reduced my standards and gave only multiple choice tests, I'd make my life easier.

Friday, November 13

Pisses me off—I'm always debriefing my Grade 9 boys when the damn PA beeps. Why does Bill Parsons make announcements with fifty-seven seconds left in the school day?

"Excuse the interruption, a couple of important announcements before you go home ..."

Collective sighs floated through the gymnasium. Gary, on the other side, looked ready to throw a basketball at the speaker.

" Remember that next week is parent-teacher interviews and, uh ..."

The bell rang, and the kids got up to leave.

" Please hold your classes until I finish this last announcement."

Gary didn't stop his Grade 11s from leaving, so I followed suit. I guess it's not wise to step in front of the mob. Bill's final announcement was inaudible.

No word from Noose-Neck about Marco.

I can retire with full pension on June 20, 2031. My letter from OTTP (Ontario Teachers' Pension Plan) says so. Because of Noose-Neck, my real retirement date will likely be January 1999.

QECO (Qualifications Evaluation Council of Ontario) also sent me a letter. The bastards assessed me at A3 instead of A4. If I had P-J (Primary-Junior) qualifications or J-I (Junior-Intermediate) I'd be at A4. I'm qualified to teach I-S (Intermediate-Senior—Grades 7–OAC), but according to QECO, this puts me at A3. Therefore, I make $34,367 this year instead of $36,805, even though I have an honours degree and the same number of credits from teachers' college. I could use that extra two grand for anti–Noose-Neck therapy.

Michel Trudeau, son of former prime minister Pierre Trudeau, is feared dead after being trapped in an avalanche.

Saturday, November 14

Mountain of marking finished!

I celebrated by going to the movies with Rick. We saw Adam Sandler's new comedy, *The Waterboy*. I wish I could tackle my adversaries the way protagonist Bobby Boucher does in the movie. He uses his medulla oblongata quite effectively.

All I need to do tomorrow is calculate midterm averages. Poppa Wib suggested I used his "trusted" old 286, the DOS-based marking program on its hard drive, and the old dot-matrix printer. I told Dad his machine was "antiquated" and that he should finally learn how to use Windows 98 on my Pentium. I downloaded some freeware mark tabulation software from Tucows.com.

Michel Trudeau confirmed dead.

Sunday, November 15

11:57 PM

Stupid freeware grading program kept crashing so I had to calculate the old-fashioned way. I refused to swallow my pride and go the 286-DOS-dot-matrix route. What the hell, at least it's done now. All I need to do tomorrow is input the marks onto the school server and add the comment codes.

Monday, November 16

Are the morning announcements not long enough? Does Bill Parsons just like to hear his own Newfie accent? Even Steph and Jamal tune him out the moment his voice repeats what's just been said. Meanwhile, I'm forced to appear interested, thinking, *Stop blathering and let me start my lesson.*

Bill's rambling continued at the staff meeting. What a snore-fest. We wasted sixty-three minutes doing a Myers-Briggs personality study and only spent five minutes at the end discussing relevant issues such as consistency with tardy students.

Noose-Neck also clarified the Late Assignment Policy, insisting that students submit work on time even if they are away for sports tournaments. "Students are not to compete if they can't submit work to teachers on time. Students can get a friend or a parent or their coach to submit the work on the due date. Otherwise, it is a 20 percent penalty per day late, no exceptions." *One of the few things Noose-Neck has ever said that makes sense.*

After the meeting, I finished inputting my grades and comment codes on the school server. "Your kid's an asshole," was not an option, so Jimmy's and Marco's reports will read, "Must take studies more seriously" instead.

Tuesday, November 17

If Andrew ever has a psychotic episode and needs to be Tasered, the cops will find it ineffective. The boy took immense pleasure in being shocked by a Tesla coil. I brought out the machine after everyone in the class tried the Van de Graaff generator (a metal ball that creates static electricity and causes hair to stand on end). Andrew challenged Chad and Daniel to see who could take the most voltage. The "low" setting, which gives a shock one would receive after shuffling along a carpet and touching a metal doorknob, wasn't enough for them. It was like some sort of macho thing. Andrew ultimately won. The kid is like Frankenstein's monster.

Noose-Neck still hasn't addressed Marco's recent misbehavior. Marco, the little bastard, now rules the roost in my Grade 9 class because his father is oblivious and Noose-Neck doesn't support me.

<u>Wednesday, November 18</u>

I confronted Noose-Neck about Marco's misbehavior.

"If he does it again," said Noose-Neck, "I'll double it."

"You promised me that last week."

"Can't you see I'm swamped with paperwork?"

"Six days isn't enough time?"

"This is why we get frustrated; you'll just have to handle it yourself."

"You're supposed to back me up when I can't handle it!"

Noose-Neck unwrapped a candy and popped it into his mouth. He leaned back in his leather chair and put his hands behind his head.

"Exactly, you can't handle it. Therefore, you don't belong in this profession."

This slur caused my medulla oblongata to trigger thoughts of homicide. I retreated to the staff room for a time out.

Lauren noticed my tension, gave my shoulders a ten-second massage, and then patted me on the back. It was enough to get me through the day without becoming psychotic.

<u>Thursday, November 19</u>

Yesterday's Grade 10 science lesson was about the relationship between electricity and magnetism.

"Electromagnetism is how we power the grid"; "don't put a magnet near a videotape or a debit card because it can erase or alter the data"; and "a strong magnet placed close to a TV screen may permanently distort the picture" were some of my comments. This last one piqued Andrew's attention and brought a mischievous smile to his cherubic face.

The look worried me.

I was right to be anxious.

The bottom right hand corner of the science department television now has a permanent distortion in it. We noticed this while viewing a

Bill Nye the Science Guy video on magnetism. Bill's head became warped whenever he moved to the right of the screen.

Donna asked, "Is that what you meant yesterday?"

Andrew sank his head into his arms. After school, I confronted him. He admitted his guilt. I phoned his mom. She asked to speak to him.

"My mom says I have to pay for a new TV or pay for the repair out of my own pocket."

"Yeah, I got that," I said. "I could hear your mom screaming through the phone."

"If I can't do it by parent-teacher interviews next week, then I can't go to Whistler for Christmas. I'm really sorry, sir; I just wanted to see if it was true."

Impeachment hearings against Bill Clinton began today.

Friday, November 20

Lorraine Coulis, the ditzy redhead in my fitness class, hunted me down after school, perplexed as to why her midterm grade was in the single digits. I guess the fact that she'd only attended six classes had escaped her.

"But it's phys ed, sir!" pleaded Lorraine. "Nobody fails phys ed."

"What is this shit?" was Marco's reaction. "All the teachers in this school hate me." His fusilli hair is getting longer.

Mrs. Yates was more constructive. She wore a pantsuit, which did little to hide her pear-shaped figure.

"Andrew has ADHD," she said, "but that's absolutely not an excuse for any of this misbehavior." With tight, pulled-back black hair and a widow's peak, the woman reminded me of Dracula.

"I'm appalled. I'll sit down with Andrew every night until he pulls up his socks. And this television incident was the last straw."

I helped Andrew carry the broken TV from the dungeon to the elevator and then out the school and into the trunk of a posh SUV. It was a Hummer.

Saturday, November 21

Casino Niagara day trip
My gambling system failed. Let's just say I didn't anticipate black hitting seven times in a row on the roulette wheel. Prior to this, I was up $95 and feeling superior. After seven successive bets on red (doubling the amount each time), I was down $159. All this in a span of forty-five minutes.

I can't believe Derek kept winning on the blackjack tables. He didn't even know that "blackjack" meant twenty-one with a face card and an ace until Rick explained it to him. Though I'm unsure of the exact figure, Derek's earnings were enough to treat Megan, Rick, and me to steak dinner and a movie (*Enemy of the State*—a "Big Brother is watching you" flick). He also covered the fine for Megan's speeding ticket, earned on the way to the falls.

Sunday, November 22

Kate isn't coming home for Christmas. Dad is devastated but unsurprised. It's been the same story for years. Unless Poppa Wib and I fly west, we don't see her during the holidays.

Our family is divided.

Monday, November 23

Jimmy didn't submit his biomechanics project today. He's at a basketball tournament today and tomorrow. I've assigned the standard 20 percent penalty. Since my dear principal Noose-Neck is Jimmy's coach, he has to back me up.

A postcard from Lisa! On the front of the card is a picture of a capybara, an Amazon mammal and the largest rodent in the world.

Dear Chud,
I'm sorry to hear you're having a difficult time.
Damian Glenn sounds like a self-involved prick.
Just take it one day at a time and remember you'll
soon be in the Amazon rainforests of Peru.
    Love Lisa
    XO
P.S. Be sure to visit the travel clinic soon to get
your vaccinations.

Tuesday, November 24

Still no assignment from Jimmy; he's now lost 40 percent on his project.

No TV from Andrew either.

Wednesday, November 25

"But I was at a basketball tournament!" fumed Jimmy. "You can't dock me 40 percent—that's retarded."

"The rules are clear," I said. "Why don't you ask your coach if you don't believe me?"

He did. I wish I hadn't made the suggestion.

Noose-Neck soon confronted me in the hallway. About a dozen students, including Jimmy, listened in.

"Why did you give Jimmy the 40 percent penalty?" asked Noose-Neck.

"Uh, that's what you said to do at the last staff meeting," I replied. I was dumbfounded but now realize I shouldn't have been surprised.

"I told Jimmy he could submit the work today."

"But you said there were no exceptions."

"Mr. Veitch, Jimmy was playing his heart out. It wasn't right to expect him to finish the work."

"You tell 'im, Coach," said Jimmy.

The crowd of a dozen students had now swelled, and each one waited intently for my retort. I knew then that Noose-Neck was laying a trap. He wanted to appear heroic in front of the students, with me playing the heel.

"Let's go into your office to talk about this," I said. Once inside, I didn't hold back. "You've superseded my authority."

"I have the right to do so."

"You could have at least contacted me before vetoing my decision."

"I'll give you that one. Now let's move on, shall we, and put this behind us."

"This isn't right."

"You're entitled to your opinion. If you don't like my decisions, you're free to leave. Finding a replacement for you shouldn't be difficult."

"Don't count on it. I'll be here until at least February."

I stormed out of the main office and then through the foyer toward the gym. Along the way, I caught a glimpse of Jimmy; he wore a sly grin, as if to say, "You lose, sucker!"

Gary was doing inventory in one of the equipment rooms. I walked in and began to vent.

"What the hell is going on?" I screamed. "I'm just following the rules he clarified and the bastard breaks it for his own gain?"

"It never used to be like this," replied Gary. "Everything's negotiable now."

"Glenn walks around with this halo over his head and makes me look like a jackass in front of the students. What good's a rule if the principal doesn't even enforce it?"

"I'm sorry to tell you this, kid, but it's only going to get worse now that Bill 160's in play."

"I'm so pissed off," I said.

Thursday, November 26

Parent-teacher interviews

Marco's dad is barely five feet tall and wears his thinning, curly gray hair in a mullet. "Hello, buddy," he said to me. "I'm Mr. Costa."

I reviewed some of Marco's antics, including the time he wouldn't stop burping in health class; the time he kept farting in the rugby scrum; the time he wore his underpants on top of his PE shorts; his obsession with smuggling Coca-Cola into the gymnasium and then spilling it; and his inability to shut up or be punctual. I also emphasized the time he nearly broke my nose with a volleyball, the time he attacked Tim in the gymnasium, and the time he slapped Tim during the assembly.

"My son? He did all that?" was all Mr. Costa could say.

The man lives in Neverland. Surely the kid is no angel at home. He must pull off some of the same shit there.

"Lemme tell you something, buddy," continued Mr. Costa. "I never had problems with Maria or Gina or Michelle. Marco's ten years younger; he wasn't planned. The rhythm method doesn't work."

I was almost relieved when Noose-Neck interrupted and shook Mr. Costa's hand.

"How you doing, buddy?" asked Mr. Costa.

"Fine, thank you. How are you, Mr. Costa?"

"I'm okay. Thanks for being so patient with my son."

"We aim to please," replied Noose-Neck.

Just then we were interrupted by Andrew Yates. "Mr. Veitch, Mr. Veitch, I can go to Whistler now," he said. "I brought the TV back."

"Excuse me, Mr. Veitch, but what is this young man talking about?" said Noose-Neck.

Oh shit.

"Um," I said, "Andrew—"

Andrew interrupted. "I broke one of the science department TVs, but don't worry, Mr. Glenn, because I fixed it and I can go to Whistler now. My mom's got it in the car."

Noose-Neck turned to me. "Mr. Veitch, why didn't you report this to me?" he said. "We have procedures for such matters. Obviously, I'll have to review them with you tomorrow. You should have sent Andrew to the office."

Yet when I send Marco down, you give him a sucker and now play buddy-buddy with his father?

"Mr. Veitch didn't need to send Andrew to the office because he dealt with me directly," said a woman. I glanced over my shoulder to see her approaching. She wore a pantsuit, so I knew it was Mrs. Yates.

"I'm Mrs. Yates, Andrew's mother," she said to Noose-Neck, before shaking his hand. I hope she squeezed hard. "We spoke in September about my concerns with Andrew and his ADHD."

"Uh, yes, I remember," said Noose-Neck, obviously lying.

"And there's no need to speak with Mr. Veitch about procedures."

Noose-Neck's neck fat began to quiver.

"Instead of wasting your time with that one, why not speak to some of Andrew's other teachers? They could learn a thing or two from Mr. Veitch on how to handle students with ADHD."

A small victory.

The rest of my interviews went smoothly. Save Marco's dad and Andrew's mom, most of the parents I spoke to were those of good students such as Jamal, Stephanie, Erwin, Tim, and Donna.

I would have liked interviews with Lorraine's mom about her daughter's lack of attendance, Jimmy's parents about his problems with authority, Bug-Eyed Zoey's dad about her potential hyperthyroid condition, and finally Brian's folks about his B.O., but none of them showed up. I guess this means I'm on the phone tomorrow.

After the interviews, some of us went to the Madison for a beer. Lauren sat beside me and kept touching my arm with her hands. Is she trying to tell me something? Does she like me? Should I have done something?

<u>Friday, November 27</u>

I'm getting sick. My voice was hoarse during today's lessons, and my head feels the size of a hot-air balloon. Worse, I was sitting on the staff room john when Parsons came on the PA. The *beep* preceding his announcement ricocheted around the concrete walls and inside my skull. I've never been in the bathroom during an announcement before. The sound created worse pain in my ears than that time I got hit driving the ball piker.

<u>Saturday, November 28</u>

Sick

I watched the Star Wars trilogy back to back to back today. That's fifty-three times now I've seen them, and I can't wait for Episode I in May. I hope George Lucas doesn't screw it up.

<u>Sunday, November 29</u>

At least the phlegm is loose now. I've been through several boxes of tissues. My nostrils are chafed from blowing my nose too much. Dad keeps finding used snot rags around the house. I leave a trail wherever I go.

<u>Monday, November 30</u>

I arrived at school looking pale, probably even whiter than Teagan in his permanently untanned state. Parsons took one glance and ordered me home.

I had to tell Noose-Neck, who was his usual sympathetic self. "Why did you even come in today? Why didn't you phone in sick? Now I have to get coverage for you at the last minute."

Poppa Wib took me to a walk-in clinic. After waiting an hour and thirty-six minutes, Dr. Thompson, whose halitosis penetrated my congestion, prescribed antibiotics for strep throat.

DECEMBER

In related news, Poppa Wib took me to see the remake of Psycho

<u>Tuesday, December 1</u>

Drugs working.
Almost human again.
Back to school tomorrow.

<u>Wednesday, December 2</u>

Though I left detailed plans for the supply teachers, including which students to look out for, which students are helpful, and where all the equipment belongs, they didn't follow them. My science class did no work, so I have to postpone the test on electricity and magnetism. At least my PE classes aren't behind—as the Grade 9s played basketball and the Grade 12s were just completing their regular fitness circuit—but Gary was pissed at me because the weight room was a mess and two basketballs are missing from the equipment room.

I can never be sick again. The only good part was that it gave me forty-eight hours without having to deal with Jimmy's smart mouth, Marco's hyperactivity, and Noose-Neck's negativity.

About the only good thing the supply teacher for Grade 12 fitness did was document Jimmy's arrival time (forty-five minutes late on Monday and forty-one minutes late on Tuesday). Jimmy was also late today, bringing his total to seventeen tardies for the semester.

Today, I told Jimmy that if he's late again tomorrow, I'm locking the weight room door and he can knock once and then wait outside quietly. I've also written him up for the eighty-five minutes of class he missed between Monday and Tuesday, though I suspect Noose-Neck will give him another "talking to," or more likely do nothing at all.

Thursday, December 3

Jimmy earned tardy number eighteen. As promised, I locked him out of the weight room. After five minutes, I went to fetch him. He was gone, so I went back in to continue my lesson. Soon after, Uncle Noose-Neck unlocked the door and let him in, stating, "This student needs to come in and get some learning done."

So how about lecturing the ogre about coming to class on time?

Thursday, December 4

"It's as satisfying to me as cumming is, you know, as in having sex with a woman and cumming," says Schwarzenegger during *Pumping Iron*. "So can you believe how much I am in heaven?"

At this point, Noose-Neck walks in.

"I am, like, getting the feeling of cumming in the gym, I'm getting the feeling of cumming at home, I'm getting the feeling of cumming backstage. When I pump up, when I pose out in front of 5,000 people, I get the same feeling, so I am cumming day and night. It's terrific, right? So I am in heaven."

I explained to Noose-Neck that the Grade 12s were watching *Pumping Iron* to study the sculpted muscles of bodybuilders (anatomy), discuss the use of anabolic steroids (sociology), and analyze the effects of endorphins on the brain (physiology).

Noose-Neck didn't hesitate to make the following comment to me in front of my students: "I'm sure to receive phone calls about the appropriateness of your teaching methods. I don't appreciate this."

Saturday, December 5

My own endorphins were released, thanks to the "runner's high" caused by my 19.2-kilometre run.

Sunday, December 6

E-mail from Teagan:

> *Carl,*
> *Flying to Oz to meet D'Souza tomorrow. Will surf on the Gold Coast then up to Cairns to do dive on the Reef. Should be some nice Australian tits to look at, and I don't mean Eric's.*
>
> *Cheers mate,*
> *Teags*
>
> *p.s. Why not join us?*

Oh how I wish I could.

Monday, December 7–Friday, December 11

I was a cafeteria Nazi (supervisor) with Gary Berg this week. All he did was bitch, moan, and whine, yet I must admit that everything the old bear said is true:

"They're all mouth with nothing good to say."

Marco to Julio: "All the teachers are against me. This school sucks ass."

"Look at what the kids do in front of the office. That's what the rules really are."

Jimmy hangs out in the main foyer, adjacent to the office, flaunting his hat and headphones while low-riding his pants. Noose-Neck walks by him and says hello.

"People turn the other cheek unless they know they'll be backed up."

Every morning, Mrs. Malone walks past several students smoking on school property yet says nothing.

"You have to handle it all yourself unless it's really serious. Like a fight, or drugs, or a kid telling you to fuck off."

I suppose this is what Noose-Neck implied a couple of weeks ago when he didn't back me up with Marco—not that Noose-Neck rushed to support me when Jimmy *did* tell me to fuck off.

"When me and your dad started teaching, the kids would stand up when we entered the room."

"You can't get fired from this job. Look at Anne Coffey—she's a doormat. The kids walk all over her."

I've also finished my Christmas shopping.

For Poppa Wib: a John Daly "Big Bertha" golf driver with graphite shaft

For Grandma Veitch: the popular *Looneyspoons* cookbook

For Aunt Pamela: *Men Are from Mars; Women Are from Venus*

For Lisa: *Lonely Planet: South America on a Shoestring* and a silver bracelet

Saturday, December 12

The travel clinic

Basically, since I'll be exposed to malaria in the Peruvian Amazon, I have a choice of the following:

1) Death by malarial fever if an infected mosquito nibbles on me
2) Death from cancer in fifteen years because I'll need to slather my skin with DEET concentrated, and thus carcinogenic, bug repellent, all to prevent the aforementioned mosquito from sucking my blood, or
3) A litany of side effects, some of which are neuropsychotic episodes, impotence, and blindness, caused from antimalarial medication.

One in 150 Mefloquine users, for example, experiences panic attacks, depressive thinking, and/or hallucinations. Symptoms may persist months after the last dose, and some individuals are so affected that they cannot work or function in normal social interactions.

Compared to Mefloquine, a.k.a. Lariam, only 1 in 1,100 Chloroquine users suffer the same fate. More commonly, Chloroquine causes vision problems. Thus, the freshwater dolphins I see when we're on the Amazon will be blurry, and I won't be able to distinguish between a piranha and a bass when fishing off an Amazon tributary. Considering my luck at casinos recently, maybe Chloroquine is the better option, but then again, some mosquitoes in South America are Chloroquine resistant.

Malarone is the best option (90+ percent effective with minor side effects), but it's not available in Canada. That leaves Doxycycline, an antibiotic, which few strains of malaria are resistant to but whose side effects only include sun sensitivity (I'll be near the equator) and gastroesophageal reflux (I'll be trying new foods).

I've also learned that antimalarial drugs don't prevent the disease but merely reduce the risk of infection. Therefore, I may suffer some of the aforementioned side effects yet still require quinine therapy if an infected female *Anopheles* mosquito bites me. Therapeutic doses of this traditional malarial terminator often cause flushed and sweaty skin, tinnitus, blurred vision, hypoglycemia, hypotension, confusion, headache, abdominal pain, rashes, vertigo, dizziness, nausea, vomiting, and diarrhea. An overdose often leads to death by anaphylactic shock, pulmonary edema, or disturbances in cardiac rhythm.

Whatever I choose, this trip better be worth it.

Sunday, December 13

Teagan and Eric phoned me from Coolangatta, a surf town on the Gold Coast of Australia. Eric used the speaker phone function on his cell phone so the three of us could all talk at the same time.

Eric: "Dude."

Teags: "Get yer feckin arse here over Christmas—forget about Lisa."

Me: "I already bought the ticket."

Teags: "Even D'Souza's pickin' up the ladies here. Well actually, not really."

Eric: "Teags is gonna get skin cancer. He's already peeled through two layers of epidermis."

Teags: "Bollocks—I'm immune te disease."

Me: "Eric, what do you know about malaria medication?"

Teags: "Ye go impotent, ye dumb fecker."

Eric: "Dude, I think that may be true."

Me: "What?"

Eric: "Don't take Lariam, especially since you've had problems with anxiety."

Teags: "And it feckin makes you impotent, too!"

Eric: "Shut up, Teags."

Me: "The doctor recommended Lariam, and Doxyclycline, too, if I don't tolerate the Lariam."

Teags: "Because it feckin makes you impotent."

Eric: "Try one or two Lariam, dude—in a couple of weeks, before you leave."

Teags: "Check out the feckin tits on that one!"

Eric: "If it bothers you, just stop. But I think it's fat soluble, so it may take a few days for any side effects to fade."

Me: "Thanks."

Eric: "Later, dude."

Teags: "Later, feck nuts."

<u>Monday, December 14</u>

Staff meeting—Another snore fest

Sixty-three minutes of multiple intelligence theory by Bill Parsons. It felt like another useless lecture from teachers' college. To survive the boredom, I doodled caricatures of Marco, Julio, Andrew Yates, Jimmy, Bill Parsons, and Noose-Neck.

Eventually, Parsons shut up and Noose-Neck concluded the meeting. He finished with a comment saying that teachers must continue with meaningful instruction every day until Christmas break.

After dismissal, I tried to reserve a TV/VCR for some *Bill Nye the Science Guy* videos next week (easy lessons *and* meaningful instruction). However, all ten machines in the school are booked, including the one in the library that I hoped no one else knew about. Lauren told me that the "gray hairs" on staff often combine their classes this time of year and show Hollywood movies. So much for meaningful instruction—I guess that's why Noose-Neck made the comment.

On my way to the parking lot, Noose-Neck stopped me and said, "I didn't appreciate you doodling during the staff meeting. I expect you to take things more seriously." I apologized but never admitted he was one of the caricatures.

In related news, Poppa Wib took me to see the remake of *Psycho*.

Tuesday, December 15

Holiday assembly
We're not allowed to say "Christmas" assembly because we're in a public and therefore secular school. However, Noose-Neck allowed a Happy Hanukkah skit, a musical Kwanzaa interlude, and a slideshow on Islamic New Year but, according to Lauren, wouldn't allow an appearance by Santa Claus or baby Jesus.

Jamal, from my Grade 12 fitness class, was the emcee and thanked everyone for their hard work and attention. Before sending the students back to class, Bill Parsons signaled for the mike.

"I guess Mr. Parsons wants to say something."

You could hear the audience of 1,100-plus emit a collective sigh. They knew as I did that Bill would repeat everything Jamal had just said and then some.

"Thank you, Jamal, and uh, thank you, Mr. Glenn, for allowing us to have this assembly, and uh, thank you, custodians, for your help, and uh, thank you, Mr. Berg, for allowing us to use the gym space, and uh, thank you, gym classes, for so willfully giving up your play time for a day and, uh …"

I didn't blame Jimmy for snoozing through this monologue. By the time Mr. Parsons thanked the tech crew for the third time, Gary was already in the PE office doing paperwork, Noose-Neck was yawning, and even Sara was spraying herself with perfume to stay awake.

The kids woke up and instantly forgave Mr. Parsons when he promised to give them all candy canes on the way out. Noose-Neck, whose office candy supplies could support a third-world country, refused to help Bill with the distribution.

Jamal, Steph, and the rest of my Grade 12s helped Jozef and the other custodians clean up the chairs. After stacking two chairs on a trolley, Jimmy said he had to talk to Noose-Neck about something (*yeah, right*) and bolted.

Jamal and Jozef worked together. Jamal, though twice as tall and three times as thin as Jozef, would pull himself and their trolley beneath the gym stage while Jozef pushed. Their system worked, mind you, because they finished two trolleys before any other group from my class finished one.

At one point, Jamal vanished beneath the stage for a few minutes. I feared that Jozef may have pushed one of the carts too hard and squished Jamal to death. However, there were no screams of terror, and Jamal reappeared a few minutes later but through the main gym doors. I never saw the beanpole emerge from beneath the mouldy stage, so he must have come out while Steph and I feebly attempted to steer our trolley that refused to go in a straight line. Either that or Jamal teleported past me or found a secret passageway.

Wednesday, December 16

A revelation about Noose-Neck

Gary, my apple fritter–addicted PE head, told me that Noose-Neck needs a promotion to boost his pension. Apparently, he's been trying to get a superintendent position for years. Sara, my perfume-addicted science head, confirmed what Gary said and elaborated on the pension structure. Noose-Neck's pension will be 70 percent of the average of his best five years' salary. Since he's only got five to go after this year, he's desperate for the promotion. Advancing from principal to superintendent increases one's salary by over $27,000, thereby boosting an annual pension by nearly $20,000.

Secret Santa

On the sign-up form, I listed sports nutrition bars, gel packs, running socks, and quick laces under "likes" and candy, junk food, and coffee mugs under "dislikes." All of my "likes" can easily be found at the Running Room and are less than the fifteen dollar spending limit. Personally, I'm happy spending more than the limit, so long as I don't draw Noose-Neck. Should this misfortune befall me, I'll give my nemesis a lump of coal.

Thursday, December 17

The sleepover: Part 1

Now I know how Jamal performed his doppelganger act two days ago. While helping Jozef trolley the chairs under the stage, he discovered a tunnel to the cafeteria.

Mr. Donahue, while preparing for tonight's opening performance of *Willy Wonka and the Chocolate Factory*, heard ruffling beneath the stage. Suspecting mischief, Donahue positioned himself so that the culprits were forced to exit by his feet, keeping the boys (Jamal and six friends) under the stage until after the performance.

The final setup for the sleepover was to take place before the play. Jamal and Co. had already trucked in two small televisions, a Nintendo 64 game system, sleeping bags, pillows, and knapsacks. They weren't expecting to be underneath for the entire performance. The only prep remaining was to buy more snacks and take a pee break.

Jamal had picked the opening night of *Willy Wonka* because the custodians wouldn't switch on the gym security system until 11:00 PM Usually, Jozef and his crew activate the alarms by 6:30 PM. This extra four hours meant the boys only had to wait seven hours to use the bathrooms after the custodians deactivated the alarm. However, once Donahue trapped them beneath the stage, their only escape was the cafeteria, where the motion sensors were already set. The boys were stuck.

Bill Parsons and Noose-Neck confiscated their bags, fearing drugs would be present, and ordered the boys home. Jamal complained that his shoes were in his bag and thus could not walk home in the snow. Parsons phoned Jamal's mom. She said Jamal could walk home in his socks.

Friday, December 18

The sleepover: Part 2

The drug dogs only sniffed out juice, potato chips, and Dr. Pepper in the bags. These kids could have been having sex or smoking up, but there wasn't even a crumb of garbage left behind.

Bill, who was having trouble keeping a straight face, asked them, "What if there was a fire alarm?"

Jamal responded, "Don't worry, sir. We tested the sprinklers under the stage and they're working."

About the only thing that created major trouble was a letter of permission for the fictional "24-Hour Famine," drafted on school letterhead. Jamal had forged Noose-Neck's signature and asked all parents for a $20 donation. This was their cover story.

Stranger still, one of the parents came in last night with twenty-four water bottles. She'd obviously expected to see the boys at the "famine" but witnessed a thrilling performance of *Willy Wonka and the Chocolate Factory* instead.

Noose-Neck wanted to suspend Jamal for five days and the rest for three. Instead, Bill proposed twenty hours of community service, to which they gladly agreed. All seven boys are honour roll students who haven't missed a class this semester. Though Jamal and Co. must clean garbage from the cafeteria and pick up cigarette butts from smoker's corner, they're strutting around the school like they won an Olympic gold medal.

I drew Sara Ross for Secret Santa. She wrote "smelly candles" and "dark chocolate" under "likes" and "ugly cottage trinkets" and "knick-knacks" under "dislikes."

Saturday, December 19

Skiing at Blue Mountain

Derek didn't plan to squander his winter vacation nursing a busted fibula. Never having skied before, he spent much of the previous two days meticulously researching the snowplow technique. None of us thought to advise him that the hardest part of downhill skiing is getting on and off the lifts. Poor bugger wasn't ready for the sudden inertia of the T-bar.

Derek tipped backward, spun around, and somehow caught the back of his right ski in the snow. We heard a sickening *crack*, like that of dried wood crackling in a fire. The lift attendant, a stubbly faced, over-the-hill ski bum, stopped the T-bar and responded with a Keanu Reeves–like "Whoa" before radioing Ski Patrol for help.

Megan and Derek returned to the resort from Collingwood Hospital a few hours later. Derek, understandably morose, rested his injured leg on the passenger side dash of Megan's car. Surrounding his right shin was a plaster cast, as white as the fresh snow now coating the ground.

Megan decided the thrill of doing a couple of donuts in the parking lot would distract her beau from his pain. It did. But after a few spins, the parking lot attendant—a puffy-faced teenage girl—scolded Megan and directed us off the resort.

Sunday, December 20

Three more days of classes.

Six days until I fly to Peru.

Eight days until I see Lisa. I hope we have sex on the first night. I suffer from MSB. Pleasuring myself (don't tell Teagan, dear diary) just isn't quite as satisfying when I know I'm so close to the real thing.

Secret Santa shopping

I bought Sara some smelly exfoliating face cream from the Body Shop, an odiferous twelve-inch candle from the Bombay Company, and Lindor dark chocolate from some kid who was fund-raising. I also bought her a card and wrote the following:

"Eating dark chocolate = endorphin release before you 'go home and make love to your husband.'"

President Clinton was impeached by the U.S. House of Representatives. That'll teach him to keep his dick in his pants.

Monday, December 21

Like the students, I silently count the hours until Christmas break. I struggle, dear diary, to deliver "meaningful instruction," especially in my science class. All this is my pathetic attempt to appease Noose-Neck.

Most of my colleagues with permanent positions simply show movies, play board games, and have parties.

Though I try not to show it, each tick of the clock seems agonizingly slow. The kids are restless, and it feels like two months ago when I had no class control. Even Donna Maclean has joined the incessant group of students pestering me.

"Are we having a party on Wednesday, sir?" they ask.

"No," I say.

"Why not? All of my other classes are."

Secret Santa

I got a Mars Bar and a box of candy canes. Did my Secret Santa not read my requests?

Tuesday, December 22

Too many kids in the hall, too many tardies, too many skips (I suspect we are at half capacity).

The clock ticks even slower. It's as if I'm back on the assembly line, earning $15.83 per sun visor. I suppose Marco, Julio, and Jimmy could thrive in that environment, but those nine weeks I spent at GM after my first year at university drained my spirit and killed my training for cross-country season.

One more day.

Secret Santa

I got a coffee mug with a smiling worm printed on the outside. Could it be Mrs. Malone?

Wednesday, December 23

Indeed, Mrs. Malone is my Secret Santa. She knew about the worm all along! She gave me a package of gummy worms with a card that said:

> *I remember my first year. Thank God this is my last. How do you think my hair got this way? I've had worse things done to me in 37 years than have an earthworm land on my head.*
> *All the best – Mona*

Took my first dose of Mefloquine. I hope I don't have a neuropsychotic episode.

Thursday, December 24

Last night I dreamt that my house was on fire. Santa Claus dropped a firebomb down the Veitch chimney and then laughed with Rudolph while my house at 355 6th Street burned to ashes. I woke up (at least I think I did) and walked downstairs for a midnight snack. Grandma lay prone on the living room carpet, head tucked in the fireplace, blowing cigarette smoke up the chimney. Grandma quit smoking years ago, so this must have been a dream, too.

Kate phoned at dinner to wish us all a Merry Christmas. For once, when she and Dad spoke, they didn't fight about Mom.

2:53 AM
Another nightmare. This time, Grandma chastised me for giving her the *Looneyspoons* cookbook—taking offense because it insinuated that she needed culinary advice. Despite my begging, Grandma refused to prepare my favourite turkey dinner and stuffing—forevermore.

3:44 AM

For once, I'm happy that Eric forgot about the time zone difference. He phoned to wish me Merry Christmas from India in the middle of the night.

I told him about my nightmares. Eric asked if I was taking Mefloquine as my antimalarial. When I said yes, Eric told me to stop the Mefloquine and try Doxycycline. He also told me it may be several days before the side effects subside and that if they don't, I'm probably truly going insane.

Friday, December 25

Grandma loved the cookbook, and her turkey dinner was heavenly. The golf driver I bought Poppa Wib was a hit, too. He kept swinging the club at an imaginary golf ball until one of his back swings punched a hole in the ceiling. Meanwhile, Aunt Pam was absorbed in the *Mars and Venus* book I gave her. She sighed and nodded her head after every paragraph. As for me, dear diary, Grandma and Aunt Pam bought me a $150 gift certificate at the Running Room, and Dad bought me Mountain Equipment Co-op four-season running pants.

After gifts, we prepared for mass.

"You're not going out like that," said Grandma to Dad.

"Like what?" said Poppa Wib.

"You look like a homeless person. Your shirt has ring-around-the-collar and that tie doesn't match your pants. Never mind that it's twenty-five years out of style."

"Mother."

"Don't 'mother' me. Mary would be ashamed of you for dressing like such a low-life."

"Tell you what," said Dad. "When you quit smoking again and stop tooting, I'll wear whatever you want."

Aunt Pam and I burst out laughing.

"Eight-six. I'm eighty-six years old, and this is the thanks I get."

Peru tomorrow.

<u>Saturday, December 26</u>

Toronto to Atlanta ➔ uneventful flight
Atlanta to Lima ➔ another story

Lucky me, I ended up beside a mom and her irritating son. The wiggly toddler kept nudging me while I tried to sleep. When I did doze, the pokes manifested themselves as piranha, munching on my body while I swam down the Amazon. I'd awake disoriented and anxious, wondering if the residual effects of Mefloquine were exacerbating my nightmares.

The final section of my six-hour, seven-minute flight was over the Andes. The snow-covered peaks looked like sugarcoated anthills from up high.

<u>Sunday, December 27</u>

First time outside North America

Aeropuerto Internacional Jorge Chávez is puny compared to Atlanta's Hartsfield-Jackson. Though I wasn't bombarded by hundreds of shops and restaurants like in Atlanta, the culture shock was instant: "No drogas" signs dotted the concourse, and armed guards, carrying machine guns over their shoulders, seemed to watch my every move. As soon as I cleared customs, everybody and their mother wanted to sell me Amazonia or Machu Picchu tours, change my money into Peruvian soles (US$1 = 3 soles), carry my luggage, or take me on a taxi ride.

Eventually, I fought my way through the touts and hopped into what looked like a reputable taxi.

"Where to, señor?" asked the driver.

"Colonial Inn," I said. "How much?"

"Twenty dollars U.S. You pay me now."

People drive aggressively, paying little attention to traffic signals and continually honking their horns. In addition, many cars spit out black exhaust. I breathed in enough fumes during the half-hour cab ride to last a lifetime.

Despite some beautiful colonial architecture, I don't find Lima attractive. There are no skyscrapers, just hundreds of buildings packed side by side like sardines. Many buildings are run down and littered with graffiti.

My hotel is in Miraflores, the section of Lima adjacent to the Pacific Coast. It's nice but smells mouldy. I ate lunch at the hotel restaurant and then walked to the coast.

Along the coast, the most common activities are soccer, surfing, paragliding, begging gringos like me for money, and making out at Parco Amor. I walked to the beach where people surfed and paid a bronzed surf boy thirty soles to teach me how to ride the waves. However, after only ten minutes, I became queasy, despite drinking agua. Humidity plus salt water plus sunlight is not a good combo for me. Adjusting from negative twenty degrees Celsius back home to twenty seven degrees Celsius here might also have had something to do with it.

Monday, December 28

Lima → Iquitos (1 hour 40 minutes)

Though a wall of thirty-degree air greeted me the instant I stepped off the plane, I knew I would like this place. Iquitos is smaller, safer, cleaner, and more relaxed than Lima.

I took an open-air bus downtown and met Lisa at the El Dorado hotel. She was in the lobby waiting for me. We greeted each other with a big hug.

"Lisa, I missed you so much!" I said. I leaned in for what I hoped would be a passionate kiss but was disappointed. Lisa turned her head so that we only exchanged a cursory peck on the cheeks.

Was that a brush-off or a tease?

"It's good to see you, Chud," she said.

We hugged again, and I gave her ass a little squeeze. She held me back slightly and rubbed my shoulders.

What is going on here? Maybe it's rude to show public displays of affection in Peru.

"Where's our room?"

I wanted her right then and there.

"Fourth floor. Drop off your stuff and come back down. I've already got the day planned."

I took the key but was disappointed to find two single beds in the room instead of a double. I moved the table that separated the beds and pushed them together.

Lisa introduced me to Percy, our guide for the day. Percy was an independent tour guide, so Lisa was able to bargain him down to US$50 for the both of us.

Percy is probably my age, but his hand-me-down white dress shirt, too big for his slight frame, made him look younger. Though oversized, the shirt was neatly tucked into properly fitting khakis. Despite the shirt, he was clean shaven and kept his black hair short, to give him a professional appearance. You knew that Percy would buy a new dress shirt as soon as he had the money.

Percy first walked us to the floating shantytown of Belen, the "Venice of the Amazon," which Lisa had described in her first postcard. Since the river is now low, the floating huts weren't floating at all; instead, they rested at ground level. Every time we passed a group of kids, the first one to notice Lisa and me would yell, "Gringo! Gringo!" to his or her friends and point in our direction.

One particular group played soccer with a ratty old ball, using rocks as goalposts. I felt compelled to join them. Lisa asked the kids, in Spanish, if I could play for a few minutes. They were delighted, and both teams fought to have me on their side. After I botched a couple of passes, mind you, I was not as desirable a teammate. Every kid—all of whom were no more than twelve—was a better player than I and stopped passing to the big gringo because they knew he might screw it up.

After Belen, Percy walked us through a crowded market—apparently built for short people. With all of my six feet, I felt like a skyscraper next to the locals. I imagine Marco would be quite comfortable here. The average human height can't be more than five foot three or four. The awnings protecting each market stall weren't much higher. I was constantly forced to duck underneath to see what was for sale.

The touts sold everything, including turtle and alligator meat, pet monkeys, medical tinctures for cancer treatment, creams for baldness, herbs for erectile difficulties, and, of course, the ubiquitous banana. I let Lisa and Percy walk ahead so I could secretly purchase the second-to-last item from the above list; I haven't had a decent erection since I took the Mefloquine and am willing to try almost anything now.

After touring the market, Percy took us to the "Anaconda place," a small private zoo Percy's friends owned. The zoo was upriver, so Percy drove Lisa and me there in his fifteen-horsepower Zodiac. During the ride, we ate lunch, a blend of spices, chicken, and rice wrapped within plantain leaves.

"I'm sick of cilantro," said Lisa. "It's in everything."

"Is that what I'm tasting?" I said. "I kind of like the stuff."

At the zoo, Percy and his friends placed one animal after another on my body. Two monkeys sat on my head, a three-toed sloth curled in my lap, and a turtle crawled on one forearm while a parrot perched on the other. The icing on the cake was the eight-foot boa constrictor and even larger Anaconda loaded onto my shoulders.

None of the animals ate one another. None of the animals ate me. Lisa was convinced the snakes would eat her and refused to try them on.

"¡*Qué lástima!*" said Percy. "You would have fun."

Our next stop was a traditional straw hut village. It was only a short walk from the Anaconda place. An intoxicated man, the chief of the village, greeted us with a handshake. The chief and his tribe reminded me of our Aboriginal Canadians back home. Indeed, they must be genetic relatives, as they looked remarkably similar.

The chief offered Lisa and me a shot of Seven Roots jungle liquor and then challenged us to target practice. We used a five-foot-long traditional blowgun and aimed at a one-sol coin several metres away. The drunken chief hit the bull's eye every time. We never came close, our darts flying off in every direction.

Percy drove us back to Iquitos in the boat and said good-bye. We gave him an extra US$10. Hopefully the tip helps him save for the new dress shirt.

We ate chicken (*pollo*) and pork (*cerdo*) for dinner. During dinner, Lisa taught me some Spanish. Now I know how to order a beer or Inca Cola (*cerveza/Inca Cola, por favor*), locate a bathroom (*¿Dónde baño?*), and say black cat (*gato negro*) and white dog (*perro blanco*). Lisa also taught me to ask how much (*¿cuánto?*) and to bargain for everything by saying it's too expensive (*demasiado*).

After dinner, we swam at the hotel *piscina*. I ordered a *cerveza,* and Lisa went upstairs to change. By the time I got to the room, Lisa was asleep in one of the beds, but she'd left them together. I'm trying to decide if this is a good sign or a bad sign. Tomorrow, I'll have to slip some of my "love potion" leaves into her tea.

Tuesday, December 29

4:32 AM: My first Spanish (almost) wet dream

I was a *perro blanco* eating *cerdo* and ordering *cerveza* from a *pollo* bartender. Soon, my bladder filled to capacity and I asked the *pollo*, "*¿Dónde baño, por favor?*" The *pollo* pointed to the *gato negro*, who looked remarkably like Lisa. The *gato negro* stuck out a paw and demanded payment for entry into the toilet. "*¿Cuánto?*" I asked.

"*Cinco (five) soles,*" replied the *gato negro*.

"*Demasiado,*" I said.

"*¡Qué lástima!*" hissed the *gato negro*.

I lifted my leg and peed on the ground. The *gato negro* meowed to the *pollo*, who got his other mafioso *pollo* friends to chase me out.

I woke abruptly, perplexed by the dream and worried that I may have peed in my underwear. Fortunately, only a couple of drops of urine had escaped my malfunctioning penis. I can't imagine having to explain to Lisa that I wet the bed.

11:15 AM: Amazonia—Explorama Lodge—80 kilometres from Iquitos

Explorama Lodge lies near a tributary of the Amazon, about eight hundred metres from the mighty river. As in Belen, huts for the dining rooms, bar, and bedroom are built on stilts. Before eating lunch, we quickly dropped off our belongings in our room. The room, unfortunately, houses two single beds. I was hoping for one double or a queen so Lisa and I could share. *Baños* and showers are a short walk away along a dirt path, each stall separated by a thick bamboo wall.

We ate a lunch of fish, rice, and beans with Luis, our guide. Short, with a pot belly and a Yankee's cap on his head, Luis reminded me of a father taking his son to a ball game. The only thing physically strange about this otherwise unremarkable man was his disproportionately large feet. I thought only adolescent boys suffered from this phenomenon. He reminded me of a Peruvian Hobbit. Luis explained that his feet grew after years of barefoot jungle walking: calluses, cuts, and more than one tarantula bite caused his feet to thicken and swell.

Joining us for lunch were Mark and Morris, two plump, thirty-something brothers from Texas. Mark, the younger (and larger) of the brothers, wore a khaki vest and cargo shorts. Hanging from his neck and shoulders were two still cameras, a video camera, and a couple of accessory bags. Mark looked like a model for the Tilley Endurables catalogue.

Morris, in contrast, dressed simply in Hawaiian shorts and a plain Texas Rangers T-shirt. He wore impossibly thick glasses that kept sliding down his sweaty, beak-like nose. Red bumps dotted his chubby forearms. The bumps were in fact insect bites. Morris stopped scratching long enough to shake my hand.

The final members at our lunch table were two gregarious parrots. I've since learned their names: Coquitta and Nikita. Fascinated by the birds, Mark videotaped the orange-winged *Amazona amazonica* opening the swinging entry doors with their beaks, eating rice off my shoulder, and shitting on my back.

"That's good luck," said Luis, before joining Lisa and Morris in laugher. I wasn't laughing and neither was Mark, who was too focused on capturing my embarrassment on tape to join in the giggles.

Nature hike—Flora and fauna

Particularly impressive were the hundred-foot trees, each one supported by thick, outstretched buttresses. Termite nests hung beneath many tree branches. Luis explained that the termites eat clay from the ground and regurgitate it en masse to form the complex, two-foot-diameter mound that is their home. Flying between the trees were macaws, toucans, hawks, and parrots. Swinging from vine to vine were small, curious squirrel monkeys. And sleeping between buttresses were hundreds of nocturnal bats.

Luis returned us to the lodge, where I had the first of my four showers for the day. Much to Lisa's dismay, I walked there with no shoes.

"You'll step on a tarantula and die," she said to me.

Not likely, I think. *I haven't seen a spider yet.*

After dinner, Luis took us back up the tributary. We watched the sunset, and I took this romantic opportunity to hold Lisa's hand. Back at the lodge, I couldn't convince her to sleep in the same bed with me.

"It's too hot to sleep in the same bed," she said. It's just as well—the "love potion" did little to activate my libido.

Wednesday, December 30

4:57 AM

I can't recall if I went to the bathroom and saw a tarantula or if I dreamt I went to the bathroom and saw a tarantula. Regardless, I checked my body for bites and there were none.

Freshwater dolphin watching

"Over there!" Morris would shout, pointing to what he thought was a dolphin. We'd all then shuffle to one side of the aluminum boat, nearly tipping it in the process, in the hopes of catching a glimpse of one. We soon learned that Morris, distracted by itchy bug bites and glasses that refused to stay on his nose, was mistakenly pointing us toward driftwood. Still, the Amazonian freshwater dolphin is bright pink, so I can't understand how he could make that error.

Eventually we enjoyed watching the real thing. Lisa and I chose not to take photos since Mark promised to send us copies next month. His camera was loaded with an exorbitant zoom lens that would make any sports photographer envious.

Piranha fishing

Luis's only fishing tool was a simple wooden rod. He used a chunk of beef for bait, connected to a hook that was, in turn, connected by a string to the rod. The piranhas couldn't resist the bloody bait. Within a minute, Luis pulled out his first catch. He unhooked the piranha without getting bitten and threw the menacing fish into a bucket. We heard the fish chomp its sharp teeth until, finally, it suffocated in the air. Turkey vultures circling above only heightened the atmosphere. We were all very impressed.

Luis parked the boat within a tributary of still, black water, beneath the outstretched limbs of several species of small Amazonian trees. The water, black from decomposition, is the ideal habitat for hungry piranha.

Morris caught five, Mark six, Luis eight, Lisa four, and I, well, none. I felt somewhat emasculated. We returned to the lodge, and Luis cooked up our catch.

While waiting, I took my second shower—still no tarantula—and then had a quick siesta, wrapped within an Incan hammock.

The native tribe

Numbering about one hundred, the tribe appeared to be a hybrid of the kind of scantily clad primitives you'd see in *National Geographic* and modern Peruvians. Some women were topless, and others wore Michael Jordan T-shirts. Some men wore nothing but leather thongs and a tube through their nose. Others wore tank tops, sneakers, shorts, and earrings. Regardless of their attire, Luis explained that all natives here rely heavily on the tourist trade for survival. I bought a six-foot blowgun, and Lisa traded her towel for a trinket made of dried coconuts. Morris was about to buy the beak of a macaw when Lisa explained the ethical dilemmas of his purchase: like coral from the Great Barrier Reef, macaw beaks are sold to rich tourists who are ignorant that the species faces extinction. Morris settled for a straw hat instead. Mark photographed everything, including the villagers beating blood from the hide of an animal, and naked kids drinking water directly from the tributary.

The rum factory

After a quick return to Explorama, Luis drove us in the boat to a small rum factory. Here, a more affluent family grinds sugar cane and uses it for sugar, molasses, and various kinds of rum. After a few samples, I purchased a bottle of ginger Amazon rum.

Incredibly, it started to rain! Imagine that—in a rainforest. It rains two hundred and fifty days a year here, but this is the first time I've experienced a downpour. While waiting for the sky to clear, Mark and Morris teased Lisa and me about our Canadian accents (eh?). Then we discussed the Furby toy phenomenon and Bill Clinton's infidelity.

Back at Explorama
Just returned from the bathroom, barefoot, of course, but have still not encountered the tarantula that Lisa warns of.

Thursday, December 31

This morning, Luis guided us through the secondary rainforest. We saw many exotic species:
- The owl-eyed butterfly, whose wings, when spread, frighten predators because they resemble the head of an owl
- The blue morpho butterfly, which, I'm told, confuses its predators because the metallic blue colour of its wings plays tricks on the retina
- The tiny and colourful but poisonous dart frog, whose secretions could paralyze or even kill an average-sized man within seconds
- A dazzling array of fungi, varied in size, shape, colour, and texture

The highlight of the morning, mind you, was watching Morris win a staring contest against a three-toed sloth.

At lunch, we met Linnea Smith, a forty-something American doctor with underarm hair and matching furry legs. The tall, slim brunette arrived in Peru nearly ten years ago for the same tour Lisa, Mark, Morris, and I are now on. She fell in love with Peru, its people, and its plants and animals, and she never left. Linnea sold her thriving practice in Wisconsin and now, in exchange for meals, gives medical advice to the Explorama staff and also serves the natives. According to Luis, she's saved many lives. I plan to buy her book, *La Doctora*, tomorrow.

Luis, by the way, is "three sheets to the wind." It's almost dinner now, and he's outside my and Lisa's room, feeding Amazon rum to a capybara, the largest rodent in the world. It's the size of a pig. Coquitta and Nikita appear to be inebriated as well. The parrots keep falling off Luis's shoulders and then awkwardly climbing back up his legs and arms for a sip of the aforementioned rum. Coquitta has not shit on Luis like she shit on me.

Mark and Morris just knocked on the door, fetching Lisa and me for dinner.

"Eh, Canadian people," said Morris. "It's a-boot time you join us for supper, eh?"

He sounds drunk, too. I suspect I'll reach the same state within a couple of hours.

¡Felíz año nuevo! dear diary.

JANUARY

Parsons said "and uh" seventy-one times during the presentation ...

<u>Friday, January 1, 1999</u>

I finally slept with Lisa but couldn't finish the damn job. What tragedy has befallen me? After thirty minutes of sex, Lisa said, "Okay now, Carlson, finish the job," and I couldn't do it. Some combination of Amazon rum, malaria medication, and pressure conspired to make me impotent!

Tomorrow is my last day with Lisa. I'm afraid we're going to have "The Talk."

<u>Saturday, January 2</u>

This morning, I stepped on a tarantula on the way to the loo. Linnea inspected my foot. She said it didn't bite me and lectured me for not wearing sandals. Lisa gave me the "I told you so" look before pulling me aside.

"Carlson," she said, "we need to talk."

It was the conversation I was dreading.

She continued. "I want you to know that last night was fun, but it was just sex."

"I, um, am a little embarrassed about my performance," I said.

"It's okay, Carlson. We were both a little drunk."

"Thanks."

"If you want to come back during March break and go to Machu Picchu, I'm up for it, but don't expect us to be more than friends. In the meantime, if someone else comes along in your life, I want you to take the opportunity."

"But I don't want someone else; I want you."

"Chud, that's really sweet."

"But?"

"But it's not fair for either of us."

"So that means that if someone else comes along in your life, you'll take the opportunity, too."

"Yes."

"These last days have been fun—just like old times."

"I won't be back in Canada for at least another year and a half. If we're truly meant to be together, it will happen when I come back home."

¡Qué lástima!

I was hoping to have an official extension of our relationship, at least until my next holiday. I could come back to Peru then and bring her back home to Canada. I know this last statement is completely selfish, but it's how I feel right now. I should just get over her and move on, but I can't seem to let go. Hopefully, by March break, my head will have cleared and I can make some good decisions about my love life.

10:03 PM

I'm back at Lima International Airport, waiting for the plane to take me to Atlanta. I overheard some American kid say to his mom, "There's snow back home." He spoke with a Southern drawl, so I assume the chubby teen is from Atlanta.

When I arrived at the airport, a friendly tout, or so I thought, offered to wrap up my blowgun. Thinking he was being nice, I let him, but then the bastard held out his hand for a tip.

"I wouldn't have had you wrap it if I knew it would cost me."

"You give me tip."

I handed the gaunt looking man three soles. He didn't return my blowgun.

"You give me ten soles."

"That's three. Now give me the blowgun."

"Ten soles, señor."

"Five."

"Okay, five."

<u>Sunday, January 3</u>

Lima to Atlanta → Peaceful. Well, sort of.

When we got close to Atlanta, the chubby teenager beside me kept yapping to his mom about how he was looking forward to finally having some "sweet tea."

9:11 AM

Five minutes after deplaning, I realized I'd left my favourite purple hooded sweatshirt on the Canadair plane. Bastard flight attendants wouldn't let me back on, nor would they get my hoodie for me. Instead, they suggested I fill out a complaint card or write a letter.

Too bad the Canadair people weren't as friendly as the U.S. customs officer who served me. "How y'all doin'?" was all he asked. I'd written on the immigration form that I was bringing in a blowgun, but he didn't even ask me about it.

I picked up my blowgun in the oversize baggage area and then decided to try some sweet tea. It's only regular tea with loads of sugar in it. I don't see why the kid from the plane made such a fuss about it.

Atlanta to Toronto flight → *delayed because of an ice storm*

11:53 PM

Finally boarding. I start work in eight hours and seven minutes.

<u>Monday, January 4</u>

2:48 AM

I smuggled my small blowgun, poison darts, and piranha jaws into Canada without detection. My six-foot-long blowgun, however, was impounded by customs.

Tired and stressed from the previous forty-eight hours, I gave the customs officer attitude. "What am I going to do?" I said. "Shoot a convenience store clerk with a poison dart and raid his cash register?"

"It's a firearm, sir," said the officer. He was one of those sweaty guys who wheezed on every comma or period. His shirt was soaked around the underarms. I wondered if the two conditions were congenital, caused by poor fitness (he was obese), caused by the stress of dealing with uncooperative idiots like me, or some combination thereof.

"Mr. Veitch, you'll need to *(wheeze)* permanently disable your firearm *(wheeze)* before Canada Customs allows it back into your possession." *Wheeze. Wheeze. Wheeze.*

"A firearm?" I said. "It's not like I can hide this in a trench coat!"

"Sir *(wheeze)*, you need to calm down."

I realized I was being a prick. "I'm sorry," I said. "I've just had a stressful day, but that's no excuse to give you attitude."

"That's fine, sir *(wheeze)*, but you'll need to come with me and complete some forms."

I became teary-eyed and launched into my sob story. "I just broke up with my girlfriend, again. The kid beside me on the plane to Atlanta kept asking for sweet tea. Then I tried the sweet tea in Atlanta and it sucked. Then my plane was delayed. Then it was delayed again. Then our plane was circling in the air in Toronto forever and I have to go to work in a couple of hours and face my boss who hates me …"

"I accept your apology, sir, and I'm sorry you're stressed," he said, before yet another *wheeze*. I could also see beads of sweat forming on his temples. He continued, "However, you'll need to come with me now and we'll complete some forms for your firearm, uh, blowgun."

4:32 AM

Forms complete. In order for me to get my "firearm," I need to return in the next twelve months with glue and wooden dowels to plug up both ends of the blowgun.

I found Poppa Wib slumped over, sleeping in a chair near the Terminal One bathroom. I didn't have the heart to tell him he was drooling.

5:08 AM
Home. Sleep.

6:13 AM, 6:18 AM, 6:23 AM, 6:28 AM, 6:33 AM, 6:38 AM
Alarm went off. Hit snooze button. Repeated cycle five more times.

6:43 AM
Jolted out of bed in a panic, remembering I had to teach sex ed to Marco, Julio, and the rest of my Grade 9 boys.

6:43 PM
I must have suffered from some sort of dissociation during the school day because I have no idea what I did in any of my classes. I hope I didn't murder Marco, Jimmy, or Noose-Neck.

Time for bed.

Tuesday, January 5

Marco, Jimmy, and Noose-Neck alive and well.

In grade 9 sex ed class, I used a technique suggested in teacher's college: the anonymous question box. I received the following queries:

"Are you gay?"

"What's a hermifrodyte?"

"I have blueballs. Does jerking off cure them?"

"Where do you buy extra large condoms?"

"When you're having sex, how does the sperm know where to go?"

"Did Adolf Hitler have three balls?"

"Are you impotent?" *(If they only knew)*

After careful consideration, I've abandoned the anonymous question box.

Wednesday, January 6

Whenever I say "penis" or "vagina," Marco and Julio laugh. If I kick them out of class, they just wander about the halls and disrupt other teachers, who, in turn, get pissed at me. If I send them to Noose-Neck, he gives them candy. My only solution, then, is to duct tape their mouths shut and glue their sorry asses to their seats.

Thursday, January 7

Marco bit Tim in health class today. Tim had refused to lend Marco paper, but Marco just grabbed it from Tim's desk anyway. Before Marco could get it away, Tim grabbed Marco's tiny wrist.

"Let go!" screamed Marco.

"Let go of my paper," said Tim.

"Let go of my arm first."

Tim complied but was poised to grab Marco's wrist again.

"Now give me my paper."

Marco lifted the paper from his desk but ripped it apart and threw it into Tim's face.

"You little turd!" yelled Tim. Then he asked me, "Sir, can I move to another desk?"

"Yes," I said.

As Tim stood up, Marco stole Tim's pen, prompting Tim to grab Marco's wrist again. This time, Marco chomped onto Tim's forearm.

"Owww!" screamed Tim. "What the hell!?" Tim let go of Marco's wrist.

"Marco's a cannibal!" somebody yelled. Everyone except Tim, Marco, and me laughed.

"Marco!" I bellowed. "Office, now!"

The little pinhead complied but not before throwing Tim's binder against the whiteboard on the way out.

"Little prick," muttered Tim. Marco gave him the finger.

I buzzed Mrs. Smith to indicate Marco was on his way.

Five minutes later, Noose-Neck arrived outside the classroom door, Marco at his side, and motioned for me to come over. I put a note on the overhead projector for the class to copy and then walked out the door to meet them.

"Marco feels you're always calling him out in class," said Noose-Neck.

No mention of the cannibal incident. Obviously Marco didn't mention this and therefore Noose-Neck's taking Marco's side.

"He's picking on me because I have ADD," added Marco.

I called Tim outside. "Tim," I said, "show Mr. Glenn your forearm."

Tim showed Noose-Neck his forearm. One of the tooth indentations was bleeding. Noose-Neck told Marco to return to his office.

"Mr. Veitch," said Noose-Neck, "why didn't you send this young man to the nurse?" Noose-Neck knew there was no choice but to suspend Marco and in the process back me up. That's something he hated to do, so the bastard was just trying for a cheap shot.

"Mr. Glenn," I said, "my understanding is that pupils in a physical altercation should be kept separate. If I'd sent them together, there may have been further complications."

"Fine," quipped Noose-Neck. "I'll take Tim to the nurse right now, but I expect the incident report after school."

<u>Friday, January 8</u>

Marco officially suspended for three days.

Ontario school boards say the funding policy of Bill 160 leaves them no choice but to increase teacher workload. Both Gary and Sara think we'll have to teach seven classes a year instead of six, with no increase in pay.

<u>Saturday, January 9</u>

E-mail from Teagan:
> Carl,
> I'm due back at Queen's next
> week. I need a ride from the
> airport. I'll call you next
> Monday when I land in Toronto.
>
> Cheers mate,
> Teags
>
> P.S. I think Eric's a poof. I
> set him up with so many women
> for an easy shag but he never
> took the bait.

<u>Sunday, January 10</u>

E-mail to Teagan:
> Teags,
> Re: Eric's "Poofiness"
> That might explain his
> obsession with Jan Ullrich. If
> he could control his farting

problem, I'm sure the bastard
would have better luck with men
than I have with women.
Re: Drive from airport
I've got two department meetings
after work that day and my dad's
looking after Grandma Veitch.
Don't just assume we can always
help you out.

Later,
Carlson

Monday, January 11

Though none will admit to it, my Grade 9 boys are fascinated by the topic of homosexuality. Maybe it's because most are still at the anal stage of Freudian development.

They wanted to know how someone becomes gay, how to tell if someone is gay, why someone would choose to be gay, and what percentage of the population was gay.

I explained that being gay or straight or bi is no more of a choice than being left-handed, right-handed, or ambidextrous.

"It's biological," I said. "It's genetic. Happens whether the person wants it or not. In fact, the percentage of the population who are gay is about the same as the percentage who are left-handed."

I explained that there is some truth to gay stereotypes, but it doesn't mean that an effeminate man is always gay, nor does it mean a masculine man is always straight.

"You can't tell if people are left-handed just by looking at them."

I thought I was reaching them.

"What would you do," I asked them, "if your best friend told you he was gay?"

The responses varied:

- "Ewww" (Tim)
- "Whatever" (Hideo)
- "I'd shoot him" (John)
- "I can tell if a guy's a faggot just by looking at him" (James)
- "I'm gay" (Julio—to a chorus of laughter)

"Stop," I said. "This discussion is over. Instead of talking about your feelings on this issue, you are to write them down and submit this journal entry to me before you leave."

Their written responses mirrored the verbal ones. I had hoped, since the first half of the class went so well and since Marco wasn't there as a distraction, that my audience would be respectful. I was wrong.

After school, we had another endless staff meeting. Bill Parsons said "and uh" seventy-one times during the presentation about cooperative learning. I kept a tally chart. Thank God I don't have any distracting habits like that.

Lauren noticed my tally and sniggered. Noose-Neck gave her the evil eye (at least it wasn't directed at me this time). Bill's presentation lasted a grueling forty-six minutes and thirty-one seconds. Gary didn't give a shit about the meeting and slumped over for a snooze.

Tuesday, January 12

Andrew asked me why I always flip the cartilage of my upper right ear inside out.

Oh shit, I thought I only did that when I was alone.

"I do that?" I asked him.

"Me and Chad counted seventeen times today."

"Seventeen?" I was shocked. Surely Andrew must have exaggerated.

"It's okay, sir. My dad picks his nose during the eulogy on Sundays. He thinks no one notices."

"Uh, I guess that makes me feel better."

"And he's a city councillor, too."

<u>Wednesday, January 13</u>

Andrew congratulated me for flipping my ear cartilage inside out only three times today.

Michael Jordan retired—again.

<u>Thursday, January 14</u>

Review day: Human sexuality test
Marco avoided his seat work by proudly telling me his mom makes his lunch, makes his bed, and brushes the tangles out of his hair. Further stall tactics included purposely dropping his pen so he needed to stand up and get it, pretending his pen ran out of ink so he had to borrow one from Julio (who sat on the opposite side of the room), and successfully engaging me in a pointless argument about his contraband Coca-Cola.

Marco had managed to sneak in a Coke, which I heard him open when my back was turned. Of course, the little pinhead hid the can behind his back when I walked by, assuming I was stupid enough not to notice.

"Give me the Coke, Marco."

"What Coke?" he said, shifting his beady eyes from side to side.

"The one you're hiding behind your back."

"Oh, you mean this Coke?" Then Marco chugged the Coke and handed me the empty can. "There you are, sir," he continued, before finishing his act with a loud belch. "Excuse me," he said, to a chorus of laughter from the class.

I sat him in the far corner, but his attention-seeking behaviour continued. He made fart noises with his underarms, which I ignored. However, Julio and some of the other boys could not, and they started laughing uncontrollably. I noticed there was a large, empty box in the room, so I put it on top of Marco's head. It also covered his shoulders and the upper part of his desk.

"I'm just going to go to sleep then, sir," said Marco, his squeaky voice muffled by the corrugated cardboard. I didn't argue.

Friday, January 15

I asked Marco if he'd gotten the tangles out of his hair. "No sir," he said. "I had to get my mom to brush them out for me again."

Saturday, January 16

Marking: Female reproductive system
- Twenty-eight of twenty-eight knew the clitoris is the only human organ designed solely for pleasure, but only Hideo, the Japanese who I suspect is gay (and who arrived in Canada two weeks ago), labelled it correctly on the diagram.
- Fifteen of twenty-eight (including Marco and Julio) thought girls "pee" out of their vagina
- Five of twenty-eight believe the "urethra" is where the baby comes out. *(Ouch.)*

Sunday, January 17

Marking: Male reproductive system
- Twenty-eight of twenty-eight labelled "penis" correctly (Marco added "the unit")
- Twenty-seven of twenty-eight labelled "anus" (not Marco)
- Twenty-one of twenty-eight labelled "scrotum" (Marco labelled it "bag" instead)
- Twenty of twenty-eight "testicles" (Marco → "the twins")

- Only Hideo knew seminal vesicle, prostate, and bulbourethral gland

<u>Monday, January 18</u>

Parental answering machines

I left voice messages on Mr. Costa's home and work machines, stating that Marco needs to score at least 80 percent on his final exam in order to receive his credit. I chose not to mention that Marco was the only student who could not label "anus" correctly on a diagram. I left similar messages for Jimmy's and Lorraine's parents.

Carlson and Wilbur Veitch's answering machine

Five messages, all from Teagan. I came home late (6:30 PM) and Dad was with Grandma Veitch during her procedure (colonoscopy), so no one was around.

#1: "Mate, you there? I'm at Pearson, come fetch me."

#2: "Poppa Wib, you there? I'm at the airport, can ye fetch me, please?"

#3: "Carlson, mate, can ye at least drive me downtown? I can take a bus to Kingston from there. Cheers."

#4: "Mr. Veitch, Carlson, anybody?"

#5: "Mate, got an idear, don't worry 'bout fetching me anymore."

I checked my e-mail.

E-mail from Teagan:
```
Carlson,
Home in Kingston.
Cheers mate,
Teagan
p.s. Bloke from customs, with
a glandular disorder, I mind,
tried to impound me didgeridoo.
Mistook it for a Peruvian
```

blowgun. Said some fool tried to
smuggle one a couple weeks ago.
Figure that gobshite was you. Am
I right? Played the bloke a few
notes from the didgeridoo. Then
he relaxed and let me through.

<u>Tuesday, January 19</u>

Noose-Neck left a note in my mailbox saying that both Mr. Costa and Mr. Frame had phoned him. I'm expected to make a list of everything the pinhead and the Jumbo-Dumbo can do to improve their grades before the exam, including photocopies of any relevant pages in the health textbook. And the bastard expects me to have everything ready by tomorrow.

Tonight, I joined Dad and Grandma at Aunt Pamela's new apartment for dinner. Her new pad is much nicer than the three-hundred-square-foot bachelorette she had to settle for after the divorce. Now, she's upgraded to a five-hundred square foot, with three rooms and her own washer-dryer. She even has a kitchen table. We ate rice and meatloaf off its polished oak surface. We were all pleased with the upgrade.

My mood changed after Poppa Wib discovered Teagan's didgeridoo in the washroom. He came into the living room holding the strange tubular instrument with an equally strange look on his face.

"What's this, Pam?" he asked my aunt.

"Oh, that's Teagan's didgeridoo," she said.

"What the hell was he doing here?" I bellowed. I feared the worst.

"Did that scrawny little Irishman hit on you?" screamed my father.

"Carlson," she said to me, before turning to my bewildered father. "Wilbur. You needn't worry. I'm old enough to be his mother. He's perfectly harmless."

"The poor boy called me from the airport, and you two weren't around, so I took pity on him. I fed him dinner and drove him to Union Station."

Grandma tooted and, completely unaware her flatulence was audible, innocently asked of the three of us, "What's going on?" It was enough to lift the tension.

E-mail to Teagan:

> Teags,
> If you try to get my aunt
> Pamela into bed I'm going to
> leak the Stages video to your
> supervisors and they'll revoke
> your grant money and you'll be
> deported back to Ireland.
>
> Carlson

Wednesday, January 20

Marco's list is forty-six items long; Jimmy's is only slightly shorter at thirty-eight. Making these lists was easy as I simply photocopied the day-by-day lesson plans I prepared back in September during the strike. Photocopying the textbook, on the other hand, was a challenge. After repeatedly jamming the machines, I chose to simply assign the two losers their own textbooks instead.

I gave the boys their lists and textbooks and also personally handed Noose-Neck his own copy, with an attached page indicating the textbook numbers I assigned.

After school, Sara told me Janis McKee will return from stress leave next semester. This means I have no job after January 29. Another desperate search for employment must begin.

E-mail from Teagan:

> *Carlson,*
> *I mind the Stages incident.*
> *You needn't worry. Your aunt*
> *is immune to my charm, and I*
> *wouldn't betray you like that.*
> *She's just eye candy for me.*
> *There's not too many fifty-year-*
> *old boers with tits like that.*
> *Cheers mate,*
> *Teagan*

E-mail to Teagan:

> *Teags,*
> *If you mention the word "tits"*
> *and my aunt Pamela in the same*
> *sentence again, I will leak the*
> *video.*
> *Carlson*

Thursday, January 21

I can now retire in thirty years and three days. Our pension plan managers, making investment choices that rival the genius of Warren Buffett, have built up a multibillion dollar slush fund. For example, OTPP owns the majority share of Maple Leaf Sports and Entertainment. We own the Leafs, an NHL hockey franchise that sells out every game but hasn't won the Stanley Cup in thirty-two years. Because of said genius, we can retire sooner than expected: teachers only need to reach an 85- (age + years of experience) instead of a 90-factor.

But for my own sake, I'll need to secure another contract in the next few days to reap these benefits. As of 3:31 PM today, there are thirty-seven job postings in the GTA. I'm qualified for eight of them, but they all expect a letter of recommendation from a current employer. I've applied for them anyway, though my efforts are likely futile.

The stork stand record

Before Jimmy and me, Stephanie held the best time in the "stork stand," a test of one's balance. Her record was two minutes and one second, a time equivalent to my personal best in the eight-hundred–metre run at Queen's and also a time that would be easy for me to beat. I had the added motivation of a one-on-one challenge from Jimmy Frame to break the class record.

In the stork stand, individuals are required to balance on one foot with the other foot resting against the opposite knee. In this position, the human body resembles the bird of birth. But this particular stork test had an additional component. Participants must do it with their eyes closed.

In high school and university, I spent many hours in physio for repeated ankle sprains. One of my rehab exercises was this very same stork stand. Crushing Stephanie's record and defeating Jimmy would be no problem.

"You'd better not be cheating," I said to Jimmy, moments after we started.

"I'm not cheating, sir," replied Jimmy.

"His eyes are closed," confirmed Steph.

"Are you cheating, sir?"

"No way. You're going down."

"Calm the testosterone, gentlemen," said Steph. "I'll see that you both play fair."

After five minutes, the remainder of the class began wagering on which one of us would win. Jamal bet a quarter on me. Jimmy's friends bet on him. Normally, the staff handbook says, gambling warrants lunch detentions, but I let this one go.

After twelve minutes, everyone in the class, save Steph, had wagered a quarter. Eleven students bet on me and the other ten on Jimmy.

After nineteen minutes, the class lost interest. Robert asked me to sign his hall pass, and Katie asked if she could turn on the TV.

"You should be studying for Monday's final exam," I said.

"You're mean," she said.

"Did you bet on me?" I asked.

"Of course," replied Katie.

"Fine, you can watch TV, but don't stop anyone else from studying."

"No one's studying, sir. Heath and Will are playing the Stop-Watch game" (a test of one's reaction time where the competitors attempt to start and stop the watch in as little time as possible), "Brianna's sleeping, Joanne's reading *Cosmo*, and Frank and Chris are playing rummy."

"Whatever, you're all seventeen or eighteen years old."

After forty-six minutes and nineteen seconds, the bell rang. Jimmy and I agreed to a draw. He shook my hand and even wished me a good weekend.

"I'll never understand men," said Steph, before leaving the classroom.

Saturday, January 23

Skiing with Derek and Megan: Round two

Derek, now recovered physically, though perhaps not mentally, from his skiing injury, successfully negotiated the chair lift at Blue Mountain. Megan taught him how to snowplow on the easy hills, leaving me by myself on the black diamond runs. Rick bailed out last night, stating, "I need to save mortgage money." Without him, I felt like the fifth wheel.

Lorraine, the carrot-topped airhead from my Grade 12 class (who will not get her credit, by the way) was also at the ski hill. I tried not to notice her (seeing students outside of school feels weird), but she noticed me near the top of Rabbit's Run.

"Mr. Veitch?" she said. "You ski?"

"Oh, hi, Lorraine."

"Shouldn't you be at home, like, marking or something?"

"I do get out once in a while." She was oblivious to my sarcasm.

Three boys, resembling the three stooges with the addition of facial piercings, arrived off the chair lift and stopped beside Lorraine and me. Curly spoke to Larry, Moe, and Lorraine in a dialect of English I still cannot understand, despite teaching teenagers for five months now and being only four-and-a-half years removed from that stage of my life. I read his body language and gathered he was jealous that Lorraine was talking to another man. Just the notion that Curly believed I was interested in his girl seemed wrong on so many levels.

The boys lit up a smoke. Judging by the smell, it was marijuana.

"Can I still pass your class?" asked Lorraine.

Curly relaxed when he realized I was Lorraine's teacher. She noticed his demeanor, as did Larry and Moe.

"You thought I was interested in him?" she said to him. "Ewww, that's, like, so gross."

"You're so fucking dumb," said Larry.

"That's her gym teacher, you idiot," said Moe, slapping Curly across the cheek.

"So, yeah, like, can I still pass your class?"

Not a chance, you airhead, was what I wanted to say. Instead, I lied and said, "You'll need to do exceptionally well on the exam, but it's possible."

"When's the exam again?"

"It's on Monday, Lorraine."

"Okay, thanks, Mr. Veitch. I'll probably come to class on Monday then."

Lorraine skied away and then took a puff of the joint, assuming I wouldn't notice—me being a distant ten metres away.

The THC did little to mar the quartet's mogul ability. They maneuvered down Rabbit's Run with ease. I did my best to match their skill but failed, repeatedly touching down with my hands to avoid a serious wipeout.

Sunday, January 24

Dear Lisa,

I've bought my ticket to Lima and then on to Cuzco. I arrive in the Andean capital on Sunday, March 21, at 8 AM, after spending the night at the Lima airport.

Still no job for second semester, however, despite many teachers taking the early retirement incentive (85-factor). Worse, Damian Glenn has hired several of them back, on occasional contracts for second semester. Gary Berg, my PE head, told me the rules allow for retired teachers to "double dip" for 90 days out of each school year and still collect full pension. Apparently, the superintendents in the board office agree with Principal Glenn's decisions. These same "grey hairs" formulate Bill 160's mandatory increased contact time with students in such a way that we teachers are forced to teach seven out of eight classes (instead of the six of eight it's been for years), as a cost-saving method. However, they contradict themselves by staffing open spots with double-dipping retirees at double my salary. It's just asinine.

Hope things are well with you. Poppa Wib says hi, by the way.

Love Carlson

XXXOOO

p.s. My blowgun is currently impounded at Canada Customs. It's considered a banned firearm. How I could rob a bank with a six-foot blowgun is quite beyond my capacity. But I want it on my wall at home, so I'll plug up both ends with wooden dowels as the law requires.

Monday, January 25

No hat.

No low-riding.

No arguments.

No attitude.

"Morning, sir," was all he said before commencing the final exam. He even brought extra pencils for the Scantron questions. I don't think this has ever happened before.

He even chastised some of his friends. "You didn't tell us there was multiple choice, sir," whined Frank, one of Jimmy's cronies.

Jimmy placated Frank by throwing him a spare pencil. "Veitch reminded us all last week, you dumbass." Shocked, Frank tacitly accepted Jimmy's order and shrank into his seat like a dying flower.

Why the change of heart? All of a sudden, when 25 percent of your mark is on the line, you behave? You think one day of angelic conduct makes me forget the previous four and a half months? I bit my tongue and enjoyed Jimmy's rare cooperation.

Lorraine arrived twenty-seven minutes late and batted her thick red eyelashes at me for the remainder of the exam period. I doubt the airhead answered more than ten questions, though half the exam (thirty multiple choice and twenty matching) was on Scantron. The remaining fifty marks were short answer. My preference was for a choice of six long answer questions, but Gary, my department head, insisted on the split after proofreading the exam.

Personally, I hate multiple choice questions. They only exist to make marking easier and are the reason I flunked two out of four biology exams in second year.

Tuesday, January 26

What sweet revenge. Though Jimmy scored 57 percent on the exam, it only raised his final grade to a scintillating 45. I refuse to bump him to 50, despite yesterday's saintly behaviour. I've recorded his final grade with the guidance department. Without the credit, Jimmy can't graduate. He'll be forced to choose between returning for another semester and taking night school, all because of me.

Dearest Marco fared even worse than Jimmy. Probably jacked up on Coke, Marco screwed up the Scantron multiple choice questions. Not only did he write in pen instead of pencil, but his answer for number two appeared in the spot for number one, and so on. When Marco scored 27 percent on the multiple choice questions, I knew I had to take a second look. After all, with only four possible answers for each question, a monkey pointing its hairy finger at random selections would score 25 percent. The irony is that when I adjusted for Marco's mistakes, it dropped him to 16 percent. Even if Marco had scored perfect on the multiple choice, he still would have failed the final exam. The only other section he completed was labelling. I suppose Marco actually learned something, however, because he labelled "anus" correctly this time.

Wednesday, January 27

I don't know which is more tedious, listening to kids whine or marking papers. Dear diary, here is but a small sample of the whining from today:

Andrew: "How many questions are on the exam, sir?"

Sparrow: "How many pages is the exam?"

Donna: "Is it hard?"

Dan: "Will you give us hints?"

Andrew: "I forgot my eraser, sir. Do you have an extra pen, sir?"

Andrew: "Can I go to the bathroom, sir?"

At least when I mark fifty billion exam questions, I can numb myself with one of Gary's apple fritters as a pseudoanalgesic. Now I know why he became addicted. I suppose it's better than smoking.

Sometime during today's marathon marking session, I looked out the PE office windows to see Noose-Neck approaching. Gary saw my nemesis, too. Suddenly embarrassed by my donut eating, I swept the crumbs off the paper I'd been marking. Gary made no such effort, despite an obvious chunk of apple that had fallen onto question seven of his current paper. Previously, I noticed this very same chunk dribble from the corner of Gary's mouth to a temporary resting place on his belly before splattering onto the paper. I hope I never regress to this heathen state.

Soon, Noose-Neck was outside the door. Though Gary could have easily opened it for him, he feigned ignorance, pretending Noose-Neck wasn't there.

Gary muttered, "Damian's got his own key; he can let himself in."

Noose-Neck opened the door just enough for his fat neck to poke around.

"Mr. Veitch," he said, "we need to speak in private." He spoke in a portentous tone. I knew it had something to do with Jimmy's final grade.

Just then, I had a fleeting image of me squishing Noose-Neck's head between the door and the door frame.

I wiped my lips to remove any residual donut that loitered on them and then stepped out to face my nemesis.

"Yes, Mr. Glenn," I said.

"I believe you're looking for a job," he said.

"I am."

"It would be in your best interest, therefore, to bump Jimmy to a 50."

"He was unsuccessful this semester. He doesn't deserve it."

"This is the only credit he needs to graduate. I hope you'll make the right decision."

"What was that about?" asked Gary, after I stepped back in the office.

I related the story. Gary recommended I bump Jimmy to 50.

"Carlson," he said, "play the game."

Poppa Wib agreed with Gary.

"Son," he said, "no one would blame you for being self-righteous, but is it worth the hassle from Jimmy's parents? Is it worth the hassle from Damian Glenn?"

Thursday, January 28

Done my marking.

Done my report cards.

Don't know why I rushed because I don't have a stinking job on Monday so I could do it then. All I need to do is decide whether or not to bump Jimmy to a 50. After all the pain he's caused me, I want Jimmy to fail. Then he'll know he *had* to come back, and he had to come back because of *me*.

Friday, January 29

I told Noose-Neck I would pass Jimmy.

Maybe, just maybe, if I bump Jimmy to a 50, Noose-Neck will hire me back. Also, Gary and Dad are right. It's not worth the hassle, and this way, Jimmy might finally leave K.S.S. after five and a half years. He'll have no purpose to return next semester except to play basketball.

"I'm glad you've come to your senses," he said. "You've done the right thing, Mr. Veitch. I didn't want to be forced to go behind your back and change the numbers."

"I don't suppose this means you'll hire me back on Monday?" I asked.

Noose-Neck spit out the candy he'd been chewing. I suppose he was surprised I even asked.

"No, Mr. Veitch, I won't hire you back on Monday."

"Maybe something will change your mind."

Saturday, January 30

Stupid me got locked inside Boyd Conservation Area today. I went there for a long, stress-relieving run. While driving through the park gates, however, I neglected to pay attention to the sign stating, "Gates locked at 4 PM daily." I guess I was dwelling on my lack of employment. By the time I finished running at 4:37 PM, my car was locked inside.

I had to run an extra fifteen minutes to find a pay phone. Poppa Wib tried to sound sympathetic, but I knew he was pissed. He regressed into his auctioneer mode, like he does whenever he's excited.

"I-know-you're-stressed-son," he said, "but-next-time-could-you-pay-a-little-more-attention-to-the-park-hours?"

Sunday, January 31

Stupid me locked my keys in the car today. Poppa Wib drove me back to Boyd Conservation Area today, and I went for another run. Before I started the workout, I tied my house key, instead of my car key, to my shoelaces, and then locked the rest of my keys in the car. Of course, I didn't realize my error until long after Dad had driven home.

I ran to the same pay phone as yesterday. Poppa Wib told me to take a taxi. Rick and Megan told me the same. I would have called Lauren, but I didn't know her number.

The thirty-three-kilometre cab ride cost $57.31. Worse, I had to borrow the cash from Poppa Wib when I got home. Dad shook his head when I asked for it.

"Yesterday, you pulled a D'Souza, and today you pulled a Teagan!" he said. "There's money in my wallet. You're cooking dinner all week."

I don't mind cooking for atonement. Without a job, what else am I going to do?

FEBRUARY

Picketing in the middle of winter sucks

Monday, February 1

Janis didn't make it past lunch. I've just gotten off the phone with Sara, who said Janis suffered a crying fit after period one. After period two, Janis told Noose-Neck she was going back on stress leave and was refusing to teach periods three and four.

In a panic, Noose-Neck called Sara and Gary into his office during lunch. His solution was to merge their afternoon classes with Janis's, doubling them in size. He even bribed them with Body Shop and Tim Hortons gift cards. However, Sara and Gary resisted the temptation of free perfume and donuts and suggested to Noose-Neck that he call me to fill in. Instead, Noose-Neck chose to teach the classes himself and will phone a supply teacher for tomorrow.

According to Sara, Noose-Neck left the period four biology class in a shambles. "None of the stools were up. There were candy wrappers in several desks, and it smelled like some of the kids had used the Bunsen burners. Even Janis would notice if a kid was using a Bunsen burner."

And this man criticizes me?

Tuesday, February 2

Thanks to Jane (my union head) and Mona (my dear Secret Santa), I have a job tomorrow. Sara phoned me with the details this afternoon.

Jane, following the lead of other union leaders in the province, instructed any teachers with a four-out-of-four timetable to refuse to teach their extra class. This applies to supply teachers as well. Therefore, when Mrs. Smith phoned to get a supply for Janis's four-out-of-four timetable, she was met with a steady stream of nos. Noose-Neck was forced to teach Janis's classes again. With half the students without a teacher during period four, Kipling Secondary was in chaos after 2 PM, and Noose-Neck can't waste any more time looking for Janis's replacement. He now has bigger problems to deal with.

One of these problems is Mona, who reaches her 85-factor in just over a month. She threatened to teach her last few weeks at another school board if Noose-Neck didn't hire me. Apparently, this wasn't enough of a threat, so Mona upped the ante. Mona, who by default became the yearbook editor again after Janis discombobulated yesterday, then refused to complete her editorial duties. Sara said Noose-Neck fielded daily phone calls from angry parents wondering when the long overdue 1997–1998 yearbook will arrive.

So, a little serendipity and a little help from my allies have made the impossible possible. Noose-Neck caved and gave me the job, but only because he ran out of options.

<u>Wednesday, February 3</u>

6:52 AM → *7:58 AM*

Amongst the usual mass of paper in my mailbox was the following handwritten note:

Your friends won't always be around to protect you. Don't expect me to grant you the second evaluation you seek.

It wasn't signed, but I think I know who wrote it.

After this warm welcome back, the photocopy machine jammed while making copies of my student questionnaires. Worse, I couldn't fix the damn thing, and several teachers were in line behind me.

"Way to go, rookie," Gary muttered. "Don't you know not to do double-sided copies on this one?"

Just then, I smelled fruity perfume. *Thank God*. It was Sara.

"Give the man a break," she said to Gary. "You know he just got his schedule last night. You've known yours since September, yet you procrastinated with your copying until now."

"Sorry, kid," said Gary. "You know I was teasing."

Sara turned to me and said, "Carlson, why don't you use the machine downstairs while I fix this one."

"Thanks," I replied.

"You'll survive this semester like you did the last one."

The queue downstairs was even longer. I felt like I was lining up for tickets to a Star Wars movie. (By the way, dear diary, it's only three and a half months till *Episode One*—wahoo!) I chose to use the office photocopier. Mrs. Smith and Bill Parsons saw me and waved a friendly hello.

Noose-Neck, however, was not so amicable. "Teachers are not to use the office machine," he said. When he made this admonition, I was already finished with my photocopying anyway, so I ignored it. I did imagine, however, giving him a face wash with today's dusting of snow.

I should have said something back. After all, I'm here until June 28 now, whether he likes it or not. I doubt anything could lessen his opinion of me.

8:15 AM → 2:45 PM

In the classroom, I was ultrastrict with my students: desks in rows, alphabetical seating ("Awww, *alphabetical*? Come on, sir."), no smiling, lots of rules, etc. I even decided on two basic penalties for misbehavior: first, "push-ups for punishment" in my gym classes. Second, "periodic tables" in my science classes: students copy out the name, symbol, and atomic mass of the first fifty elements, or more for worse behaviour.

Andrew Yates, now in my Grade 10 PE class (with none other than Dan and Sparrow), already did an extra thirty push-ups for speaking out of turn. Jamie, a skin-headed kid in my Grade 11 bio class, has half a periodic table due tomorrow for saying "shit."

"It just slipped out, sir," was his explanation.

Poppa Wib was proud of my autocracy. "Keep it up," he said. "And most of them will turn into putty."

Oh, yes, how could I forget? I got the sniffles again during every class. I shall ask Ronda if this is some sort of psychosomatic nervous response when I go for my next session.

Thursday, February 4

Jozef again broke the news to me. He was shoveling snow in the empty school parking lot when I pulled up to him.

"*Jak się masz?*" (How are you?) I asked.

"*Dobry,*" (Good) he answered.

"Where is everyone?"

"No school—lockout."

"Lockout?" I said.

"Maybe you go to Poland now?"

The radio confirmed Jozef's story: "High school teachers in the Metro West School Board refused to teach the extra workload yesterday. Therefore, superintendents unanimously agreed to lock teachers out until the dispute ends."

Friday, February 5

Can't write much. Hands frozen. Damn cold out there. I vow to give homeless people more respect in the winter. Just came out of bathtub and still can barely move fingers. Want to open letter from Lisa but fingers won't allow it. I'm writing this entry with gloves on. Would ask Poppa Wib to open envelope, but I know his big nose would snoop into my business.

Picketing in the middle of winter sucks.

Letter from Lisa

> Dear Chud,
>   I'm looking forward to visiting Cuzco and the surrounding area with you. We'll see you in March.
>   Lisa

No love Lisa? And what is this "*We'll* see you" business?

And how the hell am I going to get the money for this trip if I'm on strike or locked out all the time?

Saturday, February 6

Eric phoned from Oz. He said his classes are going well and hinted that he'd met someone. I didn't probe, so I'm not sure if the "someone" is a man or a woman. I figure he'll tell me when he's ready.

Sunday, February 7

E-mail from Teagan:
        You on strike again?

E-mail to Teagan:
        We refused to teach the extra class the school board dumped on us, so they locked us out for "safety reasons."
        You on reading week?
        Carlson

E-mail from Teagan:

> `Yep. Taking the Queen's`
> `Climbing Club to Red Rock`
> `Canyon in a week. Wanna come?`

E-mail to Teagan:

> `Don't tempt me.`

Monday, February 8–Thursday, February 18

Lockout continues

What I've discovered during the past ten days:

1. I walked/ran at least four hundred kilometres during the lockout. It was all I could do to keep warm. It was too crowded around the oil barrels.
2. Snowballs fly farthest when the relative humidity is 81 percent.
3. Lauren is addicted to Oreos.
4. Lauren doesn't like it when I throw snowballs at her.
5. Premier Mike Harris, who appears to have won the battle of public opinion, intends to call another election soon.
6. Sara, Gary, and Jane are no longer fond of Kelly Turner. As a superintendent, Kelly sits on the opposite side of the bargaining table and is thus now one of "them."
7. Sara is on a peanut-butter-and-potato diet.
8. Simcoe settled for a six-and-a-half-out-of-eight timetable.
9. Sara wonders why her peanut-butter-and-potato diet isn't causing weight loss.
10. Metro East Public (me) and all the Catholic secondary school boards in Ontario are the only remaining school boards that haven't settled contracts.
11. If and when we do go back, all remaining PA days will likely be cancelled and the school year will probably be extended at least one extra week.

12. I can go on unemployment insurance after my contract expires at the end of the semester. I may need this for a long time since nobody will hire me now that Noose-Neck has essentially blacklisted me from teaching.
13. Mona plans to show as many videos as possible to her classes until her retirement in another month. She teaches math, so I don't know how this will work out.
14. The people in the BMW who threw tomatoes at us in September were Jimmy's parents.
15. Jane started smoking again.

Friday, February 19

The provincial legislature met today and voted to force us back to work. Our contract will be settled through arbitration. If arbitrators favour the school board, I'll be making $18,000 per semester teaching four classes a day, whereas in neighbouring Peel District, a fellow rookie teacher will be earning the same teaching three.

At least I won't be stuck picketing in this damn cold.

We're continuing our protest, however, with a "work-to-rule campaign." All voluntary activities (formerly called "cocurricular" or "extracurricular") will cease to exist. This means no sports teams, no drama clubs, no band, no art club, no peer tutoring, nothing. Essentially, the school shuts down fifteen minutes after dismissal.

I wonder if the long overdue yearbook will ever see print.

Saturday, February 20

I have four different preps in four different rooms in four different areas of the school. Between periods one and two, and again between three and four, I somehow have to lock up the gym equipment rooms, monitor the boys in the change room, switch from PE clothes to a shirt and tie, pick up any necessary lab equipment, and travel to a portable or another floor through a mob of students—all in the span of five minutes.

I spent the afternoon sketching travel routes, but none seemed to work. Kipling Secondary School is a labyrinth to begin with. I don't know if I can pull this miracle off.

"If you're five minutes ahead of the students, then you're doing okay," said Poppa Wib. The only way I'll be five minutes ahead of the students is if I somehow develop the ability to teleport between classrooms and change my clothes like Superman along the way.

Sunday, February 21

The Denver Broncos won Super Bowl XXXIII, their second in a row. Dad, Derek, and I watched the game with Rick at his bachelor pad. Actually, they watched the game while I attempted to solve my school travel maze conundrum.

My latest diagrams repeatedly failed to solve the problem. Therefore, using empty beer boxes, I went three-dimensional and constructed a crude corrugated cardboard model of Kipling Secondary. Using Rick's old Star Wars figures to represent me, Noose-Neck, and the crowds I am to face, I almost had the puzzle figured out. I even included pathways that would allow me, represented by Han Solo, to completely avoid Noose-Neck, who was represented by Jabba the Hutt. And then disaster struck.

After a Denver touchdown, the boys stood up to cheer. One of them bumped into the table full of beer. Several bottles tipped over and spilled onto my model. The corrugated cardboard soaked up the beer, wilted, and then fell apart. I gave up after that.

Monday, February 22

No, no, NOOOOOOOOOOOOOOOOOO!!

I wish I were locked out again!

Guidance placed Marco Costa in my Grade 9 boys PE class. Why didn't I just pass him last semester?

Jamie and the rest of my Grade 11 general students looked especially pissed off to be back in the classroom. Jamie now wears a chin-strap beard to go with his bald head. He's also shaved three slits out of his right eyebrow.

The thug still owes me a periodic table for his prelockout cuss word.

"Come on, sir, that was three weeks ago," he said.

"Exactly," I replied. "You've had plenty of time to finish it."

"Aww, shit."

"I'll expect two now, Jamie."

Tuesday, February 23

Teleisia Campbell, an athletic looking African-Asian girl with large breasts, transferred into my Grade 11 general biology class. "Te-lee-sha," I said. "Welcome to class."

She kissed her teeth (I presume this is a rude gesture) and said, "It's Te-lee-see-uh, sir."

"Okay, then, have a seat behind Akeel."

Akeel, who barely passed my first semester Grade 10 science class, waved at Te-lee-see-uh and pointed her toward the seat behind him.

"Whatever," said Teleisia. She walked behind Akeel, threw her oversized leather purse on the desk, and then used it as a pillow.

<u>Wednesday, February 24</u>

Teleisia kept misting Akeel with perfume today. Perhaps Mrs. Ross would have appreciated her choice of scent, but not I. "Teleisia, stop spraying Akeel! Akeel, stop turning around."

"She keeps spraying me," said Akeel.

"Maybe if you would stop turning around, she wouldn't spray you!"

Still no periodic table from Jamie. He owes me three now.

In PE, Marco earned sixty push-ups for punishment and only did seventeen of them. I called his dad again. Mr. Costa said, "Listen, buddy, you look after him there, and I'll look after him here."

I think Marco's looking for another foreign thug like Julio to be his bodyguard. Fortunately, no Grade 9s in his current class share Julio's mental incapacity or his overdeveloped adolescent physique.

<u>Thursday, February 25</u>

Jamie submitted three colour photocopies of the periodic table.

"These are supposed to be handwritten," I said.

"You never specified that, sir," said Jamie.

"You know what I meant."

"Whatever, sir."

Jamie spent the rest of the class writing out his periodic tables.

"Jamie," I said, "you're supposed to do these at home."

"I ain't doin' them at home. I'll sit here, be quiet, and do my periodic tables, but I ain't doin' them at home."

I figured this was a fair trade-off so long as Jamie kept his promise. I did phone home, however, detailing to Jamie's mother how it all began with the word "shit."

"Shit, shit, shit," was her response. "That little shit is at it again."

I will turn the other cheek the next time Jamie swears.

<u>Friday, February 26</u>

Changing from PE gear to a shirt and tie keeps making me late for periods two and four. Of course, Noose-Neck has noticed. After school today, he hauled me into his office.

"How can we expect students to be punctual when our teachers cannot even do it?" he said.

<u>Saturday, February 27</u>

E-mail from Teagan:
> Your aunt Pamela has nice tits.

E-mail to Teagan:
> You're dead, you scrawny Irish
> bastard. I'm coming to Kingston
> next weekend to leak the video.

E-mail from Teagan:
> Bring your aunt Pamela.

<u>Sunday, February 28</u>

E-mail to Teagan (I used Poppa Wib's e-mail address and pretended to be him):

> Teagan,
> Please cease making comments
> to and about my sister/
> Carlson's aunt. However
> jokingly they appear to you,
> they are hurtful. Pamela is
> just recovering from a divorce

and doesn't need a scrawny,
freckled Irishman drooling over
her. Carlson is stressed with
his job and cannot waste time
processing your feeble attempts
at humour.
Should you not comply, I'll
join my son in Kingston this
weekend and help him distribute
the "Stages" video.

Yours,
Wilbur Veitch
BPHE, University of Toronto
MA, University of Ottawa

MARCH

*Thank God there was a layer of clothing between his
parts and the mouth of the mannequin he was humping*

<u>Monday, March 1</u>

Poppa Wib was confused about the following e-mail from Teagan:

> *Mr. Veitch,*
> *Please accept my humblest*
> *apologies. There is no need to*
> *distribute the "Stages" video.*
> *Yours truly,*
> *Teagan*

I explained the joke to Dad. After we had a good chuckle, I asked Dad for advice on the clothing situation at work. He told me to forget about changing between classes and wear my gym clothes for the entire day.

<u>Tuesday, March 2</u>

"I see you've regressed into your old clothing style," said Noose-Neck. "Shall I expect a scruffy bear and Birkenstocks next?"

This time I fought back. "Damian, you're expecting me to complete my duties in the gymnasium and change for science class at the same time. You can't have it both ways. If you want me to change between classes, I'll do it, but you can expect me to be late for periods two and four."

"Surely, Mr. Veitch, you can find a way to be more punctual."

"Of course I can," I replied. "But that would mean the gym storerooms would be left unlocked and equipment would be stolen. When the boys change, that's what I'm doing. But I have to do it quickly, or some of them will leave the change room early and wander the halls. I believe this is a safety concern? Therefore, I cannot in good conscience get changed until after the dismissal bell. But if I get changed, I'm late. So which is it, Mr. Glenn? Do you want me on time or in a shirt and tie?"

"Fine," he snipped, tightening the double-Windsor knot around his fat neck. "Don't change, but I expect you to at least wear cargo pants and a golf shirt. And I expect you to wear a shirt and tie when you're in health class."

"Fair enough."

"And don't expect me to grant you the re-evaluation you seek because you won't get it. I know you're colluding with others behind my back, and I don't appreciate it."

Noose-Neck stormed off.

After checking the hallway for witnesses, I gave him the finger. Just then Jozef turned and drove around the corner in the floor-scrubbing Zamboni.

"Did anyone else see me?" I asked.

Jozef winked at me. "*Nikt*," (nobody) he replied.

Wednesday, March 3

Teleisia Campbell threw a hissy fit when I woke her up. My only intention was for her to work on the circulatory system questions.

"Why did you wake me up? I'm tired. Leave me alone," she said.

"Fine," I replied. "We'll deal with this a different way."

After class, I held Teleisia back and assigned her a periodic table for punishment. She kissed her teeth at me and said, "I won't do it, sir," before storming out.

Thursday, March 4

Sara, being West Indian herself, said that when a Caribbean kid kisses her teeth at another person, it's considered rude. Some even feel it's as offensive as saying, "Fuck off."

No periodic table from Teleisia, by the way, so I've called home. However, when I asked for "Mr. or Mrs. Campbell," a groggy woman told me I had the wrong number.

<u>Friday, March 5</u>

Teleisia (still no periodic table) refused to sit behind Akeel today.

"Te-lee-see-uh," I said, "please sit at your assigned desk."

"No, sir."

"Te-lee-see-uh, move!"

"Don't yell at me, sir."

"Did anyone tell you you have Buddha ears?" asked Akeel of Teleisia.

"What!" she said. "I don't have Buddha ears."

"Who the hell is Buddha?" asked Lorraine. Yes, dear diary, *the* Lorraine from my first semester PE class. She needs this science credit to graduate.

"He's the God I worship, and he has long earlobes," said Akeel.

"I don't have long earlobes," said Teleisia.

In fact, she did. The immense weight of Teleisia's giant hooped earrings stretched out her earlobes. She did have Buddha ears, but I wasn't about to say so. The class was unfocused already, and Mr. Veitch coming in on the joke would only make it worse.

At least Akeel's comment diffused the tension between Teleisia and Akeel and between Teleisia and me. Or so I thought.

"Teleisia, please sit at your assigned desk," I said again.

"I'm not sitting behind Akeel."

"Why not?"

Dumb question.

"Are you sure you want to know?"

"Yes, Te-lee-see-uh. Please tell me."

Dumber statement.

"He fucking smells like curry every day." Class erupts into hysterics.

"It's, like, true, sir," said Lorraine.

"I can't help it if my parents feed me curry," cried Akeel.

"You could brush your teeth before you leave the house," added Cindy, between chews of her bubble gum.

"I do brush my teeth before I leave the house!" pleaded Akeel. "The smell gets stuck in my clothes."

Teleisia sprayed Akeel with her perfume. More hysterics.

"Class," I said. "Enough! Te-lee-see-uh, please step outside."

"Gladly," she said. "I won't have to smell Akeel anymore." She lifted one of his underarms and sprayed him in the armpit. "You should wear some deodorant, too. Ever heard of bathing?" Teleisia stormed out of the classroom.

When I went out to diffuse the bomb that was Teleisia, she was nowhere to be found. I buzzed Mrs. Smith to indicate that Teleisia had gone for a walkabout. We soon heard Mrs. Smith over the PA:

"*Telesha* Campbell to the main office, please. *Telesha* Campbell to the main office."

I heard Teleisia kiss her teeth, all the way from the bathroom down the hall. "It's Te-lee-see-uh!" she screamed. She walked back into the hallway and saw me.

"I was just in the bathroom, sir."

"Please go to the office," I said.

"For going to the bathroom?"

"For vulgar language, for insulting another student, and for not doing your periodic tables."

"Whatever." Teleisia walked north toward the exit sign instead of south toward the office.

"You're going the wrong way," I said.

"I'm going home."

<u>Saturday, March 6</u>

Kingston

Another feeble attempt by Teagan to complete a Beer Mile. At least he finished one out of four laps without the puke penalty this time. Hoover, McCraken, Bobo, and I all finished without penalty, but none of us broke the six-minute barrier like in the fall. During tonight's drunken talk, Teagan apologized for the "Aunt Pamela" comments and made me promise not to distribute the Stages video.

<u>Sunday, March 7</u>

Derek and Megan phoned to ask if I would be in their wedding party.

"I would be honoured," I said.

The wedding is June 12, my twenty-fifth birthday. I'll find out in a couple of weeks if Lisa will be my date.

<u>Monday, March 8</u>

Teleisia lives with her Aunt Veronica, who does not share the Campbell surname. That's why the groggy woman told me I had the wrong number last week. Mrs. Smith informed me of Teleisia's housing status when I double-checked my records with her this morning.

I introduced myself as "Mr. Veitch, Teleisia's science teacher" this time and then asked, "Could I speak with the aunt of Teleisia Campbell?"

"That's me," said the woman. She still sounded half asleep. "What did she do *now*?"

I related the issues yet ended up spending the bulk of the call listening to Veronica's complaints about life:

"Teleisia's parents live in Jamaica ..."

"I work a twelve-hour night shift to support her and my own three kids ..."

"My husband left me ..."

"What's wrong with kids these days ...?"

"I tell them to follow the rules of the institution but they don't listen ..."

After thirteen minutes and forty-four seconds, I'd had enough.

"Veronica," I said, "I'm sorry to hear things aren't so great right now, but will you talk to Teleisia for me?"

"I'll talk to her," said Veronica. "But it won't do anything."

Tuesday, March 9

Freezing rain. School at half capacity.

Some dumb bastard pulled the fire alarm, and we had to evacuate.

I wish I'd stayed in, like that time me and D'Souza did in first-year university. In residence, at least once every Thursday, Friday, and Saturday, some drunken fool would pull the fire alarm, just as a joke. D'Souza and I vacated the dorm every time except once, that being the only time, of course, the alarm was for real. There was a gas leak at Leonard Hall.

Firefighters, wearing First World War–style gas masks, knocked on our door and then came in to see two dumb nineteen-year-olds wearing earmuffs (to dampen the sound of the alarm), playing Super Tetris on a computer.

"Get the hell out of here!" they screamed. "What do you think you're doing?"

Lisa's reaction was more fierce. She was in the co-ed wing of Leonard. When D'Souza and I approached, she screamed, "What the hell were you thinking?" I asked her out the next day.

Unlike the Leonard Hall incident, today's was a false alarm. Noose-Neck and Bill Parsons now hunt for the culprit.

Wednesday, March 10

I believe that the pea-brained Marco Costa pulled the fire alarm yesterday. He had a blue stain on his left hand. Our alarms are designed such that the "puller" gets a squirt of blue dye on the hands upon triggering the switch. In addition, Marco was present in my period one class but absent during Lauren's period four class. Therefore, I've deduced that Marco pulled the alarm with his left hand during period three, got it sprayed blue, panicked, and then ran home.

After school, I reported this info to Noose-Neck. How foolish of me to believe he would support my hypothesis. If any other teacher had done the same, or if Marco's last name had begun with a letter between M and Z and I was dealing with Bill Parsons instead, the kid would've been suspended for three days and his parents would've paid the $500 fine for triggering a false alarm. Noose-Neck is so blinded by his distaste for me that he's oblivious to the truth.

"How am I going to sell this suspension to the parents?" asked Noose-Neck. "Marco says the blue on his hands is just from an exploded pen—today—and he ran home after the alarm yesterday because he was cold."

"Can you not at least call Mr. Costa and ask if Marco had the stain on his hand last night?"

"I'm not going to waste Mr. Costa's time with your drivel."

Thursday, March 11

I phoned Mr. Costa at home. One of his daughters answered.

"Is Mr. Costa available?" I asked.

"No, who's calling?" she said.

"It's Mr. Veitch. I'm Marco's PE teacher."

"What did he do now?"

"Well, I'd prefer to speak with your father, but can you tell me one thing?"

"Sure."

"Did you notice a blue stain on Marco's hand yesterday?"

"Yeah, I did. He said his pen exploded."

"Thanks. Could you have your dad phone the school as soon as possible?"

"Will do."

After classes, Noose-Neck hauled me into his office. He was so angry with me that he couldn't suck on his candy properly and had to put the semidissolved sugar ball in an open wrapper until after scolding me.

"I don't appreciate you going behind my back. Mr. Costa is very upset that you've concocted this fantasy about his supposed delinquent son."

"Mr. Glenn, I was just trying to help."

"You're not helping. In fact, Marco thinks you're picking on him again. Stay out of my way, and don't even bother to let Aunt Sara come and rescue you again."

"Fine, but I'm wondering if you'll grant me one request."

"And what is that, Mr. Veitch?"

"For Marco's sake and for Mr. Costa's sake, why don't you switch Marco out of my class?"

In reality, I was thinking that having Marco in my class was not safe for my already fledgling career. *Should Marco's antics keep escalating, I don't want to be there when he does something even more stupid.*

"Mr. Veitch, no teacher has the right to choose his or her students like candy, nor does any student or parent have the right to choose a teacher. It doesn't work that way. Besides, it would be an administrative nightmare."

Friday, March 12

After fruitlessly trying to repair the staff room photocopier and vowing to God never to use the double-sided function again, I confessed my sins to Mrs. Smith. She laughed it off and let me use the office machine.

I saw Teleisia in the office detention room. I presume she was there because of her recent misgivings. The detention couldn't have been much of a deterrent because during her custodial punishment, Teleisia ate fries, fiddled with her hooped earrings, and played cards with three other female malcontents. A fifth student lay prone on the old carpet floor, attempting to get comfortable and have a snooze. Teleisia threw a French fry in his hair and the girls giggled.

Noose-Neck, peeking through the glass window of his office, saw me using the copy machine and shook his head. Marco and Mr. Costa were also in his office. One by one, they emerged from Noose-Neck's lair.

"Mr. Costa," I said, extending my hand. "I see you got my message." Marco slumped against the wall, sucking on one of Noose-Neck's candies.

"Listen, buddy," said Mr. Costa, "I understand you're trying to help, but don't accuse my son of things you can't prove."

Saturday, March 13

Skiing: Round three
Poppa Wib came with Megan, Derek, and me, so I didn't feel like the fifth wheel this time. Derek skied on the intermediate hills with Dad while Megan and I tackled the black diamonds. This time, I negotiated Rabbit's Run without touching down with my hands. Unfortunately, Lorraine and her three stooges weren't around to witness my brilliance.

During a lunch break, the four of us played euchre. Poppa Wib and Derek were partners. Megan and I crushed them. Dad was pissed. He later told me, "Derek had no interest whatsoever in winning the game. When it's time to play, play. When it's time to flirt with your fiancée, flirt with your fiancée."

About an hour before leaving Blue Mountain, snow began to fall, leaving a thin layer of dust on the hills and in the parking lot. Before leaving, much to my father's delight, Megan did a few more donuts in the parking lot. She didn't hit any lampposts or other cars, but on the way out, she ditched the car in a snow bank. Derek, Poppa Wib, and I had to dig her out.

<u>Sunday, March 14</u>

We start CPR training in Grade 9 health class tomorrow. So it was convenient when Eric phoned from Sydney. I quizzed the future Dr. D'Souza about any updates to the ABCs of CPR.

"Dude," he said. "Just make sure those kids do the chest compressions deep and fast enough."

"Thanks," I said, before changing the subject.

"So are you still with that special someone?" I asked.

Long pause.

"Oh, that? Uh, it didn't work out," he said.

I wanted to probe but let it go when Eric quickly changed topics.

"So I'm thinking about taking another trip in July," he said.

"Eric, you're in Australia," I said. "You're whole life is a trip."

"Teags and I are thinking about Africa. Wanna come?"

"I think Lisa's coming home. I want to spend time with her."

"Dude, did you ever think that maybe your relationship with Lisa is over?"

"No," I said, before listing a dozen reasons why Lisa should come back to me. But maybe Eric was right. I guess I'll find out in another week.

<u>Monday, March 15</u>

Big sign above office photocopier: "FOR OFFICE STAFF ONLY."

At home, I mailed my reply to Megan and Derek's wedding. I ticked the check box indicating I would be bringing a guest. Hopefully, Lisa will be home by then and will join me. Otherwise, I'll have to bring Grandma Veitch as my date.

<u>Tuesday, March 16</u>

Letter from Lisa:

> Dear Chud,
>   I want you to know that I think we should see other people. It's time for you to move on. Please, then, when you arrive in Cuzco, don't expect us to be more than friends.
>   Lisa

Oh shite.

<u>Wednesday, March 17</u>

Marco gave himself a blow job with a CPR mannequin. Thank God there was a layer of clothing between his parts and the mouth of the mannequin he humped. I'll spare you the details, dear diary, but imagine having to write up that incident report.

Thursday, March 18

Mr. Costa doesn't believe Marco had "sexual relations" with the CPR mannequin. Noose-Neck, therefore, asked me for witnesses. Several boys, all trustworthy, agreed to corroborate my story. Normally, students are reluctant to rat on their peers, especially when it's not anonymous, but I think they're as fed up with Marco as I am.

Friday, March 19

Noose-Neck suspended Marco for the five days after March break. Lauren told me the pinhead bastard is on vacation in Italy that week anyway. How convenient.

Saturday, March 20

What to do if, as I suspect, Lisa has a boyfriend:
1) ~~Acceptance~~ Murder.
2) Set boyfriend up with Peruvian prostitutes, take clandestine photos of their sexual orgy, and then bribe him to leave Lisa forever.
3) Become a destitute hobo on the streets of Cuzco.
4) Dare boyfriend to run across congested streets of Peru buck naked, after secretly putting extra coca in his coca tea.
5) Defect to Peru and propose marriage to Lisa. If she refuses, kidnap her to some Andean highland hut until she develops Stockholm syndrome for me.

I wrote these ideas during my overnight stopover at Aeropuerto Internacional Jorge Chávez in Lima.

Sunday, March 21

Lima → Cuzco, the Incan capital:
A stunning, early morning flight through the Andes

As scheduled, I met Lisa at Hotel Ruines, in Plaza de Armas (the central square). She gave me a polite hug and told me her boyfriend Norman was sleeping in a triple room upstairs. I welled up with tears but nodded.

"I'm sorry, Carlson, but you must have known this was coming," she said.

I nodded again but was unable to make eye contact. "Can you take my bag upstairs?" I said. "I need to go for a walk before I'm ready to meet him."

"I understand."

"Thanks."

"Take your time. Norman is having problems with the altitude [3,326 metres]. We're going to take it easy until he's acclimatized."

It was dinner time before I returned. During my walkabout, the touts of South America's oldest continually inhabited city offered cheap massages; a multitude of discount bus, horse, train, and boat tours; altitude sickness pills; alpaca wool sweaters; Inca Colas and Pisco Sours. Unfazed, I ignored their pleas for business (even the massage with a free "happy ending") and weaved through the narrow, often stepped streets of beautiful Cuzco. Sitting on an Incan-built stone wall is where I finally accepted that Lisa and I are no more.

Monday, March 22

I now write, alone, from a Korean restaurant near Gringo Alley. Mr. Kim and his wife (I think her name is Adjima because he keeps yelling it to her) prepare my bibimbap (fried egg, veggies, and rice in a stone pot) while I make this entry.

Norman, so decimated by the altitude, still needs help walking more than ten metres and rests at the hotel with Lisa. Last night, for example, Lisa and I practically dragged the poor sod up and down the stairs at the restaurant (Victor Victoria) because he was so out of breath. I suppose this means that no "south of the equator" exploring of the tenderloins is possible until he adjusts to the thinner air. This thought is somewhat satisfying.

However, I decided to find my own room this morning. After inspecting several one-star hotel rooms (some without toilet seats and others where the aforementioned "happy endings" probably occur), I've chosen to remain at Hotel Ruines, down the hall from Lisa and Norman.

I'm also going paragliding after lunch.

11:12 AM
Kimchi (appetizers)—très hot. And miso soup fails to neutralize my burning tongue. I've asked Mr. Kim for more water.

"Adjima!" he's just screamed, followed by several Korean words, all of which seem to end in "oh" or "yo."

11:14 AM
Mrs. Kim presently serves me water to cool my tingling taste buds.

11:15 AM
Water ineffective.

11:16 AM
Mrs. Kim now walking toward me with bibimbap.

11:18 AM
Bibimbap full of red-hot chili pepper sauce; I sweat more heavily than a morbidly obese man after ten jumping jacks.

11:19 AM

Mr. Kim sensed my peril and just served me soju, a common potato or grain vodka from Korea. It's working.

11:24 AM

Mr. Kim asked me what I do "for a profession."

"I'm a teacher," I said.

"If you ever teach overseas, I have some business cards for you."

"Adjima!" he yelled, followed by something in Korean that I couldn't understand.

Adjima brought me three business cards:

Sejong Restaurant Cuzco

세종

Owner
Mr. Kim Young Min
(Peter Kim)

☎ 97-1973

Namhansanseong International School

국제학교남한산성

Headmaster Kim Young Bae
B.Sc. Ph.D. Stanford University

✆ (82-031) 206-1970

Namhansanseong International School

국제학교남한산성

Headmaster Dr. E. Williams
B.Ed. Ph.D. Princeton University

✆ (82-031) 206-1970

Mr. Kim said that teachers are highly regarded in Korea, as well respected as physicians. Kim Young Bae is his older brother. Namhansanseong International School is located in Songnam, a suburb of Seoul, Korea, where he and his wife used to live. They offer a K–12 U.S. curriculum.

If by happenstance (yeah, right) I ever need them, these three cards are now taped to the pages of my diary.

11:27 AM
Mr. Kim ordered his wife to cook me a new batch of bibimbap, without the red-hot chili pepper sauce. He also yelled at Adjima to phone the paragliding company (Andean Adventures) to fetch me from the restaurant instead of the hotel.

1:12 PM
Bibimbap finished. Bottle of soju finished, and I can now read and write Korean. It's simple to learn: only one sound per letter, and three letters together making a symbol. Mind you, though I can say the sounds and hear them, I have no clue as to what I'm saying or hearing.

1:19 PM
Now in the Andean Adventures car, I'm feeling a little tipsy from the soju.

One other tourist, an older, butchy-looking South African woman, joined me on the day trip. Maxine had a black eye. It matched her dark roots, visible beneath short, bleach-blonde hair. Maxine's shiner reminded me of Teagan's, back in the summer. Mind you, hers was caused by a recoiling bungee cord rather than an angry fist. Andean Adventures gave Maxine a free paragliding adventure after she threatened to write to Lonely Planet about the accident.

Our gear consisted of a helmet and a harness. The harness felt like a chair with a giant diaper attached, thick enough to absorb even the worst incontinence. Attached behind me was Leo (pronounced Lay-oh), my pilot.

Two minutes later, Maxine, Leo, and I ran off the cliff in tandem and then rode the thermals several hundred feet above the ground. The ride, with a majestic view of the Andes, was a thrill until the soju spoke to me.

"You are going to barf," it said.

I tried to resist, but alas, I soon puked. First, some partially digested kimchi dribbled down my chin and onto my floating feet. The rest, along with the bibimbap, heaved out from my stomach in one final shot to the farmland below. My only solace was that some of the barf sprinkled a bird, which had been, until that time, also enjoying the thermals beneath us. *How does it feel to be shit on, Mr. Bird?*

I begged Leo to land after a mere twenty-three minutes in the air. Some forty-one minutes later, Maxine landed, grinning.

Returning to Cuzco, Maxine mentioned a downhill mountain biking trip planned for tomorrow and Wednesday and invited me to join. I put my arm around her and agreed.

"You do realize I'm a lesbian?" she said.

Tuesday, March 23

My guide Raul picked me up from the hotel lobby at 5 AM. He was chipper. Raul wore a red fleece hat that made him look like a court jester.

"How you doing, Mr. Carlson?" said Raul. "We go to five thousand metres today, then straight down to Lares. It's fun, hehehe." Raul took my backpack. He walked me to the car. There stood Maxine, leaning against the vehicle, smoking a fag. The old white Toyota spewed exhaust from a rusted tailpipe. Both grey (from the cigarette) and black (from the car) clouds floated upward, toward the dark sky. Maxine snuffed out her cigarette on the ground.

Just then, a shaggy derelict, probably inebriated from a night of drinking, walked straight into her. Maxine shoved the man onto the hood of the car. He stumbled off the hood and fell to the ground, picked himself up, and then walked away.

"Too many Pisco Sours," said Raul, giggling.

We met René, Raul's brother, at the bus stop. René stood above a blue city bus, securing four mountain bikes to its roof. He waved at Maxine and me, followed by a friendly greeting. "*Buenos*," he said.

Our first stop was Calca, a small Incan town where only the most adventurous travellers visit. Maxine and I purchased some chicken-rice-carrot stew from a sturdy looking native woman.

The woman's hands were heavily calloused, and her dark face was deeply wrinkled. However, despite being in the face of two white tourists, she didn't act like the touts in Cuzco. She didn't beg for extra money, try to sell us trinkets, or overcharge for food. Instead, the woman just smiled at Maxine and me. I think she was just happy that we gringos took the time to see how the average Peruvian lived.

Maxine finished her plate and walked off to have a smoke. The native woman gave me a smile and dumped another serving on my plate.

The brothers moved our bikes from the bus to the roof of a minivan. After lunch, this van, meant to seat eight, weaved up the switchbacks carrying twelve passengers and a chicken.

One hundred metres from the summit, René told the driver to stop. We unloaded and then began our ride. Raul and René pedalled easily to the top. Maxine and I struggled behind. Indeed, the air was thin. I have more sympathy for Norman's plight now.

I was panting heavily. "Why I'm doing this," I said to Raul, "I don't really know."

He chuckled and said, "There is only 54 percent oxygen here. Now we go down."

What a thrill! The brothers often rode between switchbacks, down forty-five degree slopes, through tall grasses, dodging shrubs, boulders, and the occasional llama along the way. Maxine and I avoided the extra danger and remained on the dirt road to Lares.

We reached the Hot Springs Resort (although it feels more like a campsite) at 2:52 PM. It is now 7:58 PM. I write this entry by candlelight inside my cozy wood hut. The mud and straw roof provides ample warmth.

About two dozen of these huts surround seven thermal pools. Each pool is a different size and temperature. Flagstone walkways connect the pools to one another, and a long stone wall, embedded into a hill, holds several shower heads. We tried each pool, including the largest, where I swam a few lengths, even though the water was as muddy as the Amazon. Raul said it was safe, but I was careful not to swallow any of the water.

There are no touts here. It is a holiday many Peruvians can afford.

After a cold shower, Raul and René led Maxine and me on a hike of the surrounding countryside. Stone huts dot the vast Andean landscape. Raul detailed how indigenous hill people move between huts every two to three months. They live off the land and their animals, and most refuse to give up this nomadic existence for city life, despite government incentives.

After a chicken and rice dinner, we sipped tea and Inca Cola while playing hearts. Maxine got so pissed at losing that she refused to finish. René, though he spoke little English, quickly learned the game from Raul's description and won.

Wednesday, March 24

Lares → Cuzco
Raul, René, and now Maxine cycled many off-road routes between switchbacks. Succumbing to peer pressure, I followed. Within seconds, my front tire hit a rock, and the resulting elevated rear wheel bucked me over the handlebars.

"Nice endo," said Maxine.

After two more endos, one of which nearly resulted in death by boulder, I chose to coast down the remainder of the mountain along the dirt and gravel roads. *Screw the peer pressure.*

Now back at Hotel Ruines, I've just finished dinner with Lisa and Norman. He's more acclimatized (I didn't need to support him up any staircases), and we're taking the train to Aguas Calientes (a Machu Picchu town) tomorrow.

Thursday, March 25

The steep climb out of Cuzco does not allow for normal railroad curves. Instead, clever engineers designed a series of zigzags, allowing trains to enter and leave. Criss-crossing out of the valley took forty-five minutes, but we didn't mind. The view was spectacular.

I now know why my flight here from Lima required such a sharp turn to land—the Andes envelop the Incan capital. A network of massive Incan-built stone walls provides the foundation for many of Cuzco's buildings. Norman said the "well-to-do" populate the solid buildings downtown. In contrast, the less fortunate inhabit thousands of aluminum shacks that litter the hillsides. The shacks are stacked adjacent to and above one another in a precarious manner.

After a three-hour ride through lush valleys, we reached Aguas Calientes, situated eight kilometres from the ruins. The Urubamba River, with its water flowing violently, dissects the little tourist town.

Feeling fidgety after the long ride, I chose to trek to the park gates. Norman and Lisa followed, but Norman struggled to keep up. They soon turned back, but I walked ahead. After a few minutes, I reached the entrance of Parque Arqueológico Nacional de Machu Picchu. The lost city of the Incas was only another three-hundred vertical metres above.

Instead of following the eleven switchbacks of the bus road, I hiked up a series of flagstone stairways that cut between them. Climbing was a challenge, and not just because of the altitude. No two stairs were the same dimensions, few were level, and many were cracked or missing. I lost my balance a couple of times. The local Quechua boys had no such difficulty.

Every few minutes, I'd see a blur of colour coming downward toward me. Dressed in yellow, red, or orange weaved clothing and wearing the thinnest of sandals, one such Quechua boy would sprint past me. Some of the older boys could even take three steps at a time.

Their objective, as Norman would later tell me, was to beat a tour bus in a race down the mountain. The boys would even stop at every crossing between the bus road and the stairway for a wave as their bus drove by. Once bus and boy reach bottom, boy climbs on bus and collects tips from impressed patrons. Then boy takes bus back up to the ruins before commencing another round.

My hiking speed must have seemed pathetic to the Quechua boys. It took fifty-one minutes and eleven seconds for me to reach the gated entrance to the ruins, though I did stop twice. The first time was to gaze at the Urubamba below, and the second was to gawk at the magnificent Andes that surrounded me.

It was 4:47 PM when I reached the gates—almost closing time— so I didn't pay to go in today. What I could see through the gates captured my soul. I can't wait to spend all of tomorrow wandering the lost city of the Incas.

Lisa, Norman, and I went to a pizza restaurant for dinner. While waiting forever for our pie, I asked them if they knew why the Incas built a city on top of a remote mountain.

"Machu Picchu was chosen because of its alignment with sacred celestial events," said Norman.

"Makes sense," I said.

"That's one of the theories, anyway," said Norman, before launching into an extensive list of several other theories.

"So how did they build it? I mean, it is a city on top of a remote mountain."

Norman didn't have a definitive answer to this one. I was happy to stump Mr. Know-it-all.

Eventually, the pizza arrived. Our waitress informed us that the cook was drunk and had screwed up the first two attempts. After dinner, we wandered the narrow streets of Aguas.

Norman held Lisa's hand and didn't have to stop every ten steps like he did a couple of days back. I guess this means he's finally adapted to the altitude. I suppose I should feel happy for him, but this means his genitals might be receiving proper blood now. He could be capable of performing in the bedroom. I accept that I'll never be with Lisa again, but I still can't imagine anyone having sex with her but me.

Friday, March 26

Thirty-seven minutes and forty-three seconds to the top. Lisa and Norman paid five gringo dollars for the ten-minute bus ride.

We paid our entry fees to the ruins and then meandered along the agricultural terraces to the mortared walls of the ancient Machu Picchu town. I often sat and simply stared at what surrounded me. For a while, I was completely at peace with myself.

That was until a brown llama sniffed my sweaty feet, interrupting my Zen-like state. A white llama, jealous of the attention my toes received, spat at the brown one, before they both sauntered off.

Norman invited me to climb Huayna Picchu (Little Peak) for an even more stunning view of the ruins. Lisa chose to remain and photograph Machu Picchu from eye level.

Well-maintained but steep steps led us to the summit of Huayna. It was another thirty-minute climb for me but longer for Norman. While waiting for him, I put my hand down on what I thought was a boulder. However, I felt the dry skin of a lizard pass across my palm. Camouflaged by the lichen-covered rock, I hadn't noticed the reptile.

Frightened, the lizard scurried into a nearby shadow. It looked unharmed, but I felt bad for nearly squashing the poor thing. To atone, I placed the remains of any mosquitoes I killed near its probing tongue. I even got it to eat right from my hand, so I knew I'd been forgiven. Eventually, my lizard friend left.

Soon after, Norman appeared. He was puffed, so I grabbed his wrist to help him up the last boulder. Silently, we took in the magnificent view. I told him to look after Lisa for me.

Saturday, March 27

On the evening train back to Cuzco, some stupid kids threw rocks at our train. Opportunistic bastards hit me when I opened the windows for fresh air while descending through the zigzags.

The rock struck me near the top of my head. Lisa checked me for cuts, but thankfully the only thing she found was a goose egg.

"You'll need to part your hair on the other side for a couple of days," said Lisa, "unless you want the bump to show through."

"It's going to hurt when I comb," I said.

Back at the hotel, she held an ice pack on the top of my head while Norman and I played rummy. A few months ago, this caring gesture would also have sent blood to my loins; any contact by her felt like electricity. But now it's just the kind touch of a friend. I think I'm over her.

Sunday, March 28

Cuzco → *Lima* → *Toronto.*

Since I'd booked the earliest possible flight to Lima (6 AM), I avoided any weather delays and made it home to Toronto on time.

At customs, I noticed the same obese officer who served me during my mini-meltdown earlier this year. I joined his line.

"*Bienvenue au Canada.* Welcome to Canada," he said between laboured breaths.

"Remember me?" I asked.

After a pause, he said, "The blowgun guy."

"I'm sorry for being such a basket case back at Christmas."

"No worries—happens every day," he said. "Get your blowgun back?"

"Naw, still doing the paperwork."

He stamped my passport and said, "Welcome home, Carlson."

Monday, March 29

Welcome back, Mr. Veitch: Teleisia accused me of being racist. All I did was wake her up and insist she complete her school work.

"What about Ramon and Angie?" she argued. "They're not doing shit either. Is it because I'm black and they're white?"

"No, Teleisia," I said. "It's because—"

"I ain't doin' no work for some racist teacher."

"Could you please step outside?"

"Sure, segregate the coloured kid," she said. Teleisia stormed out.

Five minutes later, we heard *thump thump thump*. It was Teleisia pounding on the door. She opened it slightly, her long, decorated fingernails leading the way, like velociraptor claws searching for prey. Next inside was her considerable cleavage—thank God, covered by a tight red shirt. Her show had the intended effect, as Jomo whispered to Mikel, "She's got a nice rack," and Lanie said to Marci, "Oh my God, what a ho."

Finally, her head appeared, and she innocently asked, "Can I come in, sir?" followed by, "I'm sorry about my outburst."

"No, Teleisia, please wait outside."

Her expression changed from a counterfeit smile to a genuine scowl. "Whatever," she said, before storming away once more.

Another five minutes later we heard *thump thump thump. What now?* I soon smelled perfume and realized it was Sara.

"Pardon the interruption, Mr. Veitch," she said, "but I caught Ms. Campbell wandering the halls. I'll be keeping her with my OACs until the end of class." *Thank God.* "I'm sure you don't mind."

The Dow Jones closed above ten-thousand points. Dad says we should buy Nortel and JDS stock.

<u>Tuesday, March 30</u>

I let Teleisia sleep in class today.

<u>Wednesday, March 31</u>

Noose-Neck inspected my Grade 11 science class today. He noticed Teleisia's slumber immediately. All eyes watched as Noose-Neck approached her and then tapped the slumbering raptor on the shoulder.

"What?" sneered Teleisia, before she realized it was Noose-Neck and not me. She quickly changed her demeanor. "I'm sorry, Mr. Glenn. I had to work last night."

"Mr. Veitch," said Noose-Neck, "please keep your students awake so they can get some learning done."

APRIL

I have no sex life, even with myself

Led by Andrew Yates, no doubt, all the boys in my Grade 10 PE class wore their Kipling HS gym shirts and shorts backward. I pretended not to notice, mind you, reversing their April Fools' Day joke. This was my only amusement in another dreary day of teaching. Don't even ask me about Teleisia.

Nunavut, the Inuit homeland of Canada, now officially exists. Politicians created it from the eastern part of the Northwest Territories.

Friday, April 2

How can I be so exhausted after just four days back in the classroom? Thank God today was a holiday.

Saturday, April 3

Eric called, asking if I would join him and Teags in Africa this summer.

I said, "Maybe, provided I do not self-detonate from my stressful job, provided I don't land in jail after murdering my bastard boss, and provided I have some money."

Sunday, April 4

Easter Sunday

Thank you, Grandma Veitch, for the turkey! As I write, dear diary, the tryptophan converts into serotonin. I feel content despite tomorrow being another day at the grind.

<u>Monday, April 5</u>

Mr. Costa insisted that Marco be switched to another PE class, once again arguing that I pick on his poor pinhead of a son. Noose-Neck caved and removed the runt from my Grade 9 class. I'm not going to argue.

Russell Henderson, the bigot who murdered gay college kid Matthew Shepard, pleaded guilty to kidnapping and felony murder. In doing so, he hopes to avoid the death penalty.

<u>Tuesday, April 6</u>

Should I be grateful? I suppose one out of four classes is better than none. My Grade 9 boys PE kids are quite malleable now that Marco is officially gone. My Grade 10 boys PE kids are okay in the gym once I get them playing. However, they also morph into assholes when we have health class. It's as if they secretly blame me for taking away gym time and exact revenge by acting out. At least Andrew Yates takes his punishment like a man. As for my science classes, dear diary, I choose not to write about those yahoos; it's too upsetting.

E-mail from Teagan:

> Carl,
> You coming to Kili with me and D'Souza? Machame Route is the most scenic but it's also the steepest. There's also the Rongai, Lemosho, Shira, Umbwe and Marungu Routes. Marungu is easiest, but it's so busy they call it the "Coca-Cola trail."

What do you think? Check out
devotionsafaris.com.
Cheers mate,
Teagan

Wednesday, April 7

Marco Costa is now in Gary's Grade 9 class, which occurs at the same time as I teach my Grade 10s. The old bear looks more grumpy than usual. Several times, I felt his piercing glare penetrate my soul; I avoided eye contact.

E-mail to Teagan:

> *Teags,*
> *About 10 climbers a year die on*
> *Kilimanjaro, mostly because of*
> *the altitude. I almost croaked*
> *while off-road mountain biking*
> *in Peru and if this fucking job*
> *doesn't kill me, I'd like to*
> *live through the summer.*
> *Carlson*

Thursday, April 8

I bought Gary a dozen apple fritters. He gave me a pat on the back.

"That Marco's a real piece of work," he said, munching on a donut. "How did you avoid killing the little fucker?"

After school, I purchased a paperback print of the *Merck Manual of Medical Information* and read about altitude sickness.

Symptoms include headache; dehydration; insomnia; nausea; loss of appetite; fatigue; dizziness; shortness of breath upon exertion (what I felt near Lares); malaise; swelling of hands, feet, and face; rapid pulse; vomiting; and drowsiness.

Life-threatening symptoms of altitude sickness are fluid in the lungs (pulmonary edema), fever, dry cough, swelling of the brain (cerebral edema), loss of consciousness (duh!), drunken gait, and severe headaches.

Friday, April 9

School still sucks.

I understand now what Gary meant when he said, "It's better to assume they're all assholes and then maybe one or two will surprise you." I've witnessed the ubiquitous "asshole" student caricature; now I await the one or two who'll surprise me.

Saturday, April 10

I gained enough energy after another long sleep (eleven hours, three minutes) to pick up the phone and call my friends to hang out. Rick is working overtime, and Megan and Derek are busy planning their wedding. I watched *Raiders of the Lost Ark* with Poppa Wib.

I wish Noose-Neck's face would melt like Colonel Dietrich's and Major Toht's did when they looked into the Ark.

Sunday, April 11

Slept all freakin' day. So tired. So stressed.

D'Souza phoned to educate me about climbing at altitude.

"Remember Professor Bob?" he asked.

"Exercise for special populations?" I replied.

"Climb high, sleep low."

"But what about …?"

"Get your doctor to prescribe Acetazolamide, too."

"What are the side effects?"

"Dude, it's not like malaria medication. This stuff just increases the acidity of your blood."

"That doesn't sound good."

"It just increases your respiratory rate. You'll be fine. Worst case scenario, we'll stuff you in a Gamow bag."

"What's a Gamow bag?"

"Forget I said that, dude. We'll take the Marungu Route. Nobody dies on that one."

Gamow bag: a portable, plastic pressure bag inflated with a foot pump; can be used to reduce the effective altitude by as much as 1,500 metres. A Gamow bag is generally used only as an aid to evacuate severe AMS patients, not to treat them at altitude.

Monday, April 12–Thursday, April 15

@%%$@#% frustration!

My Grade 11 science class is driving me bananas. Why do I spend so much time obsessing over them? Why do I keep shuffling through the same thoughts over and over?

What a bunch of whiners, especially Annette. ("Sir, why do we have to …?"), Akeel ("That's not fair!"), Teleisia ("You're picking on me because I'm black").

Grow the fuck up, Jomo, Mikel, Vincent, Pino, Jamie, Sean (the axis of assholes) and also Lanie, Marci, and Larissa (such spoiled brats—they are all gum-chewing pseudo–valley girls).

Teleisia Campbell, you are the biggest bitch I've ever encountered in my life. If you don't have anything good to say, don't say it. Didn't your mother ever take you to see *Bambi*?

Pino, shut the fuck up. The world does not revolve around you. Lose the attitude. Also, *you are not cool.* Can't you see the other kids don't like you?

Jamie, you are so callow. You think you can swear in my class and then have the gall to refuse my consequence? You are paying for it now. How's that three days in Mrs. Ross's OAC class feel? And shave that chinstrap off your face.

Why are these kids so immature? I was never like that—never. Apparently, I am the enemy because I actually follow through. I actually tell students what to do, unlike some other colleagues of mine who are doormats.

Hmm, what kids do I actually like in that class? Kyle, yeah, and Simon, because he never shows up. Leah is tolerable, but she still occasionally mutters things under her breath. Caroline is okay because she doesn't bug anybody. I don't mind Patrick, when he keeps his mouth shut, that is.

Must call the parents of ~~Pino (again), Teleisia (again), Jamie (again),~~

EVERYONE!

Friday, April 16

Mike Harris called a provincial election for June 3. If the most recent polls are correct, Harris's right-leaning Progressive Conservative party will easily win, maintaining its stranglehold on teachers and nurses.

According to our union leaders, the only way to defeat Mike Harris is through strategic voting. The anti-Conservative vote is 58 percent right now. However, this vote is split between Liberal and NDP supporters. If the centre and centre-left Liberal and NDP supporters cannot cooperate to select the most appropriate candidate in each riding, Mike Harris will rule again. Should his hairy ass win, the teaching situation in Ontario may get worse … if that's even possible.

At this point, only one thing is certain: I'm guaranteed a way out of this mess if I realize my dream of teaching overseas. To do so, however, is next to impossible without a recommendation from a current principal. I must convince Noose-Neck to re-evaluate me. How can you make a blind man see?

Saturday, April 17

Mom died fifteen years ago today. Dad, Grandma Veitch, Aunt Pamela and I visited her grave. Mom's buried beside Babcia (grandma) and Dziadzia (granddad) Golembieski. Coicia (Aunt) Alina and Wujek (Uncle) Marcin met us there as well. Coicia gave me a hug and said, "All I can think is that the house was her dream and it turned into a nightmare."

My cousins, Stan and Tola, arrived with their spouses as we left. We used to play together all the time as kids. After Mom got sick (and especially after her death), we cousins saw less of each other. Back then, most people could accept that animals could be poisoned by our man-made toxins and pollutants. Few, Mom's sister's family included, acknowledged that the same was true for humans. Maybe they thought my mom was crazy? I don't know, but I wish Stan, Tola, Kate, Coicia, Wujek, and I could see each other more than just once a year at Mom's grave.

At home, Kate called to say hello. Her chat with me and Grandma Veitch and Aunt Pam was pleasant. Her conversation with Dad, as always, degenerated into a shouting match. At least Dad opened up to me afterward.

Before going to the Clinical Ecology Hospital in Chicago, Mom pleaded with Dad to ensure that Kate and I didn't stay in the toxic house. He was very reluctant—the divisive point between Kate and my father—

but he caved. (Maybe if Dad had listened to Mom sooner, she'd still be here, argues Kate.) Poppa Wib couldn't fathom that his then ninety-two-pound, skeletal spouse became ill because of UFFI. Mom didn't want the same thing to happen to us and fought with Dad until we left the nightmare house. Ultimately, Mom ended up in Chicago's Henrotin Hospital, about the only medical facility in North America that acknowledged the existence of environmental hypersensitivity. It was there that she died.

Kate is also bitter because Dad dropped the ensuing lawsuit against the Canadian government and Rowland Insulation. Dad told Kate and me that he had to "let go and move on," and that's why he settled the lawsuit.

Our father did his best with what he knew at the time, so why can't Kate forgive him?

<u>Sunday, April 18</u>

Wayne Gretzky played his last hockey game today, retiring after twenty NHL seasons. Imagine that—living your passion for twenty years and becoming a multimillionaire.

My passion certainly is not teaching. Save for the occasional moment in my PE classes, I dread every minute of every day. Retirement sounds good to me. I want to retire from this misery. Two more months and I'm rid of Noose-Neck and this Bill 160/four-out-of-four nonsense. I only hope I can make it that far without having a nervous breakdown like Janis McKee. Then maybe I can recover and figure out what the hell to do with the rest of my life.

<u>Monday, April 19</u>

I've just reread much of my diary for the last few months. My entries have become increasingly negative. This is not the person I want to be. What the fuck am I doing?

2:19 AM

I can't sleep. My mind keeps going in circles.

2:37 AM

Ronda always says, "Write it down and it becomes a *problem,* not a *worry.*"

Here goes:

My three best friends from last year (Lisa—now my ex-girlfriend; Teagan the Irish hedonist, and absent-minded Eric) currently pursue their passions. My friends in Toronto are too busy to hang out (so am I, I guess). My dad finds it increasingly difficult to cheer me up. My sister rarely calls, and my mom's no help because she's dead.

At work, when not on strike against the provincial government, deflecting tomato projectiles from angry parents, or picketing the school board for three weeks during a harsh winter, and when not being bullied by my boss, I try to tell horny, smelly teenagers what to do.

At home, I'm marking, preparing lessons, sleeping, or watching TV because I'm too tired to do anything else. I have no sex life, even with myself.

2:42 AM

That didn't help.

3:01 AM

I'm in the middle of my worst panic attack since second-year university. I dare not sit still since I fear my head will explode. I'm walking around the block now while writing this entry. My heart races (141 beats per minute at last count), and I have cold sweats. I feel like I'm going to die. I know that it's just a panic attack, and it will pass.

3:33 AM

Back home. Still panicking. Ronda would tell me to slow down my breathing, but I just can't seem to do it. I'm going to wake Poppa Wib.

4:11 AM

Dad convinced me to take a Xanax. Initially, I didn't want to because BZs are habit-forming. What if I have to use higher and higher doses until the strongest dose possible doesn't work? I *am* feeling better now. My mind is less obsessive. I think I can sleep.

Tuesday, April 20

I was terrified today that I'd have another panic attack, especially during a lesson. Though I was in a constant state of anxiety, like I feel the night before a race or before asking a girl on a date, I did not succumb to panic.

Instead, I kept blinking, like my eyes were dry. The kids didn't seem to notice (I'm invisible to them anyway), but Lauren did. When she asked about my eyes, I lied and said it was my contacts.

"Holy darn, you wear contacts?" she asked. "I never noticed. Is that why your eyes are so gorgeous?"

I perpetuated the myth and said, "Yes."

I returned home to discover that two teens in Littleton, Colorado, shot dozens of their classmates. Dylan Klebold and Eric Harris, supposed "social pariahs" at Columbine High School, killed twelve peers and one teacher before committing suicide.

This news triggered another panic attack. I took a Xanax after five minutes. The attack subsided, mind you, within another five minutes of doing my breathing exercises. My understanding is that the Xanax pills take at least fifteen minutes to enter the bloodstream, so I must have, hopefully, diffused my panic through breath control.

<u>Wednesday, April 21</u>

Poppa Wib made me take a Xanax before school.

"It's only half a milligram," he said, the lowest possible dose. On a day like today, I might have taken more if he pressed me.

Both student and staff were stoic today. I threw out my lesson plans (they weren't good anyway) and just let the kids talk. Nobody truly understands why yesterday's massacre happened, though rumours abound: violent video games, Marilyn Manson music, antidepressant side effects (I think both killers were on SSRIs), revenge for bullying, and neglect from their yuppie parents.

<u>Thursday, April 22</u>

I took the day off. I fear I will lose control in front of my classes. The only place I feel safe is at home, on the couch eating Pringles or in my bed. I only get up to eat or use the loo. I'm shitting and pissing so much; my nerves only allow me to stomach liquid power shakes or else I will vomit.

I phoned my therapist. Ronda reiterated that avoidance of work will only reinforce the patterns of anxiety. She also reminded me to "let it come and let it go."

My sister helped me out as well. Dad phoned her, knowing that if he couldn't calm my nerves, she probably could.

"Kate," said my father, "it's Dad. Your brother is having trouble with anxiety again. I need you to talk him down."

Thank God they didn't start arguing like normal—I think that would have triggered another panic attack. Dad brought her up to speed on my struggles of late and then passed me the phone.

"Hi, Kate," I said. "I'm a bit of a basket case right now."

"I'm doing this for you Carlson, not for Dad," she said.

I told Kate I was terrified to go outside in case I lost control and pulled a Columbine or jumped off a bridge.

"Do you want to kill somebody?" she asked.

Just then, a commercial for the new Star Wars flick came on. I can't wait.

"Only my principal. And only with a lightsaber," I responded, with a slight chuckle. "But not really, I just want to humiliate him."

"There. You laughed. That's good."

"I haven't laughed in days."

"And do you want to jump off a bridge?"

"Only if it was into a lake full of naked women with big tits. Sorry, breasts."

"So go outside and walk to the end of the driveway and back. I'll wait."

I did.

"I'm back."

"Did you die?"

"No."

"Then you can go to school tomorrow."

Friday, April 23

"Carlson, the easiest lesson in PE is to play dodgeball," said Poppa Wib. He chuckled. "Those kids love beaning each other in the head."

I took Dad's advice. It worked. So did his suggestion about watching videos in science.

"I need a VCR for today," I said to Sara. She knew I'd been struggling with something. She was unaware, however, that the "something" was a relapse of severe anxiety disorder.

"You can use the VCR I booked," she said.

"Are you sure?" I asked.

"Of course."

Lauren helped me find some Bill Nye videos. I desperately wanted to confide in her but felt too embarrassed to do so.

<u>Saturday, April 24</u>

I am to write only positive things in my diary. Otherwise, Ronda promises to hunt me down and whack my cranium with a metal ruler.

"You're just overtired and overstressed," she said. "Once your system has a chance to rest, the anxiety will subside. Practice your breathing exercises and seriously consider taking that trip to Africa."

She also told me to masturbate.

<u>Sunday, April 25</u>

Today's positive:
It felt good taking a dump.

<u>Monday, April 26</u>

Today's positive:
No Xanax required. Ronda's breathing exercises allowed me to survive the following calamities:

1. Three floors of photocopier malfunction (none of them my fault)
2. Noose-Neck's evil stare when I used the office machines
3. Teleisia refusing to clean gum off desks
4. Sparrow breaking his forearm in half after tripping on Andrew Yates's oversized foot
5. Explaining to Sparrow's dad that his son's ulnar bone had protruded from the skin
6. Noose-Neck's accusatory glare when I completed the accident form for Sparrow's injury

<u>Tuesday, April 27</u>

One step back: I read all about anxiety disorders and other mental illnesses in my Merck manual. Dad told me to "stop obsessing" over it when he caught me filing through the useless information.

"If you don't, I'll swat that thing with my driver until the words are unrecognizable," he said. "Besides, I need to work on my stroke."

"Allow me," I said, before retrieving the club I gave him for Christmas (it was in the garage). Dad was proud of me until one swing caused the shaft of the John Daly club to split in two, unleashing a sickening *crack* that reminded me of the sound when Sparrow broke his forearm.

<u>Wednesday, April 28</u>

Add Juliette Pinkerton to my revolving shit list. Mind you, at least she's in the minority in my Grade 10 advanced science class. I've managed to get most of the students on board. The stupid carrot top arrives ten minutes late and then has the gall to ask me to use the can two minutes later.

"Mr. Veitch, can I go to the bathroom?" she asks.

"No," I say.

"Mr. Veitch, can I go to the bathroom?" I ignore the second request. "Mr. Veitch, can I go to the bathroom? Mr. Veitch, can I go to the bathroom?" etc. etc. until I respond, thinking, *This girl is almost as immature as Marco.*

"No! And stop asking me."

Juliette continued, so I kicked her out of class. When I went to retrieve her, she had left the vicinity of the portables, presumably to use the toilet.

<u>Thursday, April 29</u>

Today's positives:
#1: How I handled Juliette's mother
#2: I'm researching overseas teacher recruitment fairs

I may soon find myself on the front page of the Toronto *Star*. If Mrs. Pinkerton has her way, I'll also be headline news at 6 PM. All this because I dared to lock her daughter out of science class and, worse, had the audacity to refuse permission for the child to use the bathroom afterward.

I was alone in the dungeon when I called her. "How can my child learn the curriculum when she's out of class?" screamed the belligerent woman.

"She can't. Juliette has to arrive on time," I replied.

"So you're refusing to teach my daughter."

"Mrs. Pinkerton, I'm not refusing to teach Juliette. But I'm not going to interrupt my lesson every time a student arrives late. It's not fair to the other students, who are punctual."

"Juliette says she was outside for ten minutes. She's missing the lesson."

Her voice was loud and squeaky, like a feline whose tail was just stepped on.

"When a student is late, the expectation is that she wait outside the portable until there is a break in the lesson. Then, I go out, retrieve the student, and set up a time to debrief. During this time, I'm not instructing anyone, so everybody loses."

"Is that a school rule or your rule?"

I turned down the volume on the phone. "Both."

"Where does it say this on paper? This is a health and safety issue. Does the Ministry of Education say that anywhere on their documents?"

"Mrs. Pinkerton, I think you'll find that I'm in line with school expectations."

"I want to see this on paper. Where does it say teachers are allowed to lock students outside of the classroom? Why can't my daughter just come in quietly?"

"Mrs. Pinkerton, Juliette socializes the moment she enters the room. She's a nice kid, but I can't have her talking to peers when I'm delivering curriculum."

"So have you phoned those other parents? Or are you just picking on Juliette?"

How cliché. Now take a couple of deep breaths before continuing.

"Mrs. Pinkerton, this is about Juliette, and Juliette has not been punctual recently. If I don't lock the door, she'll waltz in and divert the class's attention from curriculum. I simply cannot allow that."

I smelled Sara's perfume.

"I'm going to the newspapers. I'm going to tell them Mr. Veitch locks his students outside and refuses to teach them."

"If you feel that's best, go ahead."

"Don't doubt me, Mr. Veitch. My daughter could get attacked or kidnapped or something out there, waiting for you to let her in. And what's this I hear about you refusing to let Juliette use the bathroom?"

Sara walked past, nodded hello, and then marked papers on her desk.

"When students are late, they lose all privileges."

"I don't want my kid getting a bladder infection. I see it every day where I work in the hospital—people coming in to get treated because they held it too long."

"Mrs. Pinkerton, a four-year-old can hold it for an hour; I'm sure Juliette can—"

"That is just rude and disrespectful. How dare you compare my Juliette to a four-year-old?"

I moved the phone from my ear into midair. Sara mouthed to me, "Is everything okay?" and I nodded. Mrs. Pinkerton's squawking continued. Every twenty seconds I brought the headset to my mouth and said "uh-huh" or "yes." Eventually, there was silence.

"I'm going to call the vice principal and the superintendent," stated Mrs. P.

"Would you like their extension numbers?" I said. Sara winked and gave me the thumbs up.

"Here's what you're going to do. You're going to make an appointment for me and my kid and you and the vice principal."

"I think that's a great idea."

"You're going to call me back in ten minutes and give me a place and time."

"No need," I said. "Meet me at 8 AM on Monday morning. I'll be in Mr. Parsons's office."

"I'll be there."

"Looking forward to it. Have a nice day."

I hung up the phone and then shook my head.

Sara said, "You handled that well."

"Thanks," I said. "What a bitch!"

"Don't take it personally."

"I'm slowly learning that in this job you can't take anything personally. I just hope Bill's available at that time. I was so sick of listening to that woman squabble that I picked 8 AM at random."

"I'm sure it's fine. Bill thinks highly of you."

"Really?"

"Not all admin is like you-know-who. Would you mind if I joined you on Monday?"

"Not at all."

"I'll see you later, then. I'm going home to make love to my husband." Sara left.

I rubbed my eyes and then stretched my arms into the air. While doing so, I failed to notice Lauren sneaking up behind me.

"Boo!" she said.

I jumped. "Lauren," I said, "you scared the shit out of me."

"You seem stressed."

"Creeping up on me didn't help."

"Are you stressed?"

"Yes, but I'll be fine after a good run."

Lauren started rubbing my shoulders and asked, "How's that?"

"Ahhhh. That helps." I felt her boobs press up against my upper back. I secretly wished she were sitting on my lap, facing me, my face buried in her cleavage.

"We should go out some time," she said.

1:03 AM

I am so stupid! Why didn't I ask her out?

<u>Friday, April 30</u>

Dad says I have to buy him surf and turf for his birthday on Sunday if I don't ask Lauren out before then.

E-mail from Teagan:

```
Carl,
I'm meeting D'Souza in Nairobi
on Monday, July 5. I expect you
there.
Cheers mate,
Teagan
```

MAY

Whoever got himself stuck in the paper shredder via a necktie is wise not to admit it

<u>Saturday, May 1</u>

Today's positive: I'm going to Africa
Two phone calls cemented my decision.

The first was from Eric. "We'll meet at Carnivore," he said. "It's a restaurant in Nairobi that only serves meat. Dude, they have crocodile, wildebeest, and camel meat. The chefs barbecue around a central grill and then cut the meat onto your plate, right off the skewer."

"Camel meat?"

"And maybe zebra, too. The next day, we'll take a bus to Arusha, meet our tour guide, and climb Kili from the Tanzanian side."

"I was also reading about gorilla trekking in Uganda," I said.

"You can also go rafting on the Nile there. Me and Teags are gonna focus on Kenya and Tanzania, though."

"What about immunization?"

"Malaria, Hep A & B, and yellow fever for sure. Oh and get some Dukarol in case you swallow Nile water. You don't want to run behind a bush for a shit when we're taking pictures of lions."

"So I can climb mountains, gorilla trek, watch the wildebeest migration, raft on the Nile, eat wild game meat, and see lions, zebra, giraffe, baboons, and flamingos all on the same trip?"

"Yes."

The second call was from Elizabeth Andrews, a representative from ECIS (European Council of International Schools). ECIS and AIS (Association of International Schools) are cohosting an overseas teacher recruitment fair in Entebbe, Uganda, in July! Entebbe is only a one-hour flight from Nairobi, where I'm to meet Teagan and Eric. Elizabeth will mail an information package early next week.

E-mail to Teagan:
> Teags,
> I'm in.
> Carlson

<u>Sunday, May 2</u>

Today's negative: I didn't ask Lauren out

After treating Poppa Wib to his surf and turf dinner, we picked up Aunt Pam and visited Grandma Veitch. Grandma had apple pie and ice cream ready for all of us. I also gave Dad a new John Daly driver to replace the one I shattered a couple of weeks back. Grandma and Aunt Pam split the cost of a new golf cart.

"Thanks, everybody," said Dad. "This means a lot."

I could tell he was missing Mom and Kate. Kate did, however, send Dad a birthday card this year, which is more than she's done in the past.

I confronted Poppa Wib about Mom's death, asking questions I'd been too afraid to ask before. Though hesitant at first, Dad told me the level of formaldehyde outgassing from the UFFI was 7.0 ppm, or seventy times higher than the maximum safe level of 0.1 ppm. He changed the subject back to golf after that.

<u>Monday, May 3</u>

Today's positive: A supportive administrator

Bill, Sara, and I reviewed the Juliette Pinkerton situation prior to admitting Mrs. P. into Bill's office. "Mrs. Pinkerton is an interesting one," said Bill. "And, uh, she's probably still angry with me for suspending the older sister last semester."

In December, Bill suspended Annette Pinkerton for bullying. After the meeting, Sara informed me that "mom" felt "daughter" was the victim, despite all evidence to the contrary.

"She's a real blow," continued Bill. "And, uh, the woman simply enables the poor behaviour of her children."

Mrs. Pinkerton is young (early thirties?), yet wears colours that even I know clash. We reviewed the school expectations with Mrs. Pinkerton, and then she went off on another diatribe.

"You're turning this all so that it's directed at Juliette," Mrs. Pinkerton said to Bill. "You always take the teacher's side."

"Mrs. Pinkerton, if Juliette simply followed Mr. Veitch's expectations, just like every other student, this would be a moot point."

"You're trying to trick me with your fancy words," she squeaked. "I never said Juliette's behaviour was acceptable, only that Mr. Veitch's consequences are inappropriate."

"I'm glad we finally agree that Juliette's behaviour was inappropriate," added Sara.

"You're picking on my Juliette, just like you did with Annette," said Mrs. Pinkerton. "She was bullied, and—"

"Mrs. Pinkerton, this is about Juliette now, not your other daughter," said Bill.

Mrs. Pinkerton turned to me and asked, "How many times has Juliette been late to class?"

"Four times," I said.

"So why didn't you call me sooner?"

"Mrs. Pinkerton, Juliette was doing well until this past week. I had no reason to call."

"How many times has Juliette asked to go to the bathroom?"

Bill and Sara attempted to hide their rolling eyes. *As if I remember the exact number.*

After a pause, I responded, "I'm not sure."

"Approximately, then," she hissed.

I turned to Juliette and asked, "Do you have your agenda?"

"Uh, yeah," said Juliette.

"May I see it?"

"What are you doing?" asked Mrs. Pinkerton.

Juliette passed me her agenda. I flipped to the end section where teachers sign the hallway pass and counted my signature eleven times.

"Eleven times," I said to Mrs. Pinkerton, passing her Juliette's agenda. "And you'll see from the agenda that I allowed Juliette to use the facilities every time, every time except Wednesday after she was already late."

Sara took over. "You see, Mrs. Pinkerton, Mr. Veitch is being more than fair."

Bill continued, "Now Mrs. Pinkerton, I understand you're worried about Juliette being outside the classroom?"

"Yes, it's a health and safety issue to have my daughter outside the portable," snipped Pinkerton. "Anyone can come along and snatch her away."

"Yet you have no problem with us allowing Juliette to walk alone from Portable 23 all the way to the bathroom inside?"

"Of course not. She's a big girl," replied Pinkerton, before realizing she'd fallen into Bill's trap.

Impressive. I guess this is why I have few problems with Bill's half of the alphabet. Remember, dear diary, that Vice Principal Parsons handles discipline issues with surnames between N and Z.

Bill's comment did not placate Mrs. Pinkerton's emotions. Instead, feeling acrimonious, she launched an all-out verbal attack on the vice principal. "How do you address the other students who misbehave, Mr. Parsons? This is bullshit. I saw ten in the hallways wearing headphones. Who's in charge of that? You? What the hell? Why don't you pick on them for a change?" However, I believe this was Bill's intention: deflect the cantankerous woman's anger from me onto him.

Bill calmly raised his hand to Mrs. Pinkerton before whispering to me, Juliette, and Sara, "You'd better get to class."

"I'm calling the superintendent. I want to speak with Mr. Glenn. I'm calling the Toronto *Star* ..." continued Mrs. Pinkerton.

Tuesday, May 4

Today's positive: My faith in parental units is restored.

From Mrs. Minchin: "Don't coddle my kid, Mr. Veitch. If Paula's late, you can lock her out of the portable for as long as you need. Your priority is the other twenty-five kids who are punctual. She knows that."

From Mrs. Ramkalawan: "I appreciate your call. He'll wash his PE shirt tonight, and I'll send him with money for another tomorrow."

From Mrs. McCarthy: "God bless you for lookin' after my child. Sheila never told me dere's 'omework every day."

Thank God not all moms are combative bitches like Mrs. Pinkerton.

Wednesday, May 5

Today's positive: I know why Teleisia's breasts are so large. She's cheating.

"To the forest and the stream we go," I announced to my Grade 11 general class. They were delighted by my spontaneous outdoor lesson plan. Delighted, that is, until I outlined the tasks for the day:

1) *Catch one water strider in the glass jar.*

"Do we have to, sir?" cried Larissa. "Can't we just sit by the ravine?"

2) *Catch one dragonfly.*

"I'm allergic to dragonflies," said Akeel. "If they bite me, my eyes puff out."

"Dragonflies don't bite, stupid!" said Pino.

3) *Complete a histogram of the vegetation within your designated 1m x 1m area.*

"What's a histogram, sir?" asked Jamie.

"A bar graph, stupid!" said Pino.

"Do we have to touch the ground?" asked Teleisia. "Because I'm allergic to grass, sir. I can't touch it or I get hives. You can call my mom."

"Don't you live with your aunt?" said Lanie to Teleisia.

"Yeah," whispered Teleisia, "but Veitch doesn't know that."

Twenty-seven teenagers, working in groups of three, trotted outside to the ravine behind the school.

"Can we have a group of four?" said Marci. "Please can you make an exception?"

I glared at Marci and shook my head no.

Outside, Teleisia was too busy doing cartwheels and tumble turns to work. Though most of the class was engaged by the activity, a few boys began to ogle her breasts. Teleisia wore a tight low-cut top, her bosom scarcely concealed. I tried not to look. Jomo and Mikel, however, were not so subtle.

"Stop looking at me," cried Teleisia. "That's harassment."

"Maybe if you put your tits away it wouldn't happen," said Marci. I pretended not to hear.

"Sir," said Teleisia, "did you hear that inappropriate language?"

"I'm sorry, Teleisia," I said. "What's the problem?"

"Never mind," she said.

Soon after, I gathered the class in a circle, reviewing how today's activity relates to habitat and niche. Teleisia was last to arrive, intent on making another grand entrance. The raptor tumble-turned toward the group from fifteen metres away.

After her first flip, two round, jellylike objects flew from her top. Teleisia didn't notice that her breast prostheses had flown the coop. The left falsie hit Akeel in the head, and the right one landed on my feet. Teleisia stopped tumbling and spread her arms wide, still ignorant to her disappearing cleavage, and announced to everyone, "Teleisia's here!"

"Actually," said Akeel, removing the falsie from his face and then holding it up for the entire class to see, "Teleisia is here."

Teleisia's eyes opened wider than the Grand Canyon. She finally realized her D cups had evaporated into As. Since no one was quite sure how to react, there was only mild, muted laughter from the class at this time.

Still resting on my foot was the other breast prosthesis. I pointed to it and said to Teleisia, "I believe that one belongs to you as well."

The class erupted into wild hysterics. We couldn't stop. Teleisia accepted her fake breasts back. Her dark skin was not enough to hide her embarrassment. Telesia's cheeks had flushed bright red.

At home, I related the tale to Poppa Wib. "Didn't I tell you just to survive the first year?" he said. "And sometimes you get a surprise like today." Dad continued by relating a story about my mom's first year of teaching. "Your mother was teaching French to an unruly group of Tech boys. Some of them were twenty, and your mom was only a couple years older. One twit decided it would be funny if he tripped Ms. Golembieski. The bastard stuck his foot out as she walked between desks. Fortunately, your mother noticed and reacted in a way that would probably cost her the job today."

"What did she do?" I asked.

"She stepped on his foot with her three-inch heel and taught the rest of the lesson from that one spot. Nobody ever gave her a problem after that."

Thursday, May 6

Some bastard put pepper spray in the air vents today. During fourth period, my eyes started hurting and my throat began to scratch. Initially, I thought it was just another reaction to my anxiety problems. However, I soon noticed others with the same symptoms.

Bill Parsons's voice came over the PA: "Attention, we seem to, uh, be having a problem with the venting systems, and, uh, we'd like everyone to leave the building for a few moments."

Led by Akeel, I was almost steamrolled by my Grade 11 bio students at the door. They rushed out and then stampeded to the hallways and outside to the soccer field.

After twenty minutes and thirty-three seconds outside, Parsons was back with further instructions. Using his megaphone, he said that the "problem" wouldn't be fixed for at least two hours and we could all go home. What followed was a collective cheer from students and staff alike.

"What about our books, sir?" asked Kyle.

Teleisia overheard his query. "Bun that, Kyle," she said. "Just go home."

<u>Friday, May 7</u>

Noose-Neck called an emergency staff meeting. Also invited were a police officer and, more important, our director of education, Mrs. Denia Thomasos.

"After Columbine," said Noose-Neck, "a kid putting pepper spray in the air vents is an even more serious matter." Noose-Neck asked the staff to inform admin if we noticed any suspicious behaviour. I'm sure he was also thinking, *If I handle this situation well, the board will have no choice but to promote me.*

I put my hand up. Noose-Neck reluctantly acknowledged me. "Yes, Mr. Veitch."

"I saw Marco Costa loitering in the halls a few minutes before Mr. Parsons called the evacuation."

"Mr. Veitch," he said, "I'm sure young Marco was just using the bathroom."

"And remember that Marco had blue stains on his hands the day after the false fire alarm."

Initially, the fat around his neck quivered with anger. However, Noose-Neck quickly regained his composure. "Mr. Veitch," he said, "while I do appreciate your concern, I think it would be best if you cast aside your negative personal feelings toward young Marco. We can't waste time on such frivolous pursuits."

You bastard, I thought. I wanted to suplex him through the table right then and there. I quickly regained my cool thanks to a few slow, deep breaths, courtesy of Ronda's training.

<u>Saturday, May 8</u>

Warner Brothers and the Jenny Jones Show found liable. Months ago, producers tricked Jonathan Schmitz (Scott Amedure's killer) into appearing on an episode called "Same Sex Secret Crushes." Distraught after Amedure revealed his affection, Schmitz shot the gay man in cold blood.

I phoned Eric and asked if he'd heard about the verdict.

"Why do people hate us?" he asked. "There, I said it. I'm gay. Do you hate me, Carlson? Do you want to shoot me now?"

"Not particularly," I said. "Then it would just be me and Teags in Africa. I can't handle him for three weeks without you there as a buffer."

"This is so hard for me, dude. I've wanted to tell you, but I was too scared. And now it just came out. Does Teagan know?"

"He suspects."

"Does he want to shoot me?"

"He tried to set you up with one of the male lifeguards on the Gold Coast."

"What?"

"So I don't think he wants to shoot you."

"You mean?"

"I think he'll be happy to hear you're not asexual."

"What?"

"He told me he tried to set you up with some of the female lifeguards, and when you rejected their advances he thought maybe you were into the men."

"So you guys don't mind then?"

"It might be a little weird at first, seeing you dating a guy, but we'll get over it."

"What about my parents? Dude, what am I going to tell them?"

"I don't know, Eric, but I'll be there for you when the time comes."

Sunday, May 9

E-mail from Teagan:

> *Your aunt Pamela has nice tits.*

E-mail to Teagan:
>   *Fuck you, asshole.*

<u>Monday, May 10</u>

I received the information from Elizabeth Andrews. As expected, both ECIS and AIS require prospective teacher candidates to have a letter of recommendation from their current principal. I have until the end of the month to convince Noose-Neck to give me the second evaluation, but how?

<u>Tuesday, May 11</u>

The 1997–1998 yearbooks finally arrive tomorrow!

<u>Wednesday, May 12</u>

I normally don't enjoy staring at someone's penis, but today I made an exception.

I wondered why the students were so secretive about the yearbooks. There was giddy laughter, darting eyes, and whispers. Every time I passed by, the yearbooks would close and students would feign innocent smiles.

Let's just say, dear diary, that I could never have dreamed a better scenario of revenge against Noose-Neck. Between this and the pepper spray incident, Noose-Neck is sinking faster than the *Titanic* and exploding like the *Hindenburg*.

First, we heard the beep for the PA system. Then, we listened to a muted exchange between Mr. Parsons and Noose-Neck.

Noose-Neck: "You make the announcement—"

Parsons: "This is your responsibility, Damian. That's not my hand on the kid's shoulder." After a few seconds of silence, we heard Mr. Parsons say, "Oh, it's already on."

Mr. Parsons came to the microphone. "Excuse me, we, and uh, Mr. Glenn, uh, would like to make a very important announcement, and, uh, it's about the yearbook."

Noose Neck's voice crackled over the PA system. "Excuse me," he said, sounding utterly humiliated. "It has come to our attention that there is a misprint in the yearbook."

Hoots and hollers from the class. Noose-Neck had the final approval on the yearbook.

Noose-Neck must have neglected to proofread a page or two. Maybe someone wrote "Fuck you" or "Eat shit" in their graduation blurb and, in his haste to get the damn yearbook in print, he didn't notice. The reality was far worse. Noose-Neck missed a big one, literally.

"That's some misprint," piped Lorraine.

"Mr. Glenn has cock breath," said Jamie.

Noose-Neck continued. "Teachers, would you be so kind as to collect the yearbooks from the students. We have a comprehensive list of which students have already picked them up. Please document whose yearbooks you collect."

After this, Akeel showed me the secret. And there it was, the yearbook photo of the senior boys' basketball team. Head coach Noose-Neck was smiling proudly behind his starting centre. He had his hand on Jimmy's shoulder. Jimmy had pulled his zipper down and was holding out his oversized penis for all to see.

Thursday, May 13

In the main office, I noticed a very somber looking Noose-Neck slumped in his chair. I was there to use the fax machine. Elizabeth Andrews needed some paperwork. Behind the windows of his office door, I could see Noose-Neck staring across the room, tapping his fingers on the desk. He wasn't even wearing his tie, and thus his characteristic neck fat wasn't spilling over the collar like normal. But there was more: the bravado was gone. Noose-Neck, for the first time, seemed vulnerable.

Why is it that when you stare at someone for more than two seconds, the person can tell? Noose-Neck turned his head toward me. Our eyes met. He stood up, walked over to his office door, and opened it, all the while maintaining a glare into my eyes.

"Mr. Veitch, I hope you're not here to use the office photocopier," he said.

"Just the fax machine, Mr. Glenn," I replied.

The fax machine beeped and the confirmation slip printed.

"It's done," he said. "Now why don't you go away and make yourself useful."

Friday, May 14

The remnants of a dapper gray and blue tie are stuck in the paper shredder. So far, every male teacher, including yours truly, denies that the chewed-up tie belongs to him. Whoever got himself stuck in the paper shredder via a necktie is wise not to admit it. The relentless teasing from fellow staff members could become unbearable. Everyone is trying to solve the mystery.

Saturday, May 15

I've decided to give a triathlon another go. I'll be racing the Muskoka short course in three weeks.

My main worry is still the swim. However, after a morning swim at Centennial Pool, I'm confident I can swim faster than last summer. I tried to remember the tips Shauna gave me back at OFSAA X-Country in November, and they worked.

For the bike and run, it's all about preventing chafing and cramping. To protect the skin on my inner thighs from rubbing, I bought eight-panel bike tights from Mountain Equipment Co-op. To shield my nipples from bleeding, I found this "Body Butter" stuff from D'Ornellas Bike Shop. The owner also said the Body Butter can be used under the arms, and Band-Aids over the nipples are a good idea as well.

Sunday, May 16

I lined up with the other Star Wars geeks at Ontario Place today, hoping for advance tickets to Wednesday's premiere of *The Phantom Menace*. Since the Cinesphere has an IMAX screen, I arrived before 11 AM, more than an hour before the box office opened. However, I was still well back in the queue. Apparently, some fanatics even camped overnight. I feared the 12:01 AM premiere (Tuesday night/Wednesday morning) would be sold out but managed to purchase five tickets. Rick, Megan, Derek, Poppa Wib, and I are going.

Monday, May 17

Rumour has it that Noose-Neck's faux pas with the yearbook photo has reached the desk of Denia Thomasos, director of education.

"It's certainly not helping his chances for a promotion," said Gary. "Especially if the false fire alarm and pepper spray incident turn out to be because of Marco, as you suggested."

I had an evil thought. *There must be some way I can take advantage of Noose-Neck's implosion.*

<u>Tuesday, May 18</u>

Rick, Megan, and Derek bailed on the Star Wars premiere. They phoned me during dinner last night.

"I need to save some cash," said Rick.

"I'll pay for it," I replied.

"Can't let you do that, man. Besides, work's piling up on me."

"Derek and I have some wedding prep," said Megan.

"Come on," I said. "We planned this."

"Sorry, Carlson, no can do. By the way, are you bringing a date to the wedding?"

"Yes." I lied. "Her name is Lauren. Lauren Weeks."

That left me and Poppa Wib. Dad took me, Mom, and Kate to the original *Star Wars* in 1977, so it would still be special.

I wore my green Yoda shirt to school today.

Stephanie noticed my outfit when she walked past me in the hallway. "Sir," she said, "that's just too much."

"I hear Jedi are vegans," I joked.

"Ha ha."

Andrew Yates made a big fuss over the T-shirt in gym class. "That's so cool, sir," he said. "Where did you get that?"

"In Florida," I replied, "before *Star Wars* became popular again."

"You going tonight?"

"Yeah."

"I couldn't get seats."

Problem solved. I offered Andrew my extra three tickets. He's going with Donna and Sparrow.

"You're the best, sir. I'm sorry for throwing worms in class and breaking the TV and all the other shit I put you through. I promise I'll pay you back somehow."

It's 8 PM now. Only four hours to go. I'm so excited, especially since Dad gave up his seat so that I could ask Lauren to go. Actually, he refused to cook dinner until I called her.

"Holy darn," she said. "I'd love to."

I shall have to overcome my emotional barrier of seeing my students in public. Who cares if they figure out I've got a crush on Ms. Weeks.

Wednesday, May 19

Jar Jar Binks must die! And who the hell is the Phantom Menace anyway: Darth Maul (whose only purpose was to look cool) or Palpatine? Who is the protagonist (Anakin? Obi-Won? Qui Gon?), and what does he need? Why did they explain "the Force"? Who made that fake-looking Yoda puppet? Why did George Lucas break his cardinal rule and spend too much screen time on special effects? Why did he and the other producers cast such a weak child actor (Jake Lloyd) for young Anakin?

I really hope *The Phantom Menace* was just a dud. Its only redeeming qualities were the pod race, the lightsaber battle, and Natalie Portman's bod. I can handle the bad haircuts and awkward dialogue, but George Lucas better deliver next time or I'll melt down my old Star Wars figures.

By the way, dear diary, Lauren loved the movie. I didn't have the heart to tell her it was a flop in my eyes.

Thursday, May 20

Andrew Yates asked me if I was going to marry Ms. Weeks.

"It was just a date," I said.

"Aww, that's so cute," said Donna. "You made him blush."

Marry Lauren? I don't know, but she did agree to be my date at Megan and Derek's wedding.

<u>Friday, May 21</u>

Will he never learn? After school, from across the parking lot, I saw Marco, who appeared to be bad-mouthing Tim. Tim was walking his dog. Marco circled around Tim and his pooch on a BMX bicycle. I later learned the dog was a young Australian Shepherd, affectionately named Moose. By the time I walked over to investigate, Moose was barking and running around, following Marco. Because of Marco's circular pattern, Moose had wound his leash around his bewildered and frustrated master. Marco laughed at the entangled Tim, who could do nothing to retaliate.

The results of this conflict reminded me of the time I kicked Terry McFayden in the head. It was grade seven. Terry already had armpit hair and was shaving. He was one of those guys who grew to five-foot six by age twelve but never another inch afterward. Regardless, Terry used to chase me down during recess and deliver kidney punches to my skinny back. Usually, because I was a good runner, I could get away or hide. However, one recess I got sick of running and just waited for the bully.

Terry was a little later than normal that day. He probably had a detention with Mr. Sheblack. When he finally ran outside the doors of St. Christopher's Catholic School, I swear he was slobbering saliva, much like Moose this afternoon. Terry spotted my five-foot one-inch frame and then ran at me like a bull in Pamplona. When he was close enough, I gave him a boot to the head just like Hulk Hogan would to King Kong Bundy. Terry collapsed on the ground. He lay there groaning for the rest of recess. I gave him a leg drop for good measure. We became friends after that.

Moose added cries and growls between his barks. Marco continued to circle Moose and Tim, like a shark surrounding its helpless prey.

Moose kept tugging at the leash and lunging at Marco, but Tim held her back.

"Marco, don't be stupid," said Tim. "I can't hold onto her when she's like this."

Marco didn't listen. Tim let go of the leash. Moose, now salivating, charged after Marco, going for his ankle. Marco didn't flinch, for he knew he was safe while Tim was wrapped within the leash.

Marco noticed me approaching. He started to pedal away.

By the time I reached Tim and Moose, Tim had almost untangled himself. The full force of the Australian Shepherd was about to be unleashed.

"Help me, sir," said Tim. "She's gonna bite him."

I was too late to grab the leash. Moose got free. He tore off after Marco like the Tasmanian devil.

"Marco! Pedal faster!" I screamed.

Marco noticed the streaking furball and pedalled as fast as he could.

"I feel humiliated," said Tim to me.

"Don't let Marco break your spirits," I said. "Look at him now."

We watched the frenzied Moose snap repeatedly at Marco's ankles, which were a blur because Marco was pedalling so fast. Marco must have been pedalling faster than Jan Ullrich on a Tour de France time trial. Moose chased Marco through stop signs, around fire hydrants, and between parked cars until we could no longer see them.

Tim and I enjoyed this little bit of justice. I only wish I could make Noose-Neck run away screaming and crying like that.

"I told him I couldn't hold on," said Tim.

"You're not going after the dog?" I asked.

"She knows the way home."

We shared a belly laugh. And then Tim let me in on a couple of secrets.

<u>Saturday, May 22</u>

Rick is plumping up. Initially, I was mad that my waist size measured at a thirty-three instead of thirty-two. However, when I saw how soft and doughy Rick's midriff had become (too much time behind a desk on Bay Street, I suppose), I felt better.

Rick, Derek, and I went to see *The Matrix*, starring Keanu Reeves. It's a real mind-fuck, but a great flick. I wish I could just plug in and kick ass like Neo in the movie. I'd never have a problem with Noose-Neck, Marco, Jimmy, or Teleisia again.

<u>Sunday, May 23</u>

Holy shit! CBC, CTV, CityTV, and Global News all reported that WWF wrestler Owen Hart just died. He plummeted to his death when a stunt went wrong. The quick-release on his harness malfunctioned, and Owen dropped nearly a hundred feet from the rafters to the ring. He died instantly. This happened in front of fifteen thousand fans and on millions of television sets whose owners had purchased the pay-per-view. Owen's brother Bret was my favourite wrestler as a kid.

<u>Monday, May 24</u>

Victoria Day Holiday

Rick, in a rare appearance, joined Poppa Wib and me for a round of golf today. We tried a new course in Ajax called Deer Creek. By the third tee, Rick was up to date on my dilemma with Noose-Neck.

"Cut him a deal," he said. "That's how business works."

Dad ripped a 250-yard tee shot with his John Daly driver. It landed in the middle of the fairway. "I love this club, Carlson."

"Mind if I try it, Mr. V?" asked Rick.

"Go ahead," replied Dad, handing him the John Daly, before turning to me.

"Carlson, you should listen to Rick," he said. "Play the game and offer Damian a trade."

Rick's tee shot flew straight for one hundred yards, before slicing off to the adjacent fairway.

"Fore!" he yelled. "Mind if I take a mulligan?" asked Rick.

"Go ahead," said Dad.

"I can't sell myself out," I said to my father.

"Do you really want a job in Europe or somewhere else overseas?" he asked.

"Yes."

"What's the only way you can get it?"

Tuesday, May 25

Marco left the school today in handcuffs. Tim, as promised, had phoned the police to admit he witnessed Marco pulling the fire alarm and also putting pepper spray in the air vents. Marco and his bodyguards had bullied him into silence. Since Marco had insulted Julio's Mexican heritage, he'd quit protecting the little pinhead and also made a statement corroborating Tim's evidence. Marco finally cracked under the pressure and confessed to what I've been telling Mr. Costa and Noose-Neck along.

It's now or never for this deal with Noose-Neck.

Wednesday, May 26

Mrs. Smith, the poodle-permed secretary, set up a formal appointment between Noose-Neck and me for tomorrow. I'm still not sure I can offer him the deal. It feels rather Faustian, but it's the only way.

<u>Thursday, May 27</u>

"Are you here to rub it in my face?" asked Noose-Neck.

"No," I answered.

"For once, you were right. There, I said it. Now go back to class and leave me alone. Aren't you teaching four out of four? Don't you have papers to mark?"

"I believe, Damian," I said, "that we may be able to help each other out."

Noose-Neck loosened his tie and then unwrapped a candy before responding. "And what could you, Carlson Veitch, possibly have that would be of assistance to me? Another tip about Marco's misbehavior? Another pleasant phone call from Celeste Pinkerton?"

"Damian," I said calmly, "I know we don't see eye to eye—"

"Really?"

"I get that, and I know it may never change."

"Tell me something I didn't know."

"The difference is that now, I can give you something you need."

"Is that so?"

"If you're interested, you know where to find me."

Then I pulled out my insurance policy. "Remember this note?" I asked.

Your friends won't always be around to protect you. Don't expect me to give you the 2nd evaluation you seek.

<u>Friday, May 28</u>

All day, word circulated throughout the staff that Noose-Neck is likely being passed over for his promotion. The rumours say that the final decision will be made at the end of the month.

Indeed, I believe this to be true, because Noose-Neck sent me a message via Mrs. Smith. She buzzed my room near the end of fourth period. "Excuse me, Mr. Veitch," she said. "Sorry for interrupting—"

"Yes, Mrs. Smith," I replied.

"Mr. Glenn needs to speak with you before you go home today."

"Oohhhhhhhhh," said the class, almost in unison.

"You're in trouble!" mocked Teleisia.

"Thanks, Mrs. Smith," I said. "I'll be there in twenty minutes."

"Okay," said Noose-Neck. "I'm listening." His face was tense, his underarms were sweating, and I could even see a vein throbbing through the fat on his neck. I could tell this wasn't easy for him. He continued, "What could you possibly have that would be of assistance to me?"

Suppressing a grin, I answered, "You need to save face, and I need a glowing teacher evaluation."

"Continue."

"I understand the school board will make a decision about your promotion by the end of the month," I said, fishing for an official confirmation of the rumours.

"How do you know that?" he replied. *It was true.*

"So it's true."

"Yes, Mr. Veitch, it's true. Now how are you going to help me?"

"In order for me to get a job elsewhere, I need a letter of recommendation and a positive teaching evaluation from you," I said, before a long pause. "It pains me to say this, Damian, but why don't you give me the positive evaluation I so desire and take credit for my transformation?"

For several seconds, there was silence. We stared at each other, like two kids seeing who would blink first. Eventually, Noose-Neck looked away.

"Mr. Veitch, if you have miraculously improved, which is unlikely, it was all because of me anyway."

I bit my tongue. I wanted to lash out, but I knew ahead of time he would say something like that. The man refuses to accept that I can solve one of his problems.

"Do we have an understanding then?"

"Perhaps I shall consider your offer. I was thinking of it myself actually. I didn't need you to tell me this is what you were after."

"I hope to see you soon then."

Saturday, May 29

Elizabeth from ECIS wants to do a screening interview with me next Sunday, the day after my race. I only hope I can produce the recommendation from Noose-Neck by then. Regardless, I refuse to go through another interview with chafed thighs and bloody nipples like last summer. The eight-panel tights, Body Butter, and Band-Aids had better work!

Sunday, May 30

We sat in the smoking section of Denny's so that Jane, my union head, could feed her addiction. I sucked it up, literally, because I knew the woman could help me.

Between bites of our Grand Slam Denny's meals, I told Jane of my plan. She'll forward me the necessary paperwork by Friday at the latest.

"All Damian will need to do," she said, "is take the trade you're offering and fill in the blanks."

Monday, May 31

No word from Noose-Neck.

JUNE

"All in one blast?"

<u>Tuesday, June 1</u>

No appearance by Noose-Neck in any of my classes.

<u>Wednesday, June 2</u>

The provincial election is tomorrow. Our unions suggest strategic voting. I hope it works. We must rid the province of the premier and his right-wing "hairy ass" policies.

<u>Thursday, June 3</u>

The Progressive Conservatives succeeded in convincing most of Ontario's voters that teachers and nurses are overpaid and underworked. I just need Noose-Neck to give me the evaluation.

<u>Friday, June 4</u>

As I approached his office, I noticed a frustrated Noose-Neck gripping the phone tightly to his ear. Papers lay scattered around his desk, and sweat was visible beneath his underarms again. Though the door was closed and his voice muffled, I knew Noose-Neck was talking to the director of education. "Look, Denia, how would you have handled these situations?" I heard him plead.

He hung up the phone and let out a big sigh. I knocked on the door.

"What?" he growled. "Come in."

I opened the door. Noose-Neck saw me and rolled his eyes. "Oh, great, it's you."

I passed Noose-Neck the manila envelope containing the files.

"Here's the package," I said. "Looks like you're having a rough day."

"Wouldn't you like to know?"

"Oh, I do know. I know very well. This year has been hell for me, and yet you've done nothing to help. Not one kind word of encouragement, not one pat on the back, not one 'Hi, how are you?' And despite all of this, and despite your multiple attempts to break me, I'm still here.

"How does it feel to be smothered by your career? How are you handling the stress? Is your heart racing? Are you having trouble sleeping? Do you question your effectiveness as a principal, or as a human being? Do you feel like a failure? Do you dwell on your decisions so much so that it's taken over your entire life?"

Noose-Neck slumped in his chair, body limp, looking like he'd hung himself in his own noose.

"Now you understand my pain. The only difference is, I've got nothing left to lose and you still do. The only way out of this for us is if we both swallow our pride. In that envelope is your only chance for recompense with me. In that envelope is your only chance to redeem yourself in front of Denia Thomasos."

"I'm not promising anything," he said.

"You know my schedule. You're welcome to visit any class, anytime." I left Noose-Neck's office, feeling somewhat vindicated and thinking, *Even if he doesn't do it, I've said my piece. I've stood up to the bully.*

Saturday, June 5

Muskoka triathlon
Swim: 17:21 → 20th/47 in my age category and 152nd/396 overall
I used an old water-ski wetsuit, which is apparently the wrong type. There was too much drag when swimming. Also, when I came out of the river, the leakage was immense; I felt like a woman whose water had just broken.

T1: 2:39
Getting out of the wetsuit was difficult. A contortion artist stuck in one of those glass boxes has an easier time escaping. Worse, one of

the Band-Aids came off my left nipple and then wouldn't stick back on my wet skin.

Bike: 37:39 → 13th/47 in age; 89th/396 overall

Hilly course, so it was a slow time (only 31.9 kilometres per hour). However, my MEC eight-panel tights prevented my inner thighs from chafing.

T2: 1:29

Stupid marshals didn't stop me from entering the transition the wrong way. There were two parallel laneways, and I chose the wrong one. They screamed at me to go back around. I just dismounted and threw my bike over the fence before leaping over myself. I was pissed. After I racked my bike, my legs cramped a bit as I bent over for my socks. Though in considerable pain, I took the extra few seconds to put my socks on before my shoes. I wasn't planning on running through bloody blisters like last summer.

Run: 21:42 → 8th/47 in my cat and 64th/396 overall

Lots of mini–leg cramps during the first 2.5-kilometre loop. I only ran it in 11:59. The lead legs then loosened up, and I ran the second loop in 9:43.

FINAL TIME: 1:20:50 → 12th/47 in my cat and 84th/396 overall

1:13 AM

I'm so tired I can't sleep. However, I was able to watch Brett Hull score the Stanley Cup–winning goal in triple overtime of game six. This is the Dallas Stars' first NHL title.

2:48 AM

Stubbed my @#$@#$ toe on the fan. Poppa Wib has to break down and get central air conditioning. It's still thirty-three degrees and humid out there. I finally fell asleep, but then my hamstring cramped. I'm up now stretching it out. When I shook out my leg in the darkness, I accidentally kicked the @#$@$# fan over. Now, my hamstring is loose but the fan doesn't work. Worse, my toe is swollen and it's throbbing with every beat of my heart.

I can't sleep and have my screening interview in Belleville with ECIS tomorrow.

Sunday, June 6

Poppa Wib drove me to Belleville because my legs kept cramping.

Upon arrival at Elizabeth's house (a cute A-frame with a second-floor balcony), I warned her that my legs might cramp. I explained that I finished the Muskoka triathlon yesterday and that my hamstrings had been seizing up all night.

Elizabeth's daughter is a triathlete, so we spent the first ten minutes of the interview talking about training. This put me at ease. Elizabeth also knew someone who knew Poppa Wib, so that was a double bonus.

I breezed through the class management and curriculum questions. However, Elizabeth advised me that I should learn about the A.P. (United States) and I.B. (International Baccalaureate) programs of study. One of these two systems is used in almost all English-speaking international schools.

After that, she asked me, "Why do you want to teach overseas?"

I told Elizabeth about my travels in B.C. and Peru and my upcoming adventures in Africa. I explained how I connected with Andrew Yates, even though he was a behaviour problem, and told her that the kid recently thanked me for keeping him in check. Finally, I said, "Teaching overseas would marry my passion for travel and my desire to reach young people."

We shook hands, and then Elizabeth said, "Carlson, if you can get me a fax of the evaluation from your principal, you're in. I'll need it by Friday."

<u>Monday, June 7</u>

Revenge of the sex ed teacher

It was the same reaction any man has when witnessing one of his brethren getting sacked. In the darkened room, and on the overhead, was a line drawing of the male reproductive system. It was a side view. This image, along with my unashamed usage of the words "scrotum," "smegma," and "testicles" already had the Grade 10 boys somewhat uncomfortable, yet listening intently.

"Does anyone know what a vasectomy is?" I asked.

Andrew raised his hand and said, "I dunno, but I think my dad had one."

There were a few giggles. To suppress them, I took a pair of scissors and held them in midair, about fifteen centimetres above the glass on the overhead. I positioned the scissors in such a way that the shadow of the blades covered the vas deferens. I snipped at the sperm-carrying tube several times. The silhouette of the scissors cutting the vas deferens quickly silenced the boys.

"You simply make an incision through the scrotum and cut the vas deferens, which, as you know, is the tube that carries sperm from the testes."

Every boy in the class crossed his legs tightly. Imagine their reaction then when I used the same shadow technique to explain a prostate examination.

<u>Tuesday, June 8</u>

Revenge of the sex ed teacher: Part 2

I made Andrew and Sparrow scream almost as loudly as my Grade 9s. Pictures of vaginal warts, gonorrhea, and penile herpes tend to have that effect on teenage boys.

<u>Wednesday, June 9</u>

Revenge of the sex ed teacher: Part 3

"All in one blast?" screamed Brendan, much to the delight of his peers. We were in hysterics—not only because of his comment, but because these were the first words Brendan had said the entire semester. Up until today, we all thought he was mute.

Why his startled reaction, you ask? It probably had something to do with my report to the class that fifty to five-hundred million sperm are released each time a man ejaculates.

<u>Thursday, June 10</u>

Lauren said that Gary and Sara had heard from Kelly Turner, who said that Denia Thomasos told Kelly she will make her decision on whether or not to promote Noose-Neck by the end of next week.

<u>Friday, June 11</u>

Wedding rehearsal

At the rehearsal dinner, I asked Lauren if she felt comfortable sharing the same hotel room to save costs. "Holy darn, no problem," she said. "Remember that I'm taking my year off beginning September, so I'll do anything to cut costs."

I told her I would sleep on the couch if it would make her more comfortable.

"We can share the bed," she said. "Or you can sleep on the couch."

I want you to put on your Catwoman costume from Halloween. Then I want to spoon with you, baby.

"Uh," I said, "maybe I'll take the couch." She looked disheartened. "Or we can share the bed."

"I won't take up much space, and I promise not to kick you. That is, unless you want me to."

Sha-wing.

I am a quarter century old tomorrow.

Saturday, June 12

Megan and Derek's wedding

Megan is inconsolable, but I think it was quite funny.

In fact, I can't control my laughter. Every time I think of the image, I start sniggering, even though I'm now in the hotel room by myself. Lauren's just called me "insensitive" and has left, presumably to go down the hall and comfort Megan. I can't understand why it's such a big deal. They're only butterflies.

Megan's intention was for everyone in the wedding party and everyone in the family to release a butterfly simultaneously, as a symbol of her and Derek's love. She'd mail-ordered fifty of them from Florida at ten bucks apiece. Apparently, these particular butterflies were specially bred to survive travel in a box from Miami to Toronto. Let's just say they weren't specially bred to survive a windy day. Less than a second after Derek opened the boxes, a big *whoosh* of air blew them away, probably into the mouths of some birds who felt as though they'd just won the lottery.

Last night

Initially, I slept on the couch in our room. However, after taking a leak in the middle of the night, I noticed Lauren sleeping totally on the right side of the bed. The sheets on the left were folded open, like an invitation. I slipped under the covers beside her but faced outward, careful not to let our bodies touch, though I desperately wanted to.

Her freezing cold toes touched my calves. "Holy shit, Lauren," I said, jolting upward. "Your feet are like ice cubes." She pushed my shoulder back down and then wedged her feet between my calves.

"Then warm them up for me," she said.

Lauren put her left arm underneath mine and around my chest, her boobs pressed against my back. I could feel her nipples getting hard through her T-shirt.

"You don't have to hide your hard-on this time, Carlson," she said.

"What?" I replied.

"Even though I'm not wearing the Catwoman costume," she continued.

She knew I was hiding my half-mast back at Halloween!

"You knew?" I said.

"I knew."

"I thought those stupid baggy low-riding pants hid my excitement."

"Nope."

Sunday, June 13

I'm no longer impotent.

"How's that for a quarter-life birthday present?" asked Lauren, after our romp in the hay.

Lisa who?

Monday, June 14

Today at work, Lauren helped me make a fireball of a different kind. All I need is Lycopodium powder and a match.

When I do it in front of my class, mind you, I'll use a longer match and stand further back. After blowing the powder from my palm into the flame, the edge of the resulting fireball singed a few strands of my finger hair.

"That's what you get for laughing at the butterfly disaster," said Lauren. "It's karma."

You can't tell by looking at me but wherever I go, it smells like something is burning. That fetid burnt hair smell followed me like a puppy clinging to its mom. Even though I scrubbed my scalp with shampoo, the odour remains. I couldn't even smell Sara's perfume when she walked past me.

Texas governor George W. Bush proclaimed he will seek the Republican Party nomination for president of the United States. I saw his announcement on CNN. There's no way this guy will win. He seems pretty dumb.

Tuesday, June 15

Alex wouldn't shut up about a misadventure he and his brother had with firecrackers last night. He and his older brother Colin thought it would be funny to play Nicky Nicky Nine Doors with a twist. It almost got them shot.

I couldn't get my Grade 10 science class to focus on me because they were so enthralled with Alex's story. They wanted details. Worse, Noose-Neck arrived in Portable 3 and was scribbling notes about me in his yellow pad.

Alex continued his story. He and Colin had targeted a random house up north in Vaughan. While his brother positioned the car for a quick getaway, Alex dug a pit for his firecracker. In it, he placed a Roman candle and aimed it toward the front door of the bungalow. The kick was to see the look on the person's face when the Roman candle fireballs bounced off the screen door.

Alex rang the doorbell several times and then ran back to light the fuse. I can imagine his chubby frame trying to coordinate these motions quickly. There was no way; he's too slow. Before the plump pyromaniac could get back in the car, a man from the house had run out in front of the vehicle, aiming a shotgun at the boys through the windshield. He threatened to "blow their @#$$#ing heads off."

At this time, it was past midnight. The man noticed the suspicious looking figure (Alex) on his front lawn, digging into his property. Instead of calling the cops, the man took the law into his own hands.

He screamed for Colin to shut off the engine and then demanded ID from the boys. They complied. Colin gave the man his driver's license and Alex his school ID. The man took the ID cards and then realized it was just a couple of kids. He told them to leave and come back the next day with their parents.

The boys drove off and made the following 9-1-1 call from a nearby gas station: "Is it a worse offense to aim a firecracker at someone's door or to point a shotgun at someone and threaten to blow their heads off?"

"We'll be right there, son," said the woman at the other end of the line.

Much to the gas station attendant's confusion, six cruisers arrived within minutes. The shotgun man was arrested, and the boys spent several hours writing statements. A court session will occur in a couple of weeks.

"Let me show you how to make a firecracker," I said, to a surprised audience. This was the teachable moment I was waiting for. I knew it was a gamble, but I had to go for it. Though I hadn't had a chance to practice my demo, the materials were waiting for me in the dungeon. I placed an overhead transparency on the projector. It contained a premade note on electron orbitals, energy levels, and surface area.

"Copy this note," I said to my students. "It explains the science behind firecrackers."

I turned toward my nemesis. "Mr. Glenn?" I asked. "Could you please watch my students while I set up the demo outside?" I didn't wait for an answer.

Instead, I sprinted to the dungeon and grabbed the following:
- A glass jar containing sodium
- A glass jar containing potassium
- Lycopodium powder
- A class set of eyeglasses
- A long match
- An X-ACTO knife

Somehow, I got back to Portable 3 quickly and without dropping anything. I was motivated. This was my chance to prove Noose-Neck wrong about my teaching skills and look into his eyes while doing so. I ran to the dungeon and back so fast, it was as if I'd finally broken the two-minute barrier for the eight hundred.

"Everyone get onto the track," I said. Though still mildly confused as to what I was up to, my students complied.

"Mr. Glenn," I said, passing him the box of safety glasses. "Put a pair of these on, and give one to every student."

Noose-Neck knew I wouldn't let him refuse. He put down his yellow pad and followed my instructions. I donned a pair before gathering everyone in a circle on the track. We surrounded a one-metre-diameter puddle. Everyone but me stood well back.

I opened the first glass jar and cut a chunk of sodium, about the size of a spoon, from the larger piece of the metal.

"Everyone have their safety goggles on?" I asked.

I threw the chunk into the puddle. It quickly formed into a sphere that sparked small white flames. The ball crackled like Rice Krispies and zipped randomly around the puddle before the final explosion—punctuated by a loud *pop*.

"Wow, that is so cool! Do it again," someone said.

I repeated the demo but with an even bigger chunk and a bigger explosion.

"Different metals," I said, "produce different flame colours, depending on the electron orbital levels. Firecrackers are designed with this in mind."

Next, I threw a chunk of potassium into the puddle. It repeated the same motions as the sodium, except with a pink flame.

For my finale, I had Noose-Neck hold the long match between two fingers at the end of his outstretched arm.

"Don't move and I'll try not to set you on fire," I said to him, to a chorus of laughter from my students. Noose-Neck didn't know how to react, so again, he did as he was told.

"Everyone else stand back."

I lit the match and then dumped a handful of Lycopodium powder into my left hand. I knelt down and held my hand beside Noose-Neck's, as close to the burning match as possible. I inhaled deeply, as if I was going to hold my breath underwater for eternity.

Mom, I sure hope you're watching over me now. I need you.

With as much force as I could muster, I blew the powder upward onto the flame. The resulting three-foot-wide fireball was spectacular. Noose-Neck and I felt the heat, but neither lost any hair.

And they all applauded. I bowed and shook Noose-Neck's hand with a bone-crushing handshake—a handshake stronger than the one he gave me way back in the summer when we first met.

Noose-Neck nodded, returned to the portable, and then left with his yellow pad.

"Wicked demo, sir," Alex said. "Where can I buy those materials?"

"I don't think it would be prudent to tell you," I said. "Oh, and Alex?"

"Yes Mr. V?"

"Next time, just go cow tipping."

<u>Wednesday, June 16</u>

Revenge of the sex ed teacher: Part 4

Grade 9 boys scream worse than girls at a horror flick. I warned them the video was graphic.

"Is that her—?" asked one boy to another.

"Yeah, I think so," said the second boy.

"It's so stretched out. That's disgusting," said the first.

I didn't warn the boys they'd be watching a vaginal birth. The comments, screaming, and yelling continued:

"Ahhhhhhhhhhhhhhhh, why are you doing this to us, sir?"

"Is that the head?"

"It looks like rubber."

"It's all bloody."

Finally, the baby was born.

"Thank God that's over," said someone from the back.

Noose-Neck was there to witness the whole thing. Perhaps he'd changed his mind about my offer and hoped that yesterday was a fluke? Maybe he'd just wanted more examples of my brilliance (due to his—ahem—guidance) for the write-up of my second evaluation. Regardless, he scribbled madly on his trusted yellow notepad. I won't know for sure if my nemesis took the offer until I have the written evidence of my successful second evaluation in my hand. I wouldn't be surprised if the bastard found a way to stab me in the back again.

"Okay, boys," I said, "you may want to look away."

"There's more?"

"Please, sir, no more."

The new mother on the video screamed as she pushed out the afterbirth. My entire class screamed with her. They couldn't look away, and some appeared queasy. Even Noose-Neck looked uncomfortable.

"Oh my God, what is that?" asked one boy as the woman pushed the jello-like, bloody red tissue from her vagina.

"That's called the afterbirth," I said to the class.

A midwife in the video took the jiggling volleyball-sized tissue and placed it on a metal tray. It was like watching a chef put half a liver in a frying pan.

I continued: "The afterbirth is the expulsion of the inner uterine lining and the placenta."

"I'm becoming a monk," said one boy.

"I'm never having sex in my life," said another.

Thursday, June 17

So successful was yesterday's screening of the birthing video that I showed it to my Grade 11 bio class. The reactions were similar.

I even heard Teleisia whisper, "I'm gonna keep my legs closed from now on."

Friday, June 18

No word or paperwork from Noose-Neck.

Saturday, June 19

A crushing blow: I don't even think Noose-Neck's evaluation, if he ever gives it to me, really matters anymore.

I just got off the phone with Elizabeth Andrews.

"There's been an attack on European foreigners in Uganda," she said. "A group of Hutu rebels hacked at least ten tourists to death in Bwindi, near the Congo-Ugandan border."

"What?"

Elizabeth said that most of the European schools backed out of the recruitment fair because of safety concerns.

"All of the African, Asian, and South American schools we represent will still be there, but I need to know, Carlson—are you sure this is something you really want?"

I've got some heavy soul searching to do in the next forty-eight hours.

Sunday, June 20

Father's Day

"Son," said my father. "You can always get a contract in Europe the next time round. Don't let this stop you from teaching overseas."

"It doesn't matter anymore, Dad. I'm gonna be stuck here."

"Please don't say that."

"But it's true. I've been dreaming of Europe for months and it's not going to happen."

Poppa Wib started weeping.

"Why are you crying? This doesn't affect you."

"My dear son, I've suppressed so much pain since your mother's death."

"Don't fucking bring her into this!"

"I have something to tell you. Something you've wanted to know for years."

"If it's about Mom, you've already told me enough. It's okay, and I understand."

"Did you ever wonder why Kate blames me for your mother's death?"

"Dad, you already explained things to me."

"Did you ever wonder why her family hardly talks to us anymore?"

"Dad, I know all about it. You were the one to choose the UFFI insulation. I get it, but you had no way of knowing it would destroy Mom's health."

"No," said my father. "That's not why."

"What?"

Between sobs, he confessed the biggest regret of his life to me: "I was afraid. And if I wasn't such a chicken-shit, your mom wouldn't have gotten sick."

"Afraid? Afraid of what?"

"Afraid of leaving home to work in another country, just like you are right now."

"I'm not afraid."

"You are, my dear Carlson, and I'm not going to let you repeat my failures. You have to go to this recruitment fair in Africa."

"But Dad, I don't care anymore. I want to stay home."

"You don't want to stay home. You need to go."

"Dad, why? What's this all about?"

"We had the contract signed."

"Dad, what contract?"

"Your mother and I were going to leave Canada for Singapore for two years. We had the contract signed, but I was too afraid to leave. I was too afraid to be away from my own mother and sister. I put them ahead of your mother, your sister, and you—my own family."

I was starting to comprehend, and I started to cry as well.

"You mean?" I asked.

"Yes. One of your mother's dreams was to work overseas, just like your dream. It was my dream, too, but I was afraid."

So Dad convinced Mom to stay in Canada. They bought what was to become their dream home. The first upgrade was to improve the insulation. Upon Dad's insistence, they used UFFI. The dream home turned into a nightmare.

"My son, don't be afraid. I will always be here and your mother will always be looking down upon you."

"I think I understand," I said.

Dad looked at me and held my hand. "Do you forgive me?" he asked. "Can you still look into my eyes and respect me?"

"I respect you more than I ever have."

<u>Monday, June 21</u>

Sitting in my mailbox after school was the manila envelope I've been waiting for.

"Under my tutelage ... Carlson learned to manage children with ADHD ... was in constant communication with myself and the parents ... as to how best to meet the needs of the student..."

"Though hesitant at first, Carlson, himself a long-distance runner ... with my encouragement ... helped coach the cross-country running team ... leading several athletes I recommended to him to qualify for the OFSAA ..."

"... has taken my advice and demonstrated that the best class management is to come up with an interesting lesson plan ... whether safely demonstrating to students, as I showed him, how to make fireballs and firecrackers with Lycopodium, sodium and potassium ... ensured proper equipment used ... well-ventilated, fireproof area ..."

"... followed my proposal when teaching human sexuality ... most effective method of promoting abstinence I've ever witnessed ... showed birthing video ... though graphic, Mr. Veitch forewarned his students, and their parents ... using consent forms I provided for him ..."

"... if Carlson wasn't so open to my suggestions ... he wouldn't have progressed so rapidly ... is a very malleable employee ... takes constructive criticism well ... follows my example and strives to improve ..."

"... well organized ... "

"... Carlson displayed his fun side to students (earlier in the year I told him he was too serious sometimes) ... chasing a student with a worm in order to motivate him to run around the track ... it worked ... this particular student made the starting line on my basketball team because of his improved fitness ..."

> "... Mr. Veitch is a competent teacher ... he belongs
> in this profession ..."

The main office was already dark and locked by the time I got there. I needed to fax Elizabeth Andrews a copy of the evaluation immediately. I'd promised she'd have this information three days ago, but I hoped she'd understand. I found Jozef to let me inside.

"You go to Poland this summer?" he asked.

"No," I said. "I'm going to Africa."

"I go to Poland in August. When you go to Poland?"

"Soon. My plan is to get a job teaching in Europe next year."

"Ah, very good. Maybe you get job in Poland?"

"Maybe."

I waited until the fax machine printed me a confirmation slip. I saw Noose-Neck leave his office. He checked to see that nobody was around and then walked up to me.

"I still don't believe you belong in this profession," he said.

"You're entitled to your opinion," I said. "By the way, I bought you something."

"You bought me a gift?"

I handed the blue gift bag to him.

"It's a tie. I heard about your little mishap with the paper shredder."

Noose-Neck was silent, like I'd been so many times before.

Tuesday, June 22

Elizabeth faxed me the confirmation: I have a place in the ECIS/AIS recruitment fair in Entebbe. I also remembered the following three business cards taped into my diary:

Sejong Restaurant Cuzco

세종

Owner
Mr. Kim Young Min
(Peter Kim)

☎ 97·1973

Namhansanseong International School

국제학교남한산성

Headmaster Kim Young Bae
B.Sc. Ph.D. Stanford University

✆ (82-031) 206-1970

Namhansanseong International School

국제학교남한산성

Headmaster Dr. E. Williams
B.Ed. Ph.D. Princeton University

✆ (82-031) 206-1970

Perhaps I shall do some research on Korea?

<u>Wednesday, June 23–Wednesday, June 30</u>

Final exams and a shitload of tedious marking

The tedium, however, was punctuated by the occasional humour break. The following examples come to mind. First, 100 percent of my Grade 10 boys know that gonorrhea is an STD causing pus to drip from the penis. Andrew Yates even drew me a diagram. Second, Andrew wrote me the following note:

> Mr. V,
> Thanks for a good year. My favrite class was when we played the Grade 9s in dodgeball, even though you kicked me out and made me write a 1000-word essay on head injuries because I beaned a couple of them minor ninors and made them cry. You should cut back on the notes and maybe take it easy on kids about lates.
> Andrew

The marking is done now. My final duty at Kipling Secondary is to attend tomorrow's graduation ceremony. This is the one time I hope Noose-Neck talks because Bill Parsons will go on forever.

JULY

Take the future by storm

Graduation was a snore fest. Bill kept reading the names too slowly, and thus it took 61 minutes and 35.5 seconds to hand out the diplomas. In fact, the first of four pages of names took 19 minutes and 11.3 seconds.

Strangely, a helium balloon, which had escaped and ascended to the gymnasium ceiling, would lower down to Bill's head whenever he read too slowly.

Everyone noticed, including Bill himself. "I guess that's a sign I should read a little faster," he said to the amused audience. Sure enough, the balloon rose when Bill increased the pace.

Lauren sat beside me and couldn't believe I was doing split times for names.

"It's the only way I can sit still," I whispered to her.

"I'm glad I won't be the one sitting beside you on the plane in two days," she said.

The subject awards took 16 minutes and 43.8 seconds and the community awards and bursaries took another 21 minutes and 2.2 seconds. Denia Thomasos spoke for only 3 minutes and 13.8 seconds but Bill Parsons's address (speaking in lieu of Noose-Neck) made up for her brevity. I counted Bill saying "and um" twenty-four times before the balloon came down again. Bill looked up at it and had another chuckle, as did the grads and everyone else.

"I'll take that as another hint," he said. "In closing, then, I say to you dear graduates, take the future by storm!"

I didn't stay for the reception. It was time to pack.

Friday, July 2

Poppa Wib, Aunt Pamela, Grandma Veitch, and Lauren treated me to surf and turf at The Keg. Afterward, we went back to Grandma's for

299

apple pie. Lauren lost to Grandma in Scrabble, falling for the "Woe is me; I'm too old" trick that Grandma plays on unsuspecting victims.

Before the night was over, they gave me presents. Aunt Pamela, Grandma Veitch, and Poppa Wib all chipped in for a new three-piece suit, so I can "wow" them at my interviews. Lauren gave me a Jar Jar Binks card and two Lonely Planet travel books: one for Asia and one for Africa. I didn't have the heart to tell Lauren that I wish Yoda had choked Jar Jar to death with the Force.

I fly to Entebbe, Uganda, tomorrow. The recruitment fair starts on Tuesday now because all the Euro schools dropped out. I'm going to use the new-found time to go gorilla trekking.

I meet Eric and Teags at Carnivore in Nairobi in one week.

Tuesday, July 5

One hour with the gorillas equals:
- US$260
- Waking up at 4:45 AM
- A good thing I checked with the travel agent, as two old bus companies shut down and a new one would take me from Kampala to Butogota
- Having peanuts for breakfast because the hotel buffet wasn't open yet
- One *boda boda* (speeder bike) ride to bus park
- Only five people on the bus (yes!)
- Dozens of touts coming on the bus to sell bread and eggs and snacks etc. to the passengers
- Loud Swahili dance music on the bus at 6:15 AM until Butogota
- Moving from one parking spot to the adjacent one for no apparent reason
- Learning that the bus doesn't leave until it's full

- Moving to another parking spot for no apparent reason
- Waiting until 7:30 AM for the bus to be full before leaving and realizing I could have had my hotel buffet breakfast instead of peanuts
- Stopping every ten minutes (give or take) for the entire ten-hour bus ride for someone to get on or off or for someone to pee or poo
- 24,235,235 million Ugandan touts shoving chicken skewers, eggs, peanuts, bananas, etc., through the windows and running beside the bus when we slowed down for one of our three billion stops
- Thirty-four times the guy in front of me closing *my* window every time I opened it two centimetres to try to rid my lungs of body odour smell from the bus (take two onions and jam them into your eyes and you haven't come close to approximating the smell)
- 124 packs of cigarettes ... or the equivalent amount of damage I did to my lungs from the exhaust fumes
- Two hundred kilometres on asphalt littered with potholes and speed-bumps
- One hundred kilometres on a bumpy, pitted dirt road at the edge of the cliff through the supposed "Switzerland of Africa"
- Two cows that got stuck on the road and ended up running ahead of the bus
- Fifty Ugandans and one white guy cheering on the cows to outrun the bus to safety
- One cow jumping off the cliff and rolling down the hill to his untimely death
- Fifteen thousand Ugandan shillings for the bus ride
- Twenty thousand Ugandan shillings for the car ride a mere seventeen kilometres to Bwindi from Butogota

- One panic attack after learning I was staying at the same homestead where the Hutu rebels murdered eight tourists last month
- Twenty armed guards patrolling Butogota
- Four people at lodging who forgot to wake me up the next morning for my wake-up call
- Peanuts for breakfast again because of the lack of wake-up call
- Stopping every ten minutes to wait for Rosie, an oversized middle-aged German woman in my tour group, to catch her breath on the trek from Bwindi to the gorillas because she was so ridiculously out of shape
- One German family who took pity on me and drove me back to Entebbe so I didn't have to take the bus again

It was all worth it. I didn't want to leave the gorillas. I hope the rest of my trip is like this.

Wednesday, July 6

I interviewed with Dr. Williams from Namhansanseong International School in South Korea. He offered me a job teaching biology. I also have offers from schools in Haiti and Kuwait. I'm leaning toward South Korea. I have until the end of the weekend to decide.

Thursday, July 7

White-water rafting on the Nile! Nuff said.

Friday, July 9

Nairobi, Kenya → *Carnivore restaurant*

Between servings of ostrich meatballs (my fave), barbecued crocodile (tastes like chicken), wildebeest (okay), camel (tastes too strong), and chicken gizzards (chewing the cartilage made me dry heave), Teagan told me everything he knew about Korea, Haiti, and Kuwait.

He thinks Haiti would be rewarding but says they don't pay well and that the country is unstable.

"Kuwait is feckin safe now," he said. They treat teachers like gold. Mate, you'd make loads of dough. But it's hot there, so I say take the job in South Korea. No rent. No taxes. Buddhist and Christian holidays? Ye could fly to Beijing, Hong Kong, Shanghai, or even Tokyo on yer long weekends and do Thailand, the Philippines, Cambodia, and Vietnam on yer holidays. I'll even feckin join ya sometime."

D'Souza finally arrived at 6:17 PM

"Sorry, dudes," said Eric. "I didn't reset my watch."

To atone for his sins, we made him pay for dessert. We begin our assault on Kilimanjaro in three days.

EPILOGUE

Sunday, September 26, 1999

Sweat, though not from my spicy Chae yuk top bap (I no longer strain the chili pepper sauce from my rice), drips from my nose as I write this entry. Restless after my flight from Beijing to Seoul, and my bus ride from Kimpo Airport to Songnam, I needed some exercise. My perspiration results from a brisk run up and down Namhansanseong, the South Han Mountain Fortress.

Five messages (four voice messages on my machine and one e-mail) waited for me back home after waving good night to Catherine, Leah, Mary, Anne, and Fleecy:

1. From Poppa Wib: "I miss you, son. Call me when you're home from Beijing. I love you."
2. From Uncle Willie: "Whatever you do, Carlson, don't step on a land mine."
3. From Eric: "Dude, I'm so proud of you for moving to Korea. We're nearly in the same time zone now!"
4. From Lauren: "I'm in Patagonia; how was Beijing?"
5. An e-mail from Teagan:
   ```
   How are the Korean lassies? Can
   I come and visit?
   Cheers mate,
   Teags
   ```

The Chusok long weekend is over. Despite returning home to Korea after four days of adventure in Beijing, I look forward to work tomorrow. My students, though not without problems, follow instructions and strive to achieve.

LaVergne, TN USA
17 August 2010
193502LV00001B/4/P